CLOSER THAN BREATHING

A Light Gay Odyssey

One

On Thursday night, as usual, I called in at the Give and Take, a West London gay bar a short walk from home. Obvious shadows under my eyes, caused by lack of sleep, might have invited comment, so I put on a pair of sunglasses. They were the kind that magically darken in bright light. I had bought them that summer, and I wore them hoping, even if it was now the middle of October, that they would conceal my tiredness. Sunglasses go well with thick, dark hair like mine anyway.

The Give and Take is not a late bar. I go there to chat with friends rather than to pick someone up – an activity the barman Miles calls 'looking for take-away'. His nickname is Smiles, because he can flash one that would cheer up a funeral.

'You okay, Ben? What's with the dark glasses?' he asked, pouring me a lager. 'Been clubbing? Too much take-away?'

'Neither. Neighbours kept me awake. Should have known the dark glasses wouldn't fool anyone.'

'The bastards. You hear some terrible stories about nuisance neighbours. Mind you, hiding your black eyes behind sunglasses is a bit transparent,' he said, flashing that smile. 'Glasses… bit

1

transparent… get it?'

'You can laugh. Perhaps I should stay away from the bar lights, and hide in the dark corners.'

'We don't have any dark corners – anyway, that's not your style, is it? Let me know if you're interested in moving. I know someone who's looking for a flatmate.'

Another customer arrived and Smiles went to serve him. Offering to put me in touch with someone who wanted a flatmate was typical of Smiles, who always knew someone or something that would solve everyone's problems. However, the earplugs I picked up during my lunch break promised to be a less drastic solution than moving home. Anyway I had shared a flat before, after university, a couple of years ago, when I first came up to London. The flat share was good in some ways, but eight months had been long enough. My current self-contained little place might be cramped and two floors up, in what my boss, Jeremy, described as a dreary Victorian terrace, but it was my release from taking turns with four others to use the bathroom and kitchen. Sharing had meant not needing to go out in search of company, but having more privacy – a few quiet hours to myself whenever I wanted – had been a big improvement.

Until the previous weekend, that is, when new neighbours moved in upstairs. On Monday night the noise of heavy objects being shifted around continued until after midnight. The next night a series of rhythmic thuds hammered through the ceiling into the early hours with nothing that, from below, sounded like a tune. I guessed that they had unpacked and were celebrating their move, so I put the covers over my head and tried to sleep, but soon felt too hot. I pushed the bedding aside, put my head under the pillow, and dozed uncomfortably as the minutes dragged by. Wednesday night, with their noise again in my ears after midnight, the racket annoyed me so much that sleep was impossible. I went up to ask them to turn the music down, banging ever more loudly on their door until a young woman wearing garish lipstick, her eyelashes also plastered with make-up, answered.

'I'm from downstairs…'

'Oh, you're one of the neighbours. Nice to meet you, like. Come on in for a drink.'

Despite my anger, meeting her for the first time and wanting to be civil, I went in. She introduced her partner, who welcomed me with an energetic handshake. Her name was Jayde and his was Jake. Everyone, she said, called them the Jays. Stupidly I let him pour me a large beer. We chatted about the rents we were paying, and moaned about the three months deposit required by the landlord. They asked if I lived on my own or with a girlfriend, so I told them I was gay. With no hesitation they both said that was great, and she joked that instead of him worrying about me fancying her, she was the one who would have to worry about me fancying him. 'You have to admit I've picked myself a looker, haven't I?'

Not sure of how to turn the conversation to the subject of noise, I smiled vaguely.

'There you are you see. Read your mind!' she said, shrieking with laughter. 'Oh dear! Have to have a bit of fun, like, don't you?'

Beer in hand, my half-hearted attempts to complain had no effect on them. When I left an hour later, they had ignored what I said about their music keeping me awake. I was seething – angry mostly with myself for not being more assertive.

Everyone has nights when their sleep is disturbed. Why should a bit of noise become such a problem for me? If you are tired enough you can probably sleep anywhere. It was not as though I was likely to fall asleep on my stool at Smile's bar and fall off onto the floor.

When Smiles had finished serving he came back over to me. 'Well? This guy I mentioned, looking for a flatmate. You might get on. He's a steady type, like you. The flat's really nice, you should see it.'

'A steady type? Me? Why? Because I work in a bookshop? Jeremy would be most put out to hear his shop spoken of as a place for steady types. He would have you know that the two of us are the cutting edge of antiquarian book retail, not to say at the coal face.'

'Ah, Jeremy… how is the old thing? Still wearing his Sherlock Holmes costume?' he teased, referring to a very old-fashioned cape Jeremy sometimes wore. 'You and Jeremy, the fearless duo of historic parchments, you pair of daredevils.'

He knew perfectly well that we sold books, not historic parchments. 'Here's someone who must be a bit parched,' I said, nodding towards another regular who had come up to the bar.

I went home at eleven o'clock. All was quiet and by half past I had got into bed. After two nights short of sleep I dropped off straight away. An hour or so later the thud of the loudspeaker upstairs woke me. Should I go up to protest? What if they welcomed me as fervently as before? Easy to tell myself to be more forceful, but hampered by lack of sleep, would they shrug away my complaints as easily a second time? If so, and were I to be swept along by their matey banter again, things would be worse than ever. To try to forget the whole issue I put in the earplugs and slept fitfully until after three when the noise at last stopped.

Getting ready for work at seven-thirty the next morning, I saw in the bathroom mirror that the shadows under my eyes were developing into bags. The dark glasses were my only hope; given

4

Jeremy's unconventional dress he was unlikely to take much notice of a pair of not-all-that-dark-really glasses.

This was wishful thinking, for he commented on them straight away, attributing my tired eyes to too much reading. He himself had been working his way through the collected works of the historian Thomas Carlyle, and at times would lapse into a paternalistic manner of speech: 'Those of us who love books must learn not to over-indulge,' he counselled, nodding his head. 'As I've learned through hard experience over the years, excessive reading puts a strain on the eyes. If we do not allow adequate time for sleep, how can the mind take in what is being presented to it, however fine the words? Now you mustn't think I am trying to lecture you, but be firm, Ben. No reading into the early hours tonight.'

He went out to collect some stock acquired through an online book auction, leaving me in charge. As the shop was empty I placed a chair by the door and sat dozing with a book open in my lap. When you are really tired, catching a minute or two of sleep makes you feel much better, and the rest helped even though I woke up a couple of times in danger of falling over sideways.

Jeremy returned about an hour later. The door latch clicked and the shop bell rang. He was carrying a box of magazines, and as he manoeuvred himself through the entrance I stirred myself and quickly climbed onto the chair to tidy the valuable old atlases on a high shelf nearby.

'Why are you using a chair to do that, Ben? You should use the steps, much safer, and easier. It's because you're over-tired. I wouldn't have been at all surprised to have come back and found you having a nap.'

Could he have guessed the real reason the chair was there? To divert him from any suspicious thoughts, I asked 'Anything interesting from the auction?'

'Oh, just some old *HIM* magazines.' Or rather that is what I thought he said, wrongly guessing he meant the gay soft porn magazine from the nineteen-seventies. I asked to have a look.

'You won't find these of any interest, they're not what you imagine. *Hymn* magazines were a nineteen-thirties Church of England series dealing with church governance. The only potential buyers are specialised archivists. Sorry to disappoint you. Cup of tea instead?'

Meticulous about keeping his stock records up to date, he had me help him make a note of the issue numbers and dates of the magazines while we drank our tea. We had almost finished when the shop bell rang.

'You go, Ben, I'll finish this off.'

I left Jeremy's little office and went to stand by the till, ready to make a sale. A man about my age or a bit older, tall and fair, tidily dressed in good casual clothes, walked towards me and said, 'Excuse me, are you Ben?'

'Yes.'

'Miles from the Give and Take suggested I drop in on you. I'm Dale. I've a flat not far from here. I'm hoping to find someone to share.'

'Were you at the Give and Take? I don't remember… You're a friend of Smiles?'

'I met him through an old boyfriend.'

'Aah…' I explained my problem with the new neighbours, but said I did not intend to be terrorized out of my flat.

He shrugged. 'Do you have a lunch break? Why not have a quick look at my place anyway. I'm in Fulrose Court… wouldn't take long… it's a really nice building and, who knows, one day you might think about a move.'

One of the words to which Jeremy's hearing is highly

6

sensitive is 'lunch'. He emerged from the back of the shop wearing a bright yellow jacket, the cloth stretched very tight over his tummy. Dale did not know what to say.

Jeremy smiled. 'You've noticed my jacket. There used to be a jazz band that played in the Gay Pride rallies; the five members each had differently coloured jackets, rainbow colours being the idea, I suppose. Some while ago I saw all five for sale in a charity shop and bought them. I assumed they once belonged to the jazz band, I don't really know.'

'They must have made quite a splash at the rallies,' Dale commented.

'Jeremy would be willing to lend you one, if you like,' I offered.

'He's making fun of me. I'll be here if you want to go out for lunch. Bring me back a sandwich and a piece of cake.'

This made it impossible for me to give Dale the excuse that I could not leave the shop, and despite not having any real wish to see his flat I found myself on my way there with him. While we were waiting in the sandwich bar he said, 'I'm putting you out, aren't I? Your boss must have thought me rude, staring at him. That jacket...'

'He thinks it's good for business, that putting on unusual clothes will make customers remember the shop. He has his quirks. Nice to get out for lunch, actually. How far away did you say your flat was?'

We walked for another fifteen minutes before arriving at the stylish white façade of a block of flats about eight floors high. Two wings containing shops came forward on either side of the main entrance to make a little open square. The corners of the building were curved rather than right-angled, and below the roof was a frieze with a motif of overlapping circles. 'There it is. What do you think?' he asked.

7

'They're luxury flats all right. A bit upmarket for me.' Inside the ornate bronze panels decorated with chevrons and semicircles on the lift doors reinforced this impression. 'How old is it?'

'Nineteen-thirties. It's period architecture.'

He lived on the fourth floor. 'I'll show you round quickly while the kettle's boiling. It's plenty big enough for two. This is my bedroom. The other is the same size.' The rooms were large and well lit, nicely furnished— nothing was showy but everything matched. In the kitchen was a small table where we ate our sandwiches.

'Do you work locally?'

'I'm a manager at the local hospital. The pay is… well, public sector rates, not fantastic. I've quite a big mortgage to pay for this place. My salary covers it, but I need a flatmate to help with the taxes and bills. I was sharing with someone, a boyfriend. We split up a few months ago.'

'Have you tried advertising?' My lack of interest disappointed him and he looked glum, or more accurately, glummer than ever; he had not smiled once since we met. The fault, though, might have been mine. Being pressed into seeing his flat made me awkward.

'There are always risks if you share with someone you don't know,' he replied. He gave me the impression of being uneasy with strangers. If so, finding a new flatmate would be hard for him.

'We don't really know each other, do we?'

'We could get to know one another, you wouldn't need to decide right away. Miles says you're steady.'

'What is all this about me being steady? Alfred the Great, Ethelred the Unready, and Ben the Steady?'

This remark, meant to be humorous, made him smile for a

8

moment, but then he must have thought he had annoyed me by calling me 'steady', and his brow sank back into a frown. 'Sorry, I didn't mean it to sound like you were no one special. Stupid of me. I'm sorry.'

'No, don't... Honestly, I really do have to go back to feed Jeremy his sandwich. I go to Smiles' bar most Thursdays, and often a couple of other evenings during the week, usually from about nine. Can I see you in there some time?'

'Yes, that would be great. It's a while since I've been there for a drink.'

Neither of us suggested a specific date or time.

The next time I walked into the Give and Take, Smiles was hurriedly keying something into his mobile phone. I had to wait for him to finish before he served me. 'You'd be surprised who came in earlier,' he said. 'Some musicians from the Gay Symphony Orchestra. They booked the room upstairs to practise, about a dozen of them. I've been flirting with a very cute flautist.'

'You've been flouncing with a flautist?'

'*Flirting* with a flautist. Hope they come again. They bring a cultural ambience to the place. As a dealer in antiquarian books, you do too of course.'

About fifteen minutes later Dale turned up. This more or less confirmed that Smiles had sent him a message to come to the bar. Though not unhappy to see him, Smiles might have asked me first. He made amends by giving us both drinks on the house.

'That's very good of you, Smiles,' I said, raising my glass. 'Is this in honour of the Gay Symphony Orchestra's visit?' I turned to Dale. 'He was flirting with a flautist.'

'Well, maybe not flirting...' Smiles explained, 'Perhaps empathizing is more the word.'

'Or fondling. Fondling a flautist?'

'Ben! No, we had more a kind of resonance at a cultural level.'

He left Dale and me together. Trying not to sound suspicious, I asked, 'Did you say you'd been here before?'

'Not recently. When I first had the flat, my partner and I often went to bars and clubs, but as time went by we went out together less and less. We were drifting apart. I've more or less lost touch with the gay scene. This is relaxed compared with most of it. So many places are just about finding someone for sex.'

Okay, I thought, so you're a nice guy, not wildly promiscuous, but whatever the faults of gay pubs and clubs, life can be very lonely without them. 'Relationships have to start somewhere,' I said. 'People need to meet.'

'People want different things. I'm not trying be judgemental.'

'You should talk to Jeremy. You wouldn't think it, the way he is now, but many many years ago he used to be in the Gay Liberation Front. He hates everything about the scene, the anonymous sexual encounters, drugs, and so on and so on.'

'It is hard to imagine your boss in GLF.'

'Well he was. He tells me about it now and again... how important it is to respect ourselves and to act towards others in the same way... we must be true to ourselves and not be pressured into becoming stereotypes... being liberated does not mean being a libertine, you know,' I said adopting Jeremy's lecturing tone, though this was unfair to him as he usually spoke moderately. 'His involvement in gay rights obviously meant a lot to him. These days he doesn't see much of other gay men. He's in his late fifties and would be out of place in the pubs and clubs where young guys go to find other young guys. Maybe even in here, where you get all ages, he wouldn't feel all that comfortable.'

Perhaps I should have emulated Smiles' practice of putting people in touch, and arranged for Dale and Jeremy to meet. They could have discussed endlessly how commercial and uncaring gay venues were. But what if, instead of the moaning session being a release for them, they made each other more miserable than ever?

'Have you known him for long?' he asked.

'Eighteen months or so. I came to London without much money, and had to find a job fast. I've always loved books, and Jeremy had a *Help Wanted* ad on a booksellers' website. When I first saw the shop you could hardly get through the door. Books were piled up everywhere.'

'That didn't put you off?'

'I always think a well-stocked bookshop is like a walk-in encyclopaedia, a massive store of knowledge, far more than any one person could ever hold in his head. Jeremy's bookshelves were crammed, everything was jumbled up, paperback novels, old leather-bound volumes, newish hardbacks, fiction and non-fiction, books stacked everywhere, including on the floor. If he had found a way to do it he would have hung them from the ceiling too. You had to sort of slalom your way through gaps in the piles of clutter. He needed help. We had to off-load hundreds of books to make room to move around properly... we even gave some away to charity shops. He found it hard to part with things, which is hardly compatible with the purpose of running a shop. Telling him they were bound for a good home made letting go of some of his precious finds easier for him. We organized what were left on the shelves, and went through and priced them all. He had a good grasp of how much they were worth. He broke his habit of indiscriminate buying, and sales picked up. He's a bit eccentric, but he's kindly and easygoing,

11

which is what you want in a boss.'

'I guessed you two were not lovers,' Dale said smiling.

'Oh no. Jeremy is too high-minded for that sort of thing. What about you? Are you courting anyone at the moment?'

'Courting? That's a word you don't hear much from gay men. Nor from straights nowadays, come to that.'

'You'll have to excuse me. It's the influence of all those Victorian novels in the shop. Lots of courting going on in them.'

'I dare say, and wooing, and swooning. Maybe if gays didn't hop into bed with one another so easily… no, you'll think I'm prudish. I'm not claiming to be better than anyone else. Working in the health service makes me aware there's a downside. Not that I see the patients myself.'

Since he was unwilling to say much about his sex life, I tried asking about his job instead. 'What do you do, actually?'

He turned his head slightly aside and said defensively, 'It's management. Right now for instance, I'm sorting out the laundry. I don't mean separating the coloureds from the whites. At the hospital, for years and years the laundry has always been in the same room with rows of big commercial machines, not very up to date, churning away. Now and again one wore out and had to be replaced, but in general the laundry remained pretty much the same. Then we had an inspection. We were told the whole set-up was obsolete, so we decided to go for a new up to date laundry on another part of the site.

'We thought we were doing well until halfway through the firm that won the contract for the building and installation work went bust. There were half a dozen subcontractors and suppliers. No one could agree who was liable for what. Now it's all going way over budget, and I spend half my bloody time trying to sort out the mess. Sorry, you must be wishing you hadn't asked.'

'No, not at all. I didn't realize you had such a responsible job. I suppose I'll have to try and talk sensibly to you now,' but jokingly I asked 'Any chance of the laundry taking a few shirts and bits of stuff for me?'

He laughed. 'Thanks Ben. Thanks for saying it's a responsible job. It can be rewarding, like finding cheaper suppliers for some of the stuff we buy, so money is released that can be put to good use elsewhere. I've managed that more than a few times.'

When Smiles began closing up we left together. Neither of us invited the other back home. Instead we exchanged phone numbers and parted at a street corner. He had been good company, but was clearly not the sort who slipped casually into bed with someone after a couple of drinks. Maybe he was a bit down-hearted having lost his boyfriend, and the problems with the laundry were clearly worrying him, but doing something as worthwhile as helping run a hospital impressed me. This time he had not mentioned wanting to find a flatmate, but the subject cannot have been far from his mind. It made me wary of getting too involved with him.

The earplugs helped me to sleep that night. The following night, Friday, was even better. My tormentors were out, and no noise intruded from upstairs. I left for work on Saturday refreshed. However in the evening, after I had eaten, Jayde knocked on my door. She wore a close-fitting dress and her face was heavily made up, as though she was about to go out, but she asked anxiously, 'You've got to help me, Ben… like, it's an emergency. I don't know anyone else to ask. Jake's collapsed.'

I followed her upstairs. 'He's in there,' she said, pointing to the door of the bathroom. He was lying in the bath, completely still, only his head out of the water, his eyes closed.

'What happened?'

'I don't know.' She hung back by the open door. 'He took some pills. We got them at a party the other night. Then he came in here for his bath. You don't think it's, like, an overdose, do you?'

I called his name loudly, but he did not stir. 'Surely he can't have drowned.' I put my hand into the tepid water and pressed on his chest, hoping to feel a heartbeat or the slight rise and fall of his ribs, but could detect nothing. She stood watching. Not knowing much about first aid, but afraid something serious was wrong, I tugged at his arms and shouted in his ears, but he remained comatose. 'Did you try mouth to mouth?' I asked.

She ignored my question, but said, 'His head's above water. He can't have drowned. '

'Maybe not, but if we tried mouth to mouth it might help.'

'You do it. I don't know how to.'

'He's your boyfriend. You must have seen it being done on TV. You hold the nose, then breath air from your lungs into his. You could try it.'

She stared at me for a few moments, then opened a cupboard, took out a shower cap, and carefully put it on to protect her hairdo. She knelt beside the bath and put her mouth over his lips.

'Hold his nose.'

She gazed at me pleadingly. 'I can't do it.'

'Okay, I'll hold his nose, you try to breathe some air into him. Make sure his tongue is not in the way.'

The atmosphere was horribly clammy. She tried, but the only noticeable result was a bright smudge of her lipstick on his mouth. 'We'll have to call an ambulance,' I said.

'No you mustn't. They'll find the pills. They'll call the police in.'

'No they won't. Anyway, is that worse than him dying?'

'You try the mouth to mouth. I might not have been doing it right.'

I wiped the lipstick off his face, and as I did felt a sensation on my wet hand that must have been caused by breath from his nostrils. 'He is breathing, at least, but he might still need medical help.'

She took off the shower cap and put it back in the cupboard. A phone was lying on the window ledge and I picked it up. 'No you don't!' she shouted, lunging at it and grabbing my fingers with both her hands. For a second her nails, decorated with silver-flecked nail extensions, cut into my skin. The pressure eased, but she held on to the phone tightly enough to prevent me using it. I wrenched myself free, put the phone back on the ledge, and moved away, intending to go downstairs to make the call. She blocked the doorway to stop me. 'Don't go. We could call a taxi. We could take him to hospital in a taxi. It would be quicker. You can wait ages for an ambulance.'

'We'd have to get him downstairs and put him in it. An ambulance crew would know what to do, they would take care of him properly.'

'You don't understand. We can't afford to get into trouble.'

'You're in trouble already.'

'Please Ben, use the phone to call us a taxi.'

A splashing sound from the bath made us look round. Jake appeared to be trying, unsuccessfully, to turn on his side, but he slipped back into the same position as before, only now his chin was under water, his lips barely clear of the surface. I went over, grabbed his arm, pulled him up a little more and shouted his name. His eyelids lifted a little, and under them I could see two slivers of moist eyeball. However, shaking him and calling his name did not bring him back to consciousness.

I gave in and called a taxi. Together we hauled him from the

15

bath and dried him. She brought some of his clothes in, and left me to dress him. She had not given me any shoes, and, searching for a pair, I found her in their sitting room, putting little plastic envelopes of white powder into a bag. 'Where are his shoes?' I asked.

'Oh, I'll get them,' she said. She stood up and swigged a clear liquid from a glass. 'It's vodka. Want some?'

'No. Come and help me, would you?'

We got him on his feet and stood on either side of him holding him up. He came round enough to make a few grunting noises, and she immediately wanted to cancel the taxi and lay him on the bed, saying he was getting better. Her attitude irritated me, and I shouted, 'I'll pay for the taxi, if that's what you're worried about. He may get better, he may get worse. We don't know.'

We manoeuvred him down the stairs, Jayde going in front to prevent him falling forwards, and me somehow hanging on to him from behind. The taxi driver said nothing and looked away as we struggled to haul him onto the back seat. At the hospital the young woman doctor asked what drugs he had taken. Jayde could not or would not say.

'Whatever it was, best if we pump out his stomach.'

'Oh no, please don't,' Jayde pleaded.

'We don't have a choice. If what he's taken has knocked him out to this extent, it may damage his brain, or his liver, or his kidneys. The sooner we clear it out of his system the better his chances are.'

They wheeled him off and sent us to sit in the waiting area. She apologized for spoiling my evening, and said there was no need for me to wait. I left her sitting with the bag full of drugs on her lap.

There would still have been enough time for an hour or more at the Give and Take before it closed, but Jake's overdose was enough excitement for one night. On my own at home I worried that not calling an ambulance straight away might have done serious harm. What if the faffing around had proved fatal? Would I be partly to blame? What had made me imagine mouth to mouth resuscitation would have been any use? How much time had that performance wasted? Then I thought that Dale might know what we ought to have done. He might not be medically trained, but working at the hospital he probably talked to people who dealt with crises like that all the time.

I rang him. At first I could hear a couple of female voices in the background; he explained that he was with some friends from work. He must have moved somewhere quieter as I told him about Jake's overdose, because the background voices faded. He said, 'What we let ourselves in for by trying to help others! There's no way that you could be blamed for anything. Suppose you *had* called an ambulance straight away, would the girlfriend have been willing to let them in? Anyway, Saturday nights are a busy time in Accident and Emergency, and an ambulance might well have taken longer than your taxi did. What could anyone blame you for? Without a crystal ball, how could you know how it would all turn out?'

'I didn't think of that. The taxi was quick. So you think we might have done the right thing?'

'I'd choose you for my team any day. You sure you're okay?'

'Yes, thanks Dale. Thanks. Sorry to interrupt your evening.'

Not long after that, Jayde rang me to say Jake had come round and was going to be all right. He was being kept in hospital for observation, and she planned to return home and go back for him in the morning. I opened my door in case she might want to call in.

I heard her go past my door and was about to close it and go to bed, but she came back down again and knocked almost straight away. I asked her in and gave her a mug of tea. 'First mug of tea I've had since I went down to my parents' last Christmas.'

'Do they live far away?'

'Kent. Near Canterbury.'

'I'm from Shoeburyness.'

'Is that in Scotland?'

'No, Essex. Not far from Southend. Is the tea all right? I could get you something else…'

'It's fine. After me ruining your evening, like, it's good of you to ask me in. You're straight, aren't you?'

'Well, I'm gay actually.'

'That's not the way I meant it. You've got a job. Straight is how you are, isn't it? Not dodgy, not iffy, straight.' She seemed not to realize that she was implying that she and Jake were, in part at least, dodgy or iffy.

He was discharged from hospital the next morning, and came down to see me in the late afternoon. He looked good, wearing a fresh white T-shirt and light blue jeans. His eyes were bright and he smelt of a sweet citrus aftershave or deodorant. His voice was soft, his eyes cast down. Coming to face me must have been embarrassing for him. 'You okay now?' I asked.

'Yes. Thanks. Thanks for all you did for me last night, taking me to hospital and everything. Jayde's good fun to be with, but not the best person at handling problems, if you know what I mean.'

'Wasn't easy to know what to do. Are you all right? Do you have to go back for a check-up or anything?'

'I'm fine now. Someone at a party we went to gave me some

18

bad stuff. Usually I get it from people I know. Should have been more careful. Sorry to mess up your Saturday night. You must think I'm a right fucking prat.'

'No… well… you weren't exactly at your best.'

'I owe you.' He hooked his left thumb into the front centre of his belt loop, with his fingers spread out over his fly. 'Can I can make up for it somehow?'

He was not unattractive. I could easily have said something like 'You're hetero, aren't you?', which would have opened the way for him to say 'bisexual' or 'versatile' if he wanted to, but sex with him as compensation for my trouble the previous night was a dubious notion. Would he lie limp on the bed, hiding his grimaces while I inflicted myself on him? Quite likely we would both end up glad when the performance was over. On the other hand if we had fun, where would that leave Jayde? She might guess how we had got on, and be seized with jealousy. If he wanted to do something for me, he could do something that had nothing to do with sex. 'There is your music. After midnight, if you could turn it down…'

'Have we had it on loud?'

'Yes.'

'You should have said something. Of course we'll turn it down.' His voice had changed, become harder. Perhaps he was feeling rejected. For maybe a minute neither of us spoke. Then he added with emphasis, 'But remember, anything you want, ask me… no, tell me… whatever you want, it's yours. I owe you, remember.'

To lighten the mood I said, 'If you ever win the lottery…'

He smiled and nodded. 'Yeah, okay mate. I won't keep you. Shake hands with me, show you've no hard feelings?'

He grasped my hand tightly, put his free arm across my shoulders, pulled us together and hugged me closely. 'You're a real nice guy, Ben. Thanks.' During that very full hug, I became sexually aroused, and I think he did too. It was only a hug, but the contact had not been completely innocent.

Two

For a short while the Jays, to use the nickname Jayde and Jake had adopted, did as he promised and quietened down. However, over a couple of weeks or so the volume crept back up. No chance meetings on the stairs provided an easy opportunity for me to mention the subject again.

Friends were sympathetic, but had no practical suggestions. Smiles described them as 'those two noisy birds roosting upstairs,' and suggested firing a shotgun loaded with blanks at them. Witty, but as I pointed out, wild birds are legally protected. Jeremy offered to put up a camp bed in the shop for me if my lack of sleep became desperate. Dale suggested complaining to the local council about noise nuisance. This might have worked, but there was an awful lot to it. A council official would come to visit, I would have to keep a diary of dates and times when the nuisance occurred, and ask other neighbours to do the same. Eventually the Jays could be served with a formal notice to stop. Ultimately they could even be taken to court. The whole process sounded as though it would take months, and did I really want to face them if threatening official notices were nailed to their door? They might retaliate by making my life even more miserable.

Once, spotting them in the supermarket, I avoided them by pretending to study the labels of the herbs and spices for ten minutes until they went to the checkout. Wimpish, maybe, but to cheerily say hello would give the impression nothing was wrong, whereas to berate them about noise in a shop full of people would be embarrassing.

Worried I would be thought an idiot, I kept that particular evasive action to myself, not even telling Dale, who was always so supportive. We met in the Give and Take at least once a week, and began to spend Sunday afternoons together. His flat was only about a mile from a stretch of the Thames where lots of rowing clubs had boathouses. He belonged to the hospital sports and social club, which had a share in one of them, and he signed me in as guest so we could take out rowing skiffs.

These little boats were so narrow they were unstable until you sat down. Fast currents and gusts of wind helped or hindered progress once you were under way; in the right circumstances they would reach exhilarating speeds, but could sometimes be difficult to control. Dale knew that stretch of river, and could find sheltered places where the current slowed and we could catch our breath.

Once a police launch passed him when he was way in front, and came speeding towards me. In a strong variable wind, I tried to move out of its way towards the river bank, but facing backwards as rowers do, misjudged my position and looked round to see the launch within a few lengths of my boat. Too late, I worked the oars frantically in an effort to turn more quickly. When the launch was almost upon me, I drew them into the sides to make as narrow an obstacle as possible. The launch passed me safely, but its bow wave sent my little skiff rocking wildly. I could imagine what the police officers on board were thinking.

Dale saw the incident, turned back, and seeing that I was all right, apart from my embarrassment, he said, 'Hoping for a lift with a nice young policeman, were you?' He was more reassuring when we talked of the incident later, saying 'They were probably more worried than you were. The newspaper headline "Police Launch Collides With Rowing Boat" is the last thing they want.'

Few of the tourist boats came up to that stretch, some miles upstream from Central London. Dale loved the river and knew lots of local history. Whilst walking the riverside paths he would tell me about how busy the waterway had been fifty years ago, with barges taking coal to power stations and gas works, grain to breweries, and merchandise to warehouses. There was a pub called The City Barge on the bank where the Lord Mayor's splendid ceremonial boat once used to be moored. Here and there were houseboats, some very smart with little gardens in containers on the roof, others neglected with peeling paint and rusting metal.

One Sunday evening, after our trip on the river, Dale cooked dinner, a stir-fry, at Fulrose Court. The Jays had disturbed my sleep badly during the preceding few nights. On Thursday and Friday they had had friends round and partied for hours. On Saturday, I stupidly stayed late in a club as a way of avoiding the noise at home, but that, of course, made me more tired than ever. Sitting at the table in the warmth of Dale's flat, full of his delicious food, I fell asleep while he was in the kitchen making coffee. He woke me by gently squeezing my shoulder. 'Haven't bored you that much, have I?'

I felt rotten. He had kept the conversation going all afternoon, and then cooked the meal. My small contribution had been bringing a bottle of wine. 'What must you think. I really enjoyed the meal, and the afternoon, and being with you. I'm worn out, that's the trouble.'

'Why don't you have a quiet night here? The bed in the spare room is made up. At least you'll be fit for work in the morning.'

The prospect of a good sleep, with no need for earplugs, was difficult to turn down. I insisted he sit and relax while I cleared the table, loaded up the dishwasher, and cleaned his wok. We watched the news on television together for half an hour then, before we turned in, he showed me where he kept a spare toothbrush and invited me to use his electric shaver in the morning.

That night was my first at Fulrose Court. A couple of weekends later when he went to visit his parents in Northampton, he asked me to water his plants, gave me a key and said I was welcome to sleep in the spare room while he was away. He was not due to return until after work on Monday. I packed a small bag and stayed in his flat all weekend. After three good nights' sleep between his sheets, I felt better than I had for weeks. I was about to say how grateful I was, but he jumped in first and thanked me for keeping an eye on the place for him!

He had not mentioned the possibility of me becoming his flatmate since the day when, months ago, he had walked into the bookshop. Now the question hung, unspoken, between us. Ignoring it I said, 'I hope everything is as you left it. Except the sheets, of course. You might want to have them sterilized... and fumigated. The hospital laundry could be the ideal place.'

'Don't remind me. It's total chaos in there. The manager is due to come to see me tomorrow. If we can't organize a laundry, how can we be trusted with people's medical care?' He paused and added softly, 'That's my worry. If you came to live here you could sort your sheets out for yourself. After all, we first met because Smiles suggested you might be interested in sharing the flat with me. I don't want to push you though, and I won't mention the subject again unless you want to talk about it. Still, in about a month's time I will seriously need to find a flatmate. If you're still not interested I'll ask around at the Give and Take, or advertise maybe.'

'What if you found you couldn't stand my personal habits? I've got some funny ways.'

'We all have them. Try living here for a couple of weeks, no commitment. If it doesn't work out, you can go back to your old place. We could still be friends.'

I took up his offer of a trial flat share, and a few weeks later left my little place in the ugly Victorian terrace and moved in with him. My possessions did not call for a big removal wagon, so we borrowed Jeremy's van and made two trips. The Jays knew nothing of my escape until they saw me in the street with my arms full of towels and toiletries. They were on their way back from shopping, and had a male friend with them. I had glimpsed him once on the stairs but not spoken to him. He was enviably good-looking, his short hair effortlessly neat and attractive, his brown eyes set back under a strong brow, his lips... the fact is, I fancied him so much it was difficult not to stare at him. The Jays said hello, and Jayde asked if I was moving. No longer caring what they might think I responded 'Yes. Found somewhere quieter.'

'Oh, I hope it's a nice place. Not, like, because of us, is it?' She laughed in her loud shrill way. The idea that they might have driven me out was evidently so absurd she thought it funny.

Jake said, 'You didn't say anything. You going far?'

'No. Well, I'll still be in West London.'

'Don't be a stranger, come and see us. You haven't been around much lately.' With emphasis he added, 'I don't forget things, you know.'

'Actually,' she said, 'funny coincidence, but Toby's, like, after a place, aren't you?'

'Yes, on and off,' he said. Those wonderful deep-set eyes now looked directly into mine. 'Round here might suit me.' He smiled. Even his teeth were perfect. He waited for an answer.

'I suppose I ought to have a final check round to make sure nothing's been left behind. You're welcome to come up and have a shufti.'

Dale, overhearing me, stepped out of the back of the van and said 'Yes, go ahead, I'll wait here.'

Toby followed me upstairs and glanced rapidly round the flat, pausing only to open the bathroom cabinet.

'Empty?' I asked.

'Yes.' He smiled. 'Nothing to reveal your secrets.'

'What makes you think I have any? Have you known the Jays for long?'

'A while. I met her not long after she came up to London, before she picked up with Jake. Wonder if having them as neighbours would be a good thing or a bad thing.'

'Depends on whether you're the party type.'

'That what you are then?'

'Only up to a point.'

He went into the main room and looked out of the window. The Jays must have told him I was gay, for he said, 'That your boyfriend down there, with the van?'

'No. We'll be sharing a flat, that's all.'

'Cosy.'

'No. It's a big place. Plenty of room for two.'

'Nice to have a big place if you can afford it. Won't keep you then. See you around, maybe?' He went off upstairs to join the Jays.

26

When I returned to the van Dale asked, 'Who was the hunk?'

'A friend of the Jays, first time I've met him. Wonder what it must be like to be so good-looking?'

'He'd turn heads at the Give and Take, yours and mine included.'

We drove on to Fulrose Court. The spare bedroom easily took most of my things, and Dale had also made space for my stuff in the bathroom and kitchen. Even in the lounge he had freed up some shelf and cupboard space, clearly wanting me to have the run of the flat. From that first day he was easygoing and adaptable. We agreed to take turns with chores like vacuuming and putting the rubbish out. During our first week together we apologized to each other a lot, for leaving dirty crockery stacked in the dishwasher because we did not think it full enough to turn it on, for being in the bathroom when the other might want to use it, or just for needing to pass one another in the hall.

'Sorry,' one of us would say. 'No, I'm sorry,' would be the reply, sometimes followed by 'Well I'm sorry you're sorry,' said with a wry smile. As well as saying sorry, we gave each other silly warnings, for instance 'Coming through with knives,' when carrying cutlery, or on the way to the wash basket 'Don't look, transferring dirty undies.' Whenever I came into the room he always smiled at me, and after a few days any lingering doubts about moving in with him had gone.

Even watching television with him in the lounge was different. For him it was not an entirely passive indulgence. At intervals he would comment on the programmes; for instance, when a wildlife documentary showed turtles in the Amazon that grew to a metre long and laid a hundred eggs, he flippantly protested that a metre long was too big for a turtle, and that a hundred eggs was 'far too many to lay. What can any one do with

27

a hundred eggs?'

Jeremy approved of him. Hearing that we would be sharing the flat but not a bed, he gave me some advice from his great store of wisdom. 'Sharing has so many advantages over being on your own. Life hasn't turned out like that for me, unfortunately, I'm probably too selfish. All the petty day to day wrangles, wanting to use the bathroom at the same time, trivial misunderstandings, knowing when to hold your ground and when to give in, I'm useless at all that. You and Dale are good friends, you're sensible people. Best of all you don't have to cope with all the complications of a sexual relationship.'

What did suffer during my first few weeks at Fulrose Court was my love life. Though in the past my visits to the Give and Take usually ended with me leaving alone, opportunities to 'score' with anyone dried up completely. Dale and I usually arrived and left together, and in between spent most of our time talking to each other, so there was little chance of encouraging anyone else to take an interest. Had he broken away from me to chat someone up, and then taken them back to the flat, it would have made it easier for me, but he never did. What if a stranger I took back stole from us, or caused other trouble? As two gay men sharing, sex with one another might look like an obvious possibility, but adjusting to each other as flatmates was demanding enough without, as Jeremy had rightly said, the complications of sex. What if one of us experienced only physical pleasure, whilst deep emotions were stirring in the other? The sensible course, surely, was for us to remain just friends.

I discovered he had an aid to relieving his sexual appetite. One day, when he had gone into the kitchen for a drink, I passed his open bedroom door. On his computer screen a hunky man in swimming trunks stood on a beach with his back to the sea, rubbing his crotch. Returning, Dale saw me looking at it.

'It's a computer game,' he said. 'An erotic computer game. You go into various scenes, a beach, a bar, all sorts of places, and these hunks appear who you can have encounters with.'

'Is that your latest conquest on the screen?'

'He could be. He won't let me down, steal my wallet or credit cards, or walk off with someone else in front of me. I decide everything he is going to do. You can try it out if you want. Were you going somewhere?'

'Only the bathroom.'

He went back to his game and closed the door. Though I had never tried an erotic computer game, pornography of one kind or another had helped me relieve my sexual needs often enough; but did I feel the tiniest niggle that he went back quite so eagerly to his game, having said so little to me? He had probably been playing it before I moved into the flat, and was simply continuing a long established habit. He had never mentioned it, and now that I had found out, my own lack of any love life felt more acute than ever.

I thought my period of celibacy was about to end when the Jays' friend, the handsome Toby, appeared at the Give and Take one evening. Dale had had to work late, and said he would call in later. Toby was standing on his own at the bar. 'Hello, we've met before, haven't we?' I said, trying not to frighten him off by being too keen.

'Ben, isn't it? Let me buy you a drink. You did me a favour showing me your old flat. I've moved in.'

'Really? Do you share the Jays' taste in music?'

'I know what you mean. No, but I do go up and get a drink out of them if I hear them bouncing around upstairs. This is not a bad place. You come here much?'

Conversation was progressing nicely until, a few minutes later, Dale came in. 'Wow,' he said to Toby. 'Haven't seen you in here before. I'm Dale, by the way.'

'Hi Dale. Toby.'

'Toby, wow, that's a great name. Were you called that for any special reason, or just because it's a terrific name?'

Dale, I thought, would never get anywhere with a tired old chat-up line like that, but to my surprise Toby switched his attention from me to him, and they were soon smiling and chatting away as if they were the only two in the bar. For Dale to move in on me like that was not like him at all. I gave him a furious look. Hiding my face from Toby by raising my hand, I silently mouthed the words 'Go away.' He took no notice, and completed my humiliation by leaving the bar with Toby. 'See you Ben,' they called out as they left. So much for me worrying about bringing a stranger to the flat who might cause trouble!

Smiles, watchful as ever, came over. 'Did I really see what I thought I saw? Dale leaving the bar with take-away? Terrific looking guy, too.'

'He moved in on me and ruined my chances.'

'That's what friends are for, Ben, to get in your way and spoil your fun. Still, first time I've seen Dale with anyone since he split up with his boyfriend.'

'What if I go back and the two of them are at it on the sofa?'

'They won't be. Anyway you always do all right. Some of the guys from the Gay Symphony Orchestra should be in later. Stick around and you might find yourself cuddling a clarinettist.'

Resentment at Dale walking out with Toby had put me in the wrong mood for chatting up anyone else. After briefly saying hello to a couple of friends, I left the bar.

When I quietly let myself into the flat, Dale's bedroom door was closed. He and Toby were presumably together in his bed. Reasoning that Dale's computer game had been his only sexual release for a long time, and that therefore it would do him good to hold a real live person in his arms, I managed to cool my temper. Yet, for the first time, he had really annoyed me. Later I heard the front door open and shut, and guessed Toby had left.

The next couple of days I spoke to Dale only when necessary. Several times he asked 'You okay, Ben?' and 'Nothing wrong, is there Ben?' Each time I shrugged and turned away. A text message from him arrived while I was at work saying *I've fucked everything up, haven't I? Sorry. My fault.* Still angry, my first impulse was to delete it straight away, but Jeremy had heard the phone ring, could tell I was annoyed and said, 'Something's happened.' After a bit of coaxing I told him about Dale walking off with Toby.

'That really doesn't sound the least bit like Dale. At times we all act as if we to have a monster lurking inside us. Mostly we have it under control, but every now and again… you've every right to be annoyed, but don't do anything in anger. Until now he has been a good friend, hasn't he?'

'So far.'

'Don't… Listen, take it easy. You're wound up now. He's said he's sorry.'

I mulled over what to do about Dale's message, and sent the terse reply *Saw him first, take-away snatcher.* He replied with *Want to be friends, am very sorry. Owe you.*

Two days later I was up on the steps, bringing down the four hefty volumes of the *Imperial English Dictionary* for a customer, when Toby walked into the shop. He made straight for me. 'Hello,' he said cheerily from the foot of the steps, clearly unaware I was still smarting over being abandoned by him the other night.

How tempted I was to drop the weighty books on his head as repayment. 'Be with you as soon as I can,' I said, pretending not to know who he was. He went to the other end of the shop and began reading the spines of the encyclopaedias. After descending to his level, and spending more time than necessary with the customer, I went over to him and asked tetchily, 'Can I help at all? Oh, it's you.'

'I saw you through the window and thought I'd say hello.'

He could not possibly have seen me through the window, rows of bookshelves being in the way, but those beautiful brown eyes focused on me, neutralizing my anger, making me wonder what it must be like to see such a handsome face gazing back at you in the mornings from the shaving mirror. 'What did you think of the Give and Take?' I asked abruptly. 'Though you weren't there for long. You walked out with my flatmate, remember?'

The comment did not throw him at all. 'Well... you introduced us.'

'Did I? You and I were talking, he came over, I blinked a couple of times and the next thing you two were going through the door together.'

'He's a fast worker. We were having a chat, you and me, but you didn't seem all that interested. When your flatmate arrived you did something weird. You sort of screwed up your face. You tried to hide it with your hand, but I could see. It's okay, your flatmate explained all about it.'

'Explained what exactly?' I asked, suspecting that Dale had told him I was cursed with an uncontrollable facial twitch.

'That you're a bit nervous with strangers and need time to relax. I know how you feel, I used to be the same. Anyway, this is the third time we've met. You shouldn't be so nervy now.'

'I'm perfectly okay.'

'Good. How about meeting me one evening?'

I should have told him to piss off, but his looks had charmed away my resentment. 'That would be nice,' was what I actually said.

We met at a pub he knew, and ate at a self-service Chinese restaurant. He said he worked as a personal fitness trainer, and had some clients at a very exclusive club, but would not say more. 'Can't talk about clients,' he said, making a gesture with an open palm suggestive of pushing away my tentative queries. Somehow he made even this negative signal appear attractive.

We finished eating and he took me back to my old flat, now his. The Jays' sound system was clearly audible. He had me lie on the bed fully clothed and lay on top of me, then after a few minutes of caressing and fondling said, 'Let's get undressed now.' He knew what he wanted sexually, and I was happy to do whatever pleased him. Afterwards, as I was getting ready to leave he asked for my phone number. This might not have meant anything – some men who have lots of casual pick-ups swap numbers after sex because it makes for an easy exit – but my spirits soared.

Three

Should I have said something to Dale about my date with Toby? He might think I was taking revenge on him for coolly charming my prize away at the Give and Take. Better surely to say nothing; Toby might have decided one night with me was enough. Although my constant hope was to find a boyfriend, for months and months my love life had not progressed further than casual one-nighters.

I left a 'See u again?' message on Toby's phone the next day. For more than a week no reply came; clearly he was not yearning for my company. Then at last he rang, and asked me to go to a club in South London with him that same evening. I said yes, trying to sound moderately pleased, while hiding the euphoria that hearing his voice again had engendered.

The club was a short walk from Brixton underground station. Mixed straight and gay, it had everything to make a great night out – good dance music, terrific lights, and an attractive crowd full of life. Not knowing who you might run into in a new club is part of the excitement. Toby had lots of friends there. He used his phone every few minutes to send or receive messages. At first I thought he was contacting people outside, but seeing so

34

many inside the club use their phones, then gesture to friends across the room, I realized that most of these messages were to other clubbers. They were the most practical way of communicating, since making yourself heard over the loud music was near impossible.

As often as not, when he received a message, he went off to see someone on the crowded dance floor, and would come back to me after ten minutes or so. Once he disappeared for about twenty minutes, and I sent him the text message 'gon ome ave u?' He came back and opened his hand to show me some pills.

'Want one?'

'What are they?'

'Specials. Like Ecstasy. New love drug.'

The incident of Jake lying unconscious in the bath did not encourage me to try suspect pills. Anyway, being with a man as stunning as Toby was enough of a love drug for me; no chemical assistance was required. 'I don't need it.'

'Suit yourself,' he said, and put one in his own mouth.

What made him so sure, I wondered, that what he was taking was a new love drug, and not something meant for worming cats? His willingness to take a god-knows-what-might-be-in-it pill surprised me.

Soon the noise and flashing lights became overpowering. The club had filled up, and the bigger crowd made the atmosphere frenetic. Up at the bar I had to shout my order several times to be heard. Beer frothed over the top of the plastic glass onto a bar surface already awash with liquid. A lad so young he was probably still at school jostled his way past me in a dash for the toilets, slopping everyone's drinks as he hurried by. He threw up, slipped over and crashed to the floor, his legs splayed out in his vomit. An older guy helped him up and pushed him towards the exit, his adventures over for the night. No one tried to clear up the mess.

Thinking this might be a good time to leave, I shouted to Toby, 'Things are getting a bit frantic.' He pulled me into the middle of the dancers, where somehow we found enough space to move our limbs a little in time with the music. Happiness at being with him returned. Everyone could see we were together, that I was with the most stunning guy in the place.

During a brief lull in the sound he said, 'There's someone I need to talk to. Shouldn't take long. After that we'll go.'

He passed the patch of vomit, now marked by a sign saying 'Danger Wet Floor', and disappeared through the doorway leading to the toilets. Beyond them, past a couple of seats, was an outdoor area for people to smoke or cool off after the heat of the club. What was he doing out there? Dealing in drugs? When he came back he said, 'Had enough of this?'

'Yes.'

Outside he asked, 'What did you think of the club?'

'Great. Exciting – a bit hectic.'

'You need to unwind more, Ben. Take an Ecstasy or have a few lagers before you go in.'

'Oh, well… I'm not dragging you away?'

'I've seen the people I came to see. So what now? My place or yours? Suppose I could say your old place or your new place?'

At Fulrose Court we might, of course, encounter Dale, so we went to the flat that had once been mine and was now his. The Jays must have gone out, for the house was quiet. In the main room Toby said 'Let me undress you,' as though I was the one whose looks made an inch-by-inch exposure of flesh thrilling. He said, 'Wide shoulders, slim hips, yes, you'll do for me.' He made me feel more attractive and desirable than anyone ever had before, but how much of his desire was due to me, rather than the 'love drug' he had taken?

'That's it, keep still,' he said as he struggled with the button on the waistband of my jeans. Though I held my tummy muscles taught, he continued to fumble. I wanted to help but he pushed my hand away and lightly smacked my thigh. 'No, keep still now. Let me.' I suppose he wanted to be in control, but as it took him about two minutes to undo that one button it was a strange bit of foreplay. Still, anything that pleased him was enjoyable for me too. Any doubts about what he had been up to in the club vanished in the glow of making love.

After sex he said, 'Now be a good boy and go and make me some coffee.' I had to hunt for the mugs and coffee jar, as they were not where I used to keep them.

Going out with him always meant spending more money than usual. He would call a cab, even when a bus would have been almost as quick. His favourite club charged admission, and their drinks were expensive compared with the Give and Take. It was not somewhere you could go wearing any old clothes. Hard up after a particularly extravagant night out, I asked Dale if he would mind waiting a week for a contribution to the kitty for cleaning materials and household items — only a few pounds. As we had a good stock of essentials this was no big problem, but it meant him knowing I was out of money. He offered me a loan, but on my modest pay, borrowing would only put off the hardship until later. Economies were the only answer. If necessary I might even have to turn down a night out with Toby.

By this time I had told Dale that Toby was my boyfriend. He did not appear surprised or concerned, but inevitably our friendship suffered. Visits to the Give and Take together became less frequent, and our once regular Sunday afternoon outings became rare. We were still good friends, but inevitably time spent with Toby was time not spent with Dale.

To save money I avoided the High Street shops, where an impulse buy might be tempting, and went more often into charity shops. Most of the men's clothing they had was not worth bothering with, but the bric-a-brac and second-hand books made interesting browsing. The volunteers were usually happy to have a few minutes chat, even without me buying anything. One, that raised funds for cats' and dogs' homes, had flimsy shelves that had bent under the weight of second-hand books, mostly crime stories and other cheap fiction. On the floor underneath the bottom shelf were some cardboard boxes, full of odd items shoved down there out of the way. From the bottom of one of these I extracted a huge old hardback. It turned out to be a *Complete Works of William Shakespeare*, printed in an antiquated style, the letter 's' confusingly like the modern 'f'. The lady behind the counter who served me checked inside the front and back cover but no price was marked, and she let me have it for five pounds. 'You don't happen to know where it came from?' I asked.

'Not the vaguest idea. People bring in all kinds of old cast-offs. A lot of them go directly to the bins. A book like that will always be useful, though. An aunt of mine used one that size for pressing flowers.'

In Jeremy's bookshop we had sold a couple of old volumes of Shakespeare to collectors for hundreds of pounds. Of course my find might not be worth much, but on the way home I began to feel guilty about the idea of making a profit at the expense of a charity shop. If it should turn out to be worth a fortune, a donation to the cause would ease my conscience.

Back at Fulrose Court I examined the illustration on the title page again. It was a head and shoulders engraving of Shakespeare, the alert eyes glancing to one side. Above the picture were the words *Mr William Shakespeares* (sic) *Comedies,*

38

Histories, & Tragedies, Published according to the True Original Copies.
Below was written *London. Printed by Isaac Iaggard, and Ed. Blount.*
1623. It could not, surely, be a genuine first folio edition? Copies
were worth hundreds of thousands, possibly millions. My spine
tingled. The book was old, but surely not that old. A hundred or
more years maybe, not nearly four hundred. The cover, a thick,
dark green woven fabric, had an elaborate embossed design,
which was very even and regular. It had surely been machined
rather than hand tooled. Imagine, if a genuine sixteen-twenty-
three folio edition of Shakespeare really had somehow been left
in the bottom of a charity shop box. If only that were possible.
My purchase might go for auction at Christie's or Sotheby's. Was
it conceivable, even, that the pages of a seventeenth century
book might have been rebound in a Victorian cover? If only.
Thinking that was as pointless as dreaming of being as
handsome as Toby or as sensible as Dale.

In the bookshop, Jeremy's professional eye quickly assessed
my discovery. He wasted no time in bringing my pipe dreams to
an end. After all of twenty seconds he said, 'It's in excellent
condition. A Victorian copy, of course. You realized that, I hope.
You didn't pay a lot for it?'

'Five pounds,' I said flatly, suddenly fearing the charity shop
might have done well to get that much for it.

'Oh, well done. It's not bad. A charity shop, eh? Always worth
keeping your eyes open. If you want to sell I'll get you at least
fifty for it, easily, at the next book fair. You're developing the
knack for this business, aren't you Ben?'

He was good-hearted, and using his knowledge of the trade
would get me a fair price, keeping nothing for himself. 'By the
way,' he said, 'The Booksellers' Guild's annual dinner is in a few
weeks' time. Be nice if you came along. Help to give you a
broader picture. As well as rare book dealers, quite a few of the

independent booksellers will be there.'

'Errrh, nice of you to ask, but I don't have clothes for a formal dinner,' I said, thinking that the event sounded boring.

'The Booksellers' Guild dinner is not an occasion for formal attire. Smart casual... newish jeans... will be fine. You really should come. The after dinner speaker will be the veteran novelist Loyd Larcher. I know him slightly.'

'Do you know many famous people, Jeremy?' I asked.

'No. I met him at a chiropody clinic.'

'A *chiropody* clinic? You've never said anything about having trouble with your feet.'

'I'd dropped a heavy box of books and broke a toe nail. At least it got Larcher and me off on a good footing,' he said laughing.

I could have followed up with a comment about *corny jokes*, but it might have sidetracked us into *hitting the nail on the head* or *needing to keep instep*. Instead I asked, 'We don't have anything of his in the shop, do we?'

'He hasn't published anything for years. I think we sold the only book of his we had. *Not a Rennie More, Not a Rennie Less,* I think it was.'

'Strange title.'

'Yes. It was about industrial espionage in the pharmaceutical industry. One of the big suppliers made a fuss, threatened a lawsuit over the use of their trade name. If you really want to read something of his, I might have his saga of North Sea fishing at home, *Not a Blenny More, Not a Blenny Less*, though it wasn't his best book, in my view.'

'Blenny? A little fish that's not much sought after?'

'Exactly.'

A few days later he proudly showed me the invitation card to the Guild's dinner. Below the details, printed in scrolled decorative letters, the words *Jeremy Stimplebaum and Guest* had been added in light blue ink in beautiful copperplate handwriting.

On the day of the event I put on a clean shirt and my newest jeans; he wore a black polo neck with a gold pendant, and amazingly baggy trousers with acres of dark twill cloth between waist and knee. I could not decide if this garment had come from an expensive boutique for more mature men, or if it had been handed down by a very elderly relative. Fortunately, among fellow members of the guild, we did not appear particularly odd. Some of the women wore necklaces with beads the size of golf balls, while others sported highly ornate spectacles that covered half their faces. The suits that some of the men wore were like heirlooms left over from the days of the Boer War. They had probably been stored in mothballs for generations. Several fifty-plus men had long hair tied back in thin greying pony-tails.

Larcher himself, like other dignitaries at the top table, wore a dinner jacket. I guessed he was in his seventies, his hair white above a very pink face. The Guild's members and their guests sat at four long tables running the length of the hall. Several same-sex couples arrived, making me worry that people would think I was Jeremy's bit of stuff.

As the meal progressed, large quantities of wine were consumed. The booksellers talked more and more freely, and the noise level rose steadily. The Guild's chairman tapped his glass and knocked loudly on the table to call for quiet. To thin applause Larcher rose to speak. He embarked on a merciless tirade against modern novelists. Among his accusations were that thin material was padded out to five hundred or more pages, as though a book's worth could be measured by the kilogram, that modern novelists had nothing to say worth the effort of reading, and that their books were mere ornaments, purchased to match the colour of the lounge curtains. Modern fiction was, he claimed, bought as a shelf-filler to impress guests, destined never be taken down and read, the output of a small and shrinking band of self-proclaimed literati, or of hacks who conspired with greedy publishers to peddle tripe to people with third-class brains.

'Wow. Is he always like this?' I asked Jeremy, after Larcher had finished speaking.

'He knows his audience.'

A sharp-faced woman opposite overheard us, gulped down half a glass of red, and leaning forwards said, tripping over her words, 'He's too soft on them. If you want my opinion of modern authors, they should be g-gutle-gulleted like fish.'

'I know what you mean,' Jeremy said. He turned quickly to me. 'Great thing about Loyd these days is, since he's no longer writing, he can say what he likes.' He grabbed my arm, accidentally bonking me on the head with his gold pendant as he stood up. 'Come on, if I know him he'll be off now he's earned his fee.' He pulled me to my feet and hurried me towards the side entrance. We were just in time catch Loyd on his way out.

'Jeremy! How long has it been? Who's this you've got in tow, you old rascal?'

'Let me introduce Ben, who works at the bookshop. He loves books. He's my right-hand man. He kindly came along to keep me company, on condition that I did my utmost to bring him before you.'

This was not true; in fact, had Jeremy not pressed me to go I would not have been there at all. A smiling Larcher grasped my hand warmly. 'Is that so? Right-hand man, no less. Lucky to have help like him Jeremy, in that wonderful cultural emporium of yours. How is business these days?'

'It's much better since Ben joined my little enterprise.'

'Matter of fact, I could use a bit of help with some work that

42

is in the offing. Just a few hours administrative, clerical type of stuff for a week or two, nothing more exciting I'm afraid, but the fee could be a couple of hundred, and the work can be fitted in to suit you. If Jeremy has no objection, Ben, dear chap, are you interested? Good. I'll be in touch.' He gave me his card and strode out through the side door.

I was so delighted at the prospect of assisting the famous Larcher that I could have given Jeremy a kiss, except that it would confirm any suspicions the diners had about us.

Telling Toby about the dinner, or meeting Loyd Larcher, would have been pointless. He was only ever interested in things relevant to his immediate needs. Even the Give and Take, with its mixed age group, he referred to as 'that old dive you used to go to, more dead than alive.' Other gay pubs, clubs and venues were an essential part of his world, but not the one where I had been a regular. To make a change from going to his favourite bars, I persuaded him to meet me at Hammersmith Bridge one Sunday afternoon, hoping he would like the busy riverside path. However he was not interested in any of the lively pubs we passed, not even those where we could have sat facing the river. After half an hour he was bored, and could not be bothered to visit the monument to the painter Hogarth in the graveyard of the old village church at Chiswick. We walked glumly on, coming to the path below terraces where, once a year, people stood to watch the 'Oxbridge' Boat Race. He asked pointedly 'Are we going anywhere, or are we just walking?'

His reaction, when I said we would reach a big pub after we crossed Chiswick Bridge, was a bored shrug. My attempts at conversation met with little or no response. Was this his way of telling me he was simply not interested in going anywhere at all that I might suggest?

When we were walking across the bridge a spectacular road accident took place right in front of us. It began when a lorry pulled forward sharply, and shed seven or eight sacks of building materials. They lay on the road and partly across the footpath at the side. Unaware of leaving this hazard behind, the driver did not stop. Cars swerved haphazardly to avoid the obstruction, and disaster soon followed. One car bounced over a sack in the road, then crossed the central white line, forcing an oncoming van to swing sharply left. Mounting the footpath, it hit a pile of several sacks and careered over the parapet, plummeting into the river. It landed in three or four feet of water. The driver opened the cab door, saw us and shouted for help.

I held up my phone and shouted back, 'I'll call 999.' After I had called the police, Toby and I rushed back along the bridge to the bank. The driver had lowered himself into the river and was wading towards us. With my camera phone I took some pictures of him, his partly immersed van in the background. His clothes were soaking wet. 'Are you all right?' I asked. 'I've called the police. Should we get an ambulance?'

'Fucking car was coming straight at me. Nothing I could do, not a fucking thing.'

I suggested he sat down on a low wall nearby. He was a fit-looking man in his late thirties. After a few deep breaths he cursed, 'Fucking bridge, fucking Sunday deliveries, fucking river, fucking soaking, fucking shite all over the fucking road.'

'You sure you're not hurt?'

'Shook up, but no. Couple of bruises maybe.' He sat quietly for a minute or so. 'Thanks for stopping. No other fucker did. You got through on the phone?'

'Yes. You see, over there, that's a police launch on its way. I got a few pictures.'

I showed them to him and he said, 'Not bad. The fucking van

44

can stay in the river for all I care. Sorry. Take no notice of me. Suppose it could have been worse. At least it was the return trip with an empty van.' When he stood up his wet trousers clung to his skin and he pulled the cloth loose. Defying misfortune he joked, 'Suppose it'll save having a bath, won't it?'

I laughed, glad he felt recovered enough to make a joke. Toby, however, was becoming edgy. He said, 'Listen mate, we're already late. Help's on its way. You mind if we…'

'Yeah, no need for you to hang about. Do you have a phone number, in case I need a witness?'

I gave him mine, and agreed to send him the pictures from my phone. We shook hands. It was mean to leave him like that, but Toby was already off over the bridge at speed. When I caught up with him he said, 'Began to think we'd be stuck there all day. The wet trousers turning you on, were they?'

How different he was from Dale, who had he been present would have taken charge of the situation, made absolutely sure the man was not hurt, and known exactly what to do. Over lunch in the pub I said, 'All of the times I've come down to the river, this is the first time anything really out of the ordinary has happened.'

'Oh, fantastic things happen to me all the time,' he answered. 'Quite sexy, the way his wet trousers clung, wasn't it?'

'How can you talk about the poor man like that? He was lucky not to have been badly injured, and all you can think about is his clinging wet trousers!'

'You were getting an eyeful too, don't pretend otherwise. Anyway, what about wet T-shirt competitions? Everyone thinks they're sexy. Wonder how you'd look in one? Have to get you under the shower in a T-shirt and a pair of white shorts. See what it does for you.'

Having my super-attractive boyfriend enjoy the idea of seeing me like that drove any doubts about his attitude to the accident from my mind. All I wanted was to get back to his flat to have sex.

Four

Dale had been raised in Northampton, where his parents still lived, but he had an elderly aunt in South London. Recently, due to failing health, she had given up her large suburban semi and moved into a care home. He was prevailed upon to clear out her belongings so the house could be sold.

His aunt was keen on crime fiction and had accumulated hundreds of books, so he asked me to go down to see if they were worth anything. He had been rather low lately because of more delays with the the new hospital laundry, and I was happy to go, if only to keep him company.

There is no real money to be made from second-hand mass market paperbacks. If she owned a good dictionary, atlas, encyclopaedia, or collectable cookery books Jeremy might get his wallet out, but he would not want ordinary detective stories. Dale knew of an old family Bible, but another relative was keen to take that as an heirloom.

We travelled by train from Victoria Station to a suburb with streets and streets of semi-detached houses. His aunt's, with a large bow window and Tudor-effect boards on the façade, was one of two hundred in a long avenue. We went in and he showed me several rooms with shelves full of books. I picked a few paperbacks out at random – some crime fiction and a romantic novel. 'Not really stuff for an antiquarian bookshop; may be more a question of someone taking them off your hands.'

He pointed to an Agatha Christie. 'She's still popular.'

'On TV, certainly. Paperback reprints of her books are common. Trouble is they're two a penny. Your aunt took good care of them, but rarity is what makes an old book valuable. These paperbacks may have been precious to the old lady, but sentimental value doesn't convert into cash.'

He pointed out some book club editions of Dickens, attractively bound in leather. 'What about these?'

'They'll fetch something, but you can probably still get the same or very similar editions new, so they're not hugely sought after. No disrespect to your aunt, but I wonder if they've ever been read?'

He was disappointed. Not wanting to be insensitive, in a more kindly tone I said, 'This place is really homely, well cared for, she must have loved it here.'

'Yes, it meant so much to her. When I was a kid I used to love coming to visit. She had things hidden away in the cupboards, playing cards, old board games, even a film projector. The garage and garden sheds were packed with stuff. She used to let me explore. Wanted to keep me out of mischief, probably.'

Part of his childhood was going with the sale of the house. No wonder he was sad. I reached out and touched his shoulder sympathetically. Suddenly serious he said, 'To change the subject dramatically, Ben, there is something…'

Before he finished, I happened to glance down, and noticed on a low shelf a hardback with Loyd Larcher's name on the spine. 'What's this?' I broke in, bending to pick up the book. It was *Not a Jenny More, Not a Jenny Less*. A quick glance inside told me it was published in nineteen-sixty-two. No reprints were listed, and I realized that in my hands was an unblemished first edition, complete with dust jacket. The first sentence of the blurb read: *When two cousins with the same name fall in love with the same man, an astonishing intrigue develops.*

'We might be on to something here, Dale, this is a first edition. I told you, didn't I, that Loyd Larcher was the speaker at that dinner Jeremy took me to? He gave me his card, though we've not been in contact again.'

'Oh yes, Loyd Larcher. He was quite famous, wasn't he?'

'Your aunt might have been one of his fans. Let's see if she has any others.' We searched the bookcases and pulled out more Larcher first editions, together with other books that ought be worth more than a pittance. Among them were a dozen or more biographies, several cookery books and some lavishly illustrated volumes on astrology. They were enough to make it worth asking Jeremy what he thought.

'I'd better let my aunt know, in case she wants to keep any. I'll ring her tonight. She doesn't have much space for her personal stuff.'

'You don't want anything yourself?'

'I'm getting the hall clock for clearing the house. It's a good one. Other members of the family have had china, bits of furniture, old family photos. When the house is sold the money will be invested to help pay for her care. She's not expecting much for the books.'

The next day I showed Jeremy the list of potentially valuable books we had found. 'Well done, Ben, this is very professional. Have a word with Dale and fix a time for us to go round. Best if it's out of shop hours. I'll offer a good price, but don't build up his expectations. The Loyd Larchers are promising. You seldom see his political novel about the population explosion, *So Very*

Many More, Not So Many Less, for sale. Most of the list, though, are not what you would call rare books… difficult to know what they'd fetch.'

We fixed up an evening for the three of us to go to the house in Jeremy's van. The passenger seat was just large enough for two. I sat in the middle, unable to move further towards Jeremy because of the handbrake, and trying not to lean too hard on Dale when we cornered. Jeremy talked all the time about how he admired people who did socially valuable jobs in the National Health Service, about how demanding the work must be, and how generally underrated the public sector was. Then he made me cringe with embarrassment by saying, 'and of course it's good to know that someone sensible and reliable is looking after Ben.'

Dale leaned comfortingly towards me and said, 'We look after each other. It's a good arrangement.'

When we reached the house we took in empty cardboard boxes and put them on the floor of the lounge. Jeremy checked through the copies of Loyd's novels. 'Yes,' he said, 'I think she has them all, every one. Splendid… every one a first edition in top condition. Not signed though.' He sniffed the pages of one of them, something he occasionally did to books in the shop. 'First editions of this one,' he continued, '*Not a Benny More, Not a Benny Less*, are very hard to come by. It's about benzedrine addiction in the nineteen-fifties. Most of the print run was lost in a fire at the distributor's warehouse. Only a few dozen survived. Reprints have sold well though, plenty of them around.'

'Do Loyd Larcher's books smell nice, Jeremy?' I asked.

'Oh, a book of that age doesn't have much smell. You would pick me up on that, wouldn't you? Now Dale will think I spend half my time sniffing books. Very occasionally, say if an old book has been rebound, you can smell the solvents from the adhesive, but not enough to give a glue sniffer a kick. Die-hard book lovers enjoy the fresh smell of a new book, it's part of the obsession, I wouldn't call it substance abuse.'

Dale said, 'I probably shouldn't ask, but would the Larchers be worth more if he could be persuaded to sign them now?'

'As a general rule a signed copy is worth a bit more, but it's something done mostly to help sales when a book comes out. Marketing people get up to all kinds of tricks. I don't know about getting him to sign them now, they've been out of print for so long. Worth letting him know this set has turned up though. I'll mention they are unsigned and see what he says. He might even know of a potential buyer.'

Having put Loyd's first editions into a box, he picked up a book on astrology and flicked over the pages. 'Ah! Someone I know will definitely be interested in this! Pack all this lot up, boys, and let me have fifteen minutes to see what's left on the shelves, in case you've missed anything.'

Dale put the kettle on for tea while I filled the boxes. Jeremy joined us in the kitchen, empty-handed and said, 'You did a thorough job, you two. I'll give you the number of a dealer who shifts a lot of old paperbacks. Tell him how many there are, and if he has space he'll make an offer. If not they will have to go to a house clearance firm. Unless you want to try selling them yourself on the internet, but I fear that would be a lot of effort for not much return.' On the way back to Fulrose Court we picked up a meal at a Chinese take-away, and Jeremy bought a bottle of good wine. By the time we had eaten we were ready to turn in.

The next day he was in a trance-like state. He must have been up half the night examining the new acquisitions. He looked as though he had slept in his clothes: his shirt was crumpled, and his tie thrown back over his left shoulder. Using the excuse that he wanted to tackle the accounts, he retired to the office once we had opened up. I checked on him after about an hour, and saw him asleep at his desk. His head, sinking down, had come to rest on top of a Loyd Larcher first edition. One of his shoe laces had come undone and straggled over the floor. I was tempted to sneak up and tie it to a leg of the desk, but chickened out, afraid he would fall and hurt himself when he stood up.

He was back to normal the next day, and rang Loyd to tell him about our discovery. The timing was bad though: a new omnibus edition of his novels due out soon and he was, understandably, too occupied with that to be much interested in our hoard. I stood by the office door hoping that my presence would remind Jeremy to ask about the work he had mentioned at the Booksellers' Guild dinner, but Loyd must have remembered it himself without being prompted, for Jeremy said, 'Yes, he is,' and waved me over to take the phone.

Loyd explained that some time ago he had agreed to judge a short story competition. He needed help as he was about to go on a lecture tour in the US to promote his omnibus edition, and would not have time to do all the work himself. He wanted me to weed out the stories that exceeded the permitted length, were in very poor English, or were religious or political tracts masquerading as stories. A few days ago the organizers had told him that several hundred entries had come in, and many more were expected before the closing date. He thought four or five days' work would be enough for me to go through and throw out the rubbish.

I had never undertaken anything like this before, but the job sounded interesting, the money would be welcome, and it would be something to add to my CV. I said, 'I'm certainly interested. What was the competition called again?'

'The Effingham and Meadowgoose International Short Story Competition.'

'Effingham and what?'

'Meadowgoose. Strange name, I know, but it is quite well known in some circles. I'm sure Jeremy will have heard of it. Have a word with him, and call me back with a definite yes or no. I'll be here the rest of the afternoon.'

Jeremy remembered seeing some leaflets about the competition years ago, in the local library. He thought lending Loyd a hand was a good opportunity for me, and offered to watch the shop for a few extra hours to free a little of my time for the work.

I called Loyd back, and he said he would bring the entries to the shop in a week's time. So that, if he happened to ask whether I had read anything of his, I could honestly say yes, I began *Not a Kilkenny More, Not a Kilkenny Less*, his novel about an Irish migrant who made a fortune in the US and named a suburb of Pittsburgh after his home town.

A week later a taxi pulled up outside the bookshop. Loyd, followed by the driver carrying three boxes of entries for the Effingham and Meadowgoose International Short Story Competition, strode into the bookshop. Jeremy, wearing a double-breasted suit, a shirt with the collar button undone and a little check scarf around his neck, fluttered around his old acquaintance. He proudly held up one of the first editions, *Not a Larceny More, Not a Larceny Less*.

'Ah yes,' Loyd said, 'the second of my two crime novels. That copy has survived the years well, better than I have.'

'You look in excellent health, everyone says so. You wouldn't care to sign it, I suppose?' Jeremy's public school accent was more noticeable than usual, his vowels somehow sounding rounded and staccato at the same time.

'Be glad to. Since you have the complete set, I may as well do them all. Give me a bit of book signing practice for when the omnibus edition comes out.'

'Gosh, that would be stupendous… I really shouldn't put you to so much trouble.' He passed Loyd the one he held in his hand; I supplied a pen. 'Such a virtuoso demonstration of how crime narrative can be used to reveal the intrinsic nature of the major characters,' Jeremy warbled as he watched Loyd sign.

The author's pink face glowed with satisfaction at this blatant flattery, and not to be outdone he responded in similarly ringing tones: 'You know I always wish I had made time to develop a little business acumen. You've achieved that rare ambience here that can be found only in a good bookshop. One has the sense of being in a treasure house where time simply melts away.'

Jeremy nodded to me and I brought the stack of first editions and put them down beside Loyd. He signed and handed each one to me after doing so. They continued to preen one another with cringe-making compliments. Then they remembered old times for nearly half an hour, until Loyd suddenly glanced at his watch and said, 'Good heavens, going to be late for a luncheon engagement. The competition! So good of you, Ben, to agree to help. If you could have a bit of a shuffle through the entries and sort out, say, eight to a dozen that are not too bad. I'll take it from there when I return from across the pond. All strictly between us, of course. One thing, no clever mummy stories please, can't abide them. Here's twenty per cent of your fee as confirmation of our arrangement, if that's acceptable?'

'Oh, yes, thank you,' I said, surprised to be paid money in advance. He handed me a cheque and headed for the door, leaving Jeremy extremely pleased with himself, and me alarmed at not knowing more about what was wanted of me. 'Why has he given me an advance?'

'He's wily. Accepting a payment means you have entered into a legally binding contract. If you changed your mind, it would be difficult for you to back out. Keep the cheque in your pocket if you're having doubts.'

'No, not doubts about taking the job on. What did he mean by "clever mummy" stories.'

'Really don't know. Something to do with Egyptian mummies coming back to life and terrorizing archaeologists, perhaps? No... he can't have meant that.'

The answer to my question became clear when I read the first few stories. Most were about, and probably written by, mothers with young children. One began *This was the first time Jemima had come home from school with green hair*, had anxious mummy and teacher discussing how Jemima was being led astray by the class minx, and ended with clever mummy inviting her daughter's errant school friend for a break in the family's holiday cottage in the Cotswolds, thereby bringing out the little tyke's better side. Oh what a clever mummy she was!

That evening I stayed behind at the flat, working on the competition entries while Dale went to the Give and Take. When he returned alone, I said cheekily, 'No luck tonight then?'

'Come on, how often have you seen me pick someone up in the Give and Take? Once, that's all. The way you talk you would think I was anybody's.'

This was a good reply, and he watched me struggle to think of a follow up that would not be another unfair dig. After a pause I said, 'No one at the Give and Take could rival those guys in your computer game, could they?'

He sat down beside me on the sofa and asked, 'How are you getting on with the competition?'

'Started on it.'

'Maybe I should put something in for it. I write stuff for the hospital newsletter.'

'You've missed the closing date for this year. Anyway, what would you call it? *Hospital Laundry Blues?*'

'I've written about much more than the hospital laundry. Finding the time would be my problem.'

'I don't really know what I'm supposed to be doing. Maybe Loyd Larcher should have asked you to help him.'

'How many stories do you have to go through?'

'Three boxes.'

'You don't know how many, do you? Suppose you aim to do ten a day, a hundred would take you ten days. If there are a thousand, you will need a hundred days. You ought to count them and draw up a timetable.'

This suggestion was so obviously sensible I felt stupid for not having thought of it. Do people like Dale understand how irritating they are when they come up with good ideas like that? Did the National Health Service run courses on how to be cleverer than everybody else? How utterly different he was from Toby, whose answer to a problem would most likely be taking some pills or snorting some coke.

Dale said he had arranged to spend the coming weekend with an old friend on the other side of London. Toby too was away visiting family. This left me with Sunday free to work on the stories, and I did as Dale suggested and counted them. There were more than eight hundred. Skimming through half a dozen quickly gave me a headache and took nearly half an hour. One of them was about a christening, two were about weddings, two about experiences in hospitals, and the last was a long address to the congregation at the funeral of 'Charlie' who in the last sentence was revealed to be a pet dog. I had a strong feeling I had read something very like it years ago.

A quicker way had to be found. Would it be fair to read only the first few sentences, and drop any without a strong beginning? Doing that all day and most of the evening got me about half way through the stack of entries. About one out of ten were good enough to be read more thoroughly.

I was thinking of going down to the Give and Take for the last hour before closing when Dale returned. He brought with him a newspaper that carried an exposé of Loyd Larcher. Under the headline 'AUTHOR ROCKED BY SEX AND MONEY SCANDALS', the article claimed that Loyd had hired a male 'model' to pose for erotic photographs, plied him with alcohol and made 'improper suggestions'. The veteran author was also said to have misled the publisher of his first novel into believing he was an Oxford don, to have got one of his books onto the best-seller list by inflating sales figures through a scam with a now defunct book club, and to have accepted a large advance from a politician's widow for her husband's biography, which he never intended to write and of which she saw only a few fragments before her own demise. The paper's picture of the male 'model', a smiling young man in a lounge suit with salon-styled hair, must have been decades old. None of the scandals was recent.

At the bookshop the next day Jeremy read the exposé and commented, 'Seeing all this old muck about Loyd in print again makes me despair of the press. He may have got up to a few tricks in his time, but this is totally misleading. I happen to know he was relying on the politician's widow for material for that biography. When she died the decision to abandon it was taken by the publisher, not Loyd, who had put in a lot of time for little recompense. None of this is new. Ignore it, that's my advice. How are you getting on with the competition?'

I told him that there was not enough time to read through all the entries. He at once suggested ringing Loyd in the US to ask his advice. He found, searching on the internet, that Loyd was due to speak at the University of Buffalo, rang their number and handed me the phone. While I was waiting to be put through, Jeremy thought it very funny to say that he did not understand why buffaloes needed a university, as he thought hunters had wiped them all out years ago.

Luckily Loyd was on the premises. He cheerfully dismissed my worries about the number of competition entries. 'Good heavens Ben, you mustn't try to read them all, you'll drive yourself mad, you silly boy. Have a shuffle through and find me about a dozen or twenty that aren't too bad, that's all I asked you to do. Throw out any that are too long, any claptrap about elves and goblins or child magicians, and then ditch all the clever mummy stories. Shuffle through the others to find me some that are written in good English, preferably a bit of variety, original fantasy, people coping with life's crises, I don't mind the odd love story, or some humour, whatever. Am I making sense?'

'Yes, of course, I've rejected quite a few "clever mummy" stories already. On a different subject, I'm not sure whether you know, but some awful stuff about you has appeared in the newspapers over here. Jeremy says it's all old gossip.'

'I knew some ancient scandals were about to get a fresh airing. You're too young to remember, but years ago some murky rumours about me were reported in the press. My publisher is responsible for reviving them. He has someone who specializes in feeding juicy titbits to journalists. The omnibus edition is due out in a couple of weeks, and with me over here out of reach they're giving the press hacks a lot of bullshit to get publicity.

'They've provided me with a statement, denying everything as stale old gossip based on malice and misunderstandings. Sad fact, but scandal has become the best way to sell books these days. A dear friend of mine came off far worse. His publisher forced him to go into politics to keep his name in front of the public. Modern publishers have absolutely no scruples about what they force us to do. Well, must go. Have to sing for my supper while I'm over here, you know.'

Over the next few weeks I continued to work on the competition as conscientiously as the time allowed. Dale offered to read through some of them, and I gave him one with gay characters, an amusing story about two men trying too hard to impress each other. He read that and liked it, and then showed me an article of his in an old hospital newsletter about the treasurer of the staff holiday club stealing the funds, as if the Effingham and Meadowgoose material was not too much to cope with already. 'If I changed the setting and the names, would it stand a chance as a competition entry?' he asked.

'You're not trying to get me to sneak it onto my shortlist, are you?'

'No. I was thinking of, perhaps, putting it in for next year.'

Five

One night Smiles turned up at Toby's South London club. By this time the faces of many of the regulars were familiar to me, though I seldom spoke to any of them. Smiles, out of his usual haunt, was relieved to see someone he knew. 'So this is where you've been choosing to spend your time – and money,' he said.

Hanging round as usual waiting for Toby, I was glad to see him. 'Toby's choice. This place is his playing field.'

'Playing the field, more like?' He nodded towards my boyfriend, who was dancing with a sweet-faced girl I had never seen before. People mostly danced without touching, in whatever little free space they could find, but Toby and the girl were holding each other close, rubbing their bodies suggestively against one another. In that place, jealousy over a bit of flirtatious showing off would be bizarrely possessive.

'He knows all the regulars. At times it's as if he knows the whole of London. A change for you, coming here.'

To talk more easily we walked past the toilets to the open area outside. He had come because the owners of the Give and Take were planning a new late night venue, and wanted him to investigate the competition.

'This place always fills up,' I said. 'It's buzzing, I'll say that for it, but how to go about creating the buzz to start with… The scene is not really for me, too frenetic, I'm not the right person to talk to about what draws people in.'

'I expect they're making money though, takings on the door are probably good… wonder what the drink sales are like. High prices. You see people come in, meet friends, dance, some of them go to the bar, some not. A venue like this becomes the place to be seen, but it won't necessarily last, a new club opens and people go there instead… or troublemakers drive away the decent customers. Late night clubs are so different to the Give and Take, where it's a friendly bar and there's hardly ever any trouble. Bet the Gay Symphony Orchestra are not coming in here to rehearse. No prospect of toying with a trombonist tonight.'

'You've moved on from the clarinettist, then.'

'There's a whole orchestra for me to play with, remember.'

'You're as bad as Toby.'

'I'd forgotten how you always take everything literally. What I'd really like now is someone steady in my life. Working at the Give and Take there's too much temptation.'

We went back inside to find the club busier than before. 'I wonder how many are crammed in tonight. Bet there are more than health and safety rules permit,' he said. 'Don't look round, but a woman over there has just pointed at you. Now she's heading this way. Boy with her is not bad.'

That the Jays should turn up was no surprise. The club was mixed straight and gay, and their type of place. I introduced them to Smiles as 'the couple with the music system'. He asked them if they missed having me as a neighbour.

Jayde said, 'He still comes round to his old flat sometimes, but he doesn't come up to see us. We get told plenty though.' She turned to me. 'No use you thinking you've got away from us that easy. Does Toby know you're here at his club with your friend?'

'He's over there,' I said, waving towards him.

'Oh yeah,' she said. 'Busy as usual.'

'Why don't we all dance?' Jake suggested.

We found enough space on the floor for the four of us. After a couple of minutes Smiles danced up close to me. Speaking loudly in order to be heard, he said in my ear, 'I wouldn't mind finding myself in a dark corner with your friend Jake. Bet she keeps him on a short lead. Guess I've seen enough of the club. Would it be okay if I leave you to it? I gave him a thumbs up and mouthed 'Yes.' The Jays were making regular eye contact with me and smiling. Even after he had gone, with them for company I felt more at ease in that place than usual. Toby, at the other end of the room, waved to us, but made off in another direction to see one of his regular contacts.

The club was always hot, and dancing made us hotter still. The Jays followed me to the bar to get drinks, and I leaned forwards so the barman could hear me. Jake was so close behind me I could feel him against my back. He reached out an arm to take his drink from the bar and leaned firmly on me. A lot of straight men think that to act a bit gay now and again shows how cool they are, so I ignored him. No one took much notice, not even Jayde who was right next to us. I turned around to face him. 'How you doing, mate?' he asked, looking me in the eye. He put his hands on either side of me on the bar surface, pinning me to the spot.

She regarded us calmly and said, 'Good in here, isn't it Ben? Like, it's a nice free and easy type of place.'

His face was two inches from mine. He said, 'You come here because Toby drags you along, don't you? Ever thought it was time to let him know he shouldn't take you for granted?'

'He's right, isn't he?' she said, putting a hand on my shoulder.

As she spoke, Toby came up behind him and startled him by saying, 'Put him down, you don't know where he's been.'

Jayde was ready with a riposte. 'You're lucky he's still here, the way you go off and leave him lying around. Serve you right if somebody took him home with them. We're not the only ones who've been eyeing him up.'

'He's saving himself for me. He's a good boy, aren't you Ben?' He enjoyed making me out to be gullible. What did the three of them really think of me? That I was too dim to keep up in their game of grab-every-thrill-that's-going?

Jake, suddenly serious, said in my ear, 'I know what you're thinking. We're crap, aren't we? You think us turning up is like finding you've got some dog shit stuck on your shoe.' Jayde and Toby, not able to make out fully what he said in the general din, laughed uncertainly.

His speculation about my thoughts surprised me, particularly on a night when, for the first time, their company had actually been welcome. 'No... why do you say that? I'm glad you're here.'

Toby cut in, 'That's enough. No more taking advantage of him, you two, not without my say so, anyway.' To me he said. 'Come on, we can go now, if you're ready.'

Despite feeling a wimp for doing so, I obediently followed him out.

Having left the hot stale air of the club we walked to a corner where it was easy to hail a taxi. For something to say I asked him about the woman he had been dancing with. 'Not going to be jealous because of that, are you? Who am I with now?' Then, as an afterthought, he added, 'Besides, I am bisexual, you know.'

I did not know, and thought it highly unlikely. He was no more bi than I was. He had said that to worry me, to make clear to me that he was the top dog. 'I only asked who she was,' I said sharply.

'Don't worry about her,' Toby replied. 'Her boyfriend wasn't far away. He's not someone you cross. You can forget about her.'

How sure of himself he was, thinking that seeing him with the girl had made me jealous. A denial, though, would have sounded hollow, so I said coolly, 'You never told me you were bi. Do you have a girlfriend at the moment?'

'What?'

'Do you have a girlfriend at the moment?'

He waggled his hand in a maybe, maybe not gesture, unable to think of a smart answer. The topic was evidently closed. This was how he was all the time. Scoring points was the closest he came to meaningful conversation. When we were back at his flat we shagged without much enthusiasm; more than ever we seemed to share nothing except sex. Being with him was, I supposed, better than having no boyfriend at all.

During the last few weeks there had been odd mornings when Dale had not been around, a sign he was staying overnight with pick-ups, or possibly that he too had found a boyfriend. He had not volunteered any information, but why should he, since I never talked to him about my relationship with Toby? We had other things to talk about; he was interested in my progress with the Effingham and Meadowgoose International Short Story Competition, at times making me feel as though he was supervising, as if it was one of his projects at work. Hearing that Loyd had told me by phone to 'shuffle through and find a dozen stories that weren't bad,' he let me know he did not approve. All of the stories, he said, ought to be read through by several people and assessed against an agreed list of criteria.

This idea was reasonable, but it would have taken lots more time than Loyd, who clearly wanted only minimum effort, had allowed. If Dale had been organizing the competition from the start he might have argued for a fairer system and talked Loyd round, but to change the process now would be impracticable.

He must have guessed what was going through my mind, for he said: 'Always so easy to tell someone else how they should do things, but nothing I have to deal with myself is ever simple. The way you're doing it is more spontaneous, perhaps it's right for the competition. The thing is… you know if you want a bit of help with anything, or just to talk to someone, do ask me if I can help, I will. Have you found any more stories with a gay theme?'

'Yes, one. And it's one of the better ones. Good enough for the shortlist, I think.'

'Changing the subject, there is something I wanted to ask you, as a favour.'

'Go on.'

'You know my aunt, the one in the nursing home whose books you sorted out? I've mentioned having a new flatmate a couple of times, and that we're friends. Well, last time I went to see her she said, if you could find time one day, she would like to meet you. I know you're busy with the competition now, and going to a nursing home to see an elderly relative of mine is lot to ask. You don't have to, I'll understand if you'd rather not.'

He must have said nice things to her about me, and of course I said yes. He took me down to the home, near Kingston-upon-Thames, on a Thursday afternoon. On our way to the front door, through the windows we could see in the sitting room several old ladies in big armchairs watching television, and others staring through the windows at the world outside. To my eyes they were not noticeably older than Loyd Larcher, who went on lecture tours in the US, had his omnibus edition coming out and was judge of a short story competition. The home's residents had, apparently, settled into a much more limited kind of existence.

Dale's aunt had her own room, on the first floor. She got up slowly from her chair to welcome us. Her hair was iron-grey and her skin sallow, but she took my hand firmly and smiled, putting me at ease. 'I'm so glad you've come,' she said, 'it's lovely to have visitors.' She had an electric kettle and some cups on a tray, and made us tea. When she sat down again she said to Dale, 'Show Ben that picture of you, over there.' On a small sideboard she had half a dozen framed family photographs, and he handed me one taken of him when he was in school uniform. 'He was in the fifth form then,' she said.

He was a good-looking boy, his eyes clear and bright, his youthful skin free of blemishes. Seeing him day after day his appearance had become familiar, unremarkable, but the photo reminded me that he was attractive, and given his personality he would surely, one day, make someone a good boyfriend. Had we not started off as friends and moved on to being flatmates, perhaps he and I might have had a fling. People you come to know as friends tend to remain friends; you think of going out somewhere together, not of having sex. Only later, on the way home, did the thought come into my mind that, should Dale one day find a boyfriend, he might no longer want me as a flatmate.

His aunt asked me about the bookshop and if many of the books from her house had been sold. She also told me of the lady in the next room, who had been headmistress of an infants' school. This heavily built woman had fallen over the day before, and three of the staff were needed to help her back on her feet. Then she asked Dale to check at reception to see if the postman had brought any letters for her, a rather obvious contrivance to enable her to talk to me alone.

'I'm so pleased that Dale has someone reliable to share with,' she began. 'He was never one for being on his own. He has

66

always been good-natured, and the trouble with being good-natured is that people take advantage of you. The world has so many people who are of the opposite kind. You moving in with him has cheered him up, you know. He needed that.'

'It's very nice of you to say that. Sharing with him has been good for me too.'

'You know I'm a great fan of crime fiction. Are you two going to be like Sherlock Holmes and Dr Watson?' she asked, laughing.

'I don't think we'll ever be as famous as that.'

'Probably better not to live so dangerously.'

Dale returned with a white envelope which he handed to her. 'Oh, that's just the bank,' she said. 'Ben was telling me how much he likes the flat. Do you know, I've never seen it. Why don't you bring me a photo of it, with the two of you, of course?'

'I'm not sure if we have one,' he said.

'Well, you could take one, couldn't you?'

He promised he would, and when she began to tire, we left. As we walked to the station I said, 'She's really nice. She cares a lot about you, doesn't she? That photograph of you she has …' I almost said *you looked gorgeous*, but realized how the comment would sound and stopped myself, embarrassed. He regarded me quizzically, but at that moment my phone rang and saved me from having to end the sentence.

Loyd enjoyed his US lecture tour, and returned in good spirits. A week later, after accepting my competition shortlist without question, he had chosen the winner. He invited me to call at his flat to thank me for my help and, as he put it, to settle my account. I was worried about leaving Jeremy on his own in the shop because in the wet and windy weather of the last few days he had caught flu. He was very sensitive to draughts, and not wanting to face customers sat all morning in the office trying to do paperwork. He had swathed himself in a thick pullover, a tweed jacket, and what Smiles calls his Sherlock Holmes cape. I made him frequent hot drinks and persuaded him to let me shut the shop for a couple of hours in the afternoon while I went to see Loyd, who lived a bus ride away in a building near Regent's Park.

'Dear boy, delighted to see you,' he said, with his customary old world charm. He left me for a few minutes to bring refreshments. I admired his Sheraton furniture and Dutch landscapes until he came back carrying a laden silver tray. He said he hoped the Effingham and Meadowgoose work had not been too onerous, and I asked him what he had thought of the story about a gay couple quarrelling all the time when they were on holiday, but beginning to behave normally towards each other during their journey home.

'Oh yes, definitely one of the better ones. Had to rule it out, of course. Have to remember the political climate at the Effingham and Meadowgoose. A story with a positive attitude to gay men would never be accepted by the Committee.

'What political climate?'

'A very fundamentalist conservative group has taken over the competition. It used to be the plain old Effingham Wayzgoose Prize for Writers, run by the owner of the nearby print works. A wayzgoose, as I'm sure you know, is the print workers' Christmas festive dinner. When the works closed down the competition was taken over by the right-wing parish council and renamed. They added *International* to make it sound more important, and Meadowgoose after the nearby Goose Meadow. Not being political myself, I was in two minds about being this year's judge, but the fee is not bad and frankly, quite a few years have gone by since my last book, so a little extra money helps... well, let's say helps me pay my tailor's bills. Of course my books provided a good living for me in their day, but thrift was never one of my strong points.' He glanced around at his expensive furnishings. 'Perhaps I should be more principled, and insist on awarding the prize to the story about the same-sex couple, but at my age the enthusiasm for fighting battles… '

'Talking of your success,' I said, 'can I ask you something? You know I'm working for Jeremy in his bookshop, and obviously the job is fine, but sometimes I do wonder if it is going to be my lifelong career. Trouble is I still haven't really worked out what I want to do in life. Your novels did so brilliantly well. Did you always know that writing was the thing for you?'

'Not really. My first taste of being published was in a local newspaper. I was a journalist for some years before my first book came out. Don't ask me why it should be, but, for me, the titles have been the key to success. Incredible, but a particular form of words proved vital. You may have noticed nearly all my books are called *Not a something more, not a something less*, with the "something" always a word ending in *enny. Enny* or *eny*, it didn't matter. So long as the title conformed to that pattern, the books were successful, from *Not a Progeny More, Not a Progeny Less* to *Not an Abergavenny More, Not an Abergavenny Less*. If I strayed from that format even a little, they didn't sell. For instance, my novel about slanderous accusations raised against a peer of the realm, *Never a Calumny More, Never a Calumny Less*, was a complete flop. That is why I dried up. If you think about it, not all that many words do end in *enny or eny*.

'Afraid you won't find what I'm saying a lot of help, but whatever field you're hoping to make your fortune in, you simply have to find something that will work for you, not necessarily a catchphrase, but some memorable, striking little thing that people will remember you by, a sort of key that will open up the gate to success. You have to open your mind to the possibilities.'

He was surely well-intentioned, but his advice was rather like telling me that the secret of success was to find something or other that would help me do well. Undeniable, but not specific enough to be any use. 'Well, thanks, have to keep hunting for that key, I suppose. By the way, you didn't ever, did you, write a novel called *Not a Halfpenny More, Not a Halfpenny Less*?'

'Good Lord, never thought of that! *Not a Ha'penny More, Not a Ha'penny Less*.' He gestured oddly with his right hand as though spotting paint onto a canvas. 'Potential! It has definite potential!' A creative gleam came into his eye. 'Well, mustn't keep you, dear boy, know how busy you are.' He got up and from his desk fetched an envelope with my name on it, and a thick book wrapped in brown paper. 'What we agreed, plus a little bonus for diligence, thought you deserved it. Also advance orders for the omnibus edition of my novels are coming in well, and here you are, you're welcome to a signed copy, well done. Perhaps you and I will co-operate again on another project in the future, you never know what will come up. *Not a Ha'penny More, Not a Ha'penny Less*. Never thought of it, I'll be damned!'

On the bus home I unwrapped the book and found that above his signature he had written the message *To Ben, may he find happiness and fulfilment in his life's Odyssey.* Then I read the long list of his novels on the dust jacket:

Not a Progeny More, Not a Progeny Less
Aristocratic Giles is heir to the family estates, but to receive his inheritance he must have exactly seven children…

Not a Blenny More, Not a Blenny Less
Ruthless competition between fishermen for the biggest catch

leads to tragedy in the North Sea…

Not a Jenny More, Not a Jenny Less

Jenny believes she has found happiness with the man of her dreams, until her cousin, also called Jenny, comes to stay…

So Very Many More, Not So Many Less

As the population rises, the government introduces restrictions on numbers of offspring. The result is turmoil on the streets…

Not a Benny More, Not a Benny Less

Emerging amphetamine addiction in the nineteen-fifties leads a fashionable Harley Street psychiatrist to the depths of depravity…

Not a Kilkenny More, Not a Kilkenny Less

An Irish emigré in the US causes consternation in the city of his ancestors when he proposes to name a suburb of Pittsburgh after his home town…

Not a Larceny More, Not a Larceny Less

Two crack jewel thieves compete with each other in a series of ever more daring raids…

Not a Rennie More, Not a Rennie Less

Giants of the pharmaceutical industry engage in a ruthless war for dominance in an effervescent market sector…

Not a Villainy More, Not a Villainy Less

In the second of the author's much praised crime fiction novels, veteran burglar Chalky Fawcentry plans to go straight after a last raid, his hundredth robbery of a stately home…

Never a Calumny More, Never a Calumny Less

Ace detective Rhombus foils a malicious plot to undermine a noble and honourable Lord of The Realm with outlandish and unfounded scandal…

Not a Fennimore, Not a Fenniless

A spoof Wild West saga. In a gold rush town pillaged by Indians and lawless gunmen, two hairdressers feud over who will tend the prospectors' coiffure, until they have to join forces to avoid losing their own scalps…

Not an Abergavenny More, Not an Abergavenny Less

Worthies of the town are astonished when a delegation arrives from South America claiming to be from a thriving Welsh colony founded over a century ago in the rain forest…

Six

Toby was keen to go to a new fetish club that the Jays had told him about where everyone dressed up in rubber, leather or 'Goth' gear. He had no strong leanings towards any of those things as far as I knew, but it was somewhere new and different. He said black jeans and T-shirt, with a little macabre touch such as skull and crossbones earrings or exaggerated black eye shadow, would do as minimal costume.

I thought the club might be a good laugh, and at least it would be a change from his usual dive. For my token fetish touch I bought two push-on vampire teeth from a fancy dress shop. They were just right, not grotesquely large, but protruding over my lower lip enough to be noticed. Wearing them I stole up on Dale when he was combing his hair in the bathroom. He looked at me in the mirror, puzzled, and I opened my mouth wide and made as thought to bite his neck. 'Do you know,' he said, unperturbed by my plastic fangs, 'that mirrors do not reflect the image of vampires? It's a well-known non-fact.'

'A well-known *non-fact*?'

'Nothing to do with people turning into vampires is fact, is it?'

'Will you still think that after I've bitten you?'

'Please don't, this is a clean shirt. You look good though… I'm not being ironic… a hint of danger can be appealing. You off out somewhere?'

I told him about the new club. At first he seemed interested, but was put off on hearing that Toby and the Jays were going. Otherwise he might have let me drag him along. He was tired anyway from working even later than usual on a reorganization in the out-patient clinics. Going with him to the Give and Take for half an hour might have cheered him up, but it was too late to change my arrangement with Toby and the Jays. Reluctantly I left him to watch television, or find relief in his erotic computer game.

On reaching Toby's flat I regretted leaving Dale on his own more than ever. Toby opened the door wearing a leather kilt, black eye-shadow and black lipstick. I felt obliged to say the effect was fantastic. He clearly thought that it was wonderful, but twirling around in his stupid kilt, his face made ugly by grotesque make-up, to me he looked awful. My usual pride over being with someone so attractive would have to be suspended that night. Increasingly, what other people thought was unimportant. Whether we were happy or miserable depended ultimately on the two of us. For me the fetish club was a sideshow, an hour or two's potentially amusing distraction. For him it was evidently a big event, worth a lot of preparation.

Used to being able to have pretty well anyone he wanted, he was always self-confidant. He pushed me onto the sofa and said, 'Fuck me, those teeth do something for you. We've got time before we go. You can give me a thrill right now.'

'What about your make-up?'

'Oh, yeah, don't mess that up, be careful.' He grabbed my hand and put it under his kilt, but as he did his phone rang. He could never resist answering it straight away. After listening for a few moments he said, 'Yes, but we don't need to rush, do we… What?… Oh, okay.' He ended the call. 'Sorry, sexy. The Jays are on their way in a taxi. They're at the corner of the road.'

Like Toby, they had dressed up far more than me. Each wore a tight-fitting black latex top. His had a hood that, pulled up, covered his head except for his eyes, nose and mouth; her top had ribbed bra cups, very low at the front, exposing the upper surface of her breasts and revealing her nipples. 'You'll do,' she said to Toby. They'll all be wondering what you've got on under that kilt. But what about him? Where does he think he's going? His aunty's Hallowe'en party? Come here.' She took a stick of face paint from her handbag and told me to sit down. I submitted to having black lines painted on my cheeks and forehead. They had let their cab go, so Toby phoned for another to take us to the club. God knows what the driver must have thought as we climbed in.

When we descended the steps to the fetish bar we found only half a dozen others. Four were wearing black clothes that might have come from any high street shop; only two were in fetish gear, a man wearing a long black priest's robe, and a woman in rubber trousers with oval openings at the back that exposed half her buttocks. All had improbably black hair. Behind the bar was a mural of a moonlit Gothic ruin surrounded by bats and howling wolves. Cocktails on promotion included a sweet, gooey green liquid called triffid juice, and a purple concoction called viper's blood.

Shortly after we sat down, Jayde took a box from her bag with the words *A Gift for You* written on it and handed it to me. 'Here you are Ben,' she said, unusually sweetly. 'We spotted this in a novelty shop and thought you'd like it.' She had no reason to give me a present, and holding it at arm's length I suspiciously tugged at a flap in the wrapping on the side. With a startling whooping sound, a three foot black balloon in the shape of a phallus rose into the air in front of me. Everyone else in the bar saw what I was holding and fell around laughing.

Concealing my embarrassment and indignation, I laughed too, pretending to find the huge dick funny, and said loudly, 'Just what I've always wanted.' In a different situation I might have thought the prank funny, but in that place, in front of strangers I felt that she had humiliated me.

Jake read my true feelings and said, 'Sorry mate.' He took the balloon from me and tugged at something inside to deflate it. He patted my knee and said, 'It's just a joke, let it go. Tell you what, come and dance with me.'

'This is not a gay club, is it?'

'Come on, who's going to worry about that? That bloke in the black frock, or that woman with her arse hanging out?'

Toby wanted to check out the group at the bar and said, 'Go on Ben, let's see how you and Jake move together. Have a try at making me jealous.'

The music, more like screams of aggression than a song, was hard to dance to. Jake pulled me to him and said, 'Let's take up his challenge… try and make him jealous, what d'you say?'

'You might be the one who should worry about being jealous. The other night Toby told me he was bisexual. Maybe he fancies Jayde.'

'Everyone's supposed to be a bit bi, aren't they? Including me, in case you're wondering. See Toby and that bloke now, is he chatting him up? It's nice to have a change, sometimes, isn't it? Loosen up, Ben, don't be inhibited. Take an 'E' to help you get into it. You don't want to miss out.'

My guess was that Toby was more likely to be selling pills to the man at the bar, not chatting him up. The music of drum beats and relentless screams ended, and I broke away from Jake's arms. We went back to the table, where Jayde hurriedly finished talking to someone on her phone. 'You two were dancing very close.' she said. 'You on the turn, Jake?'

'What of it? Suppose he is someone I could go for?'

She laughed. 'Oh, get you. You'll be painting your nails next. Come and have a dance with me now, Ben. Ought to be turn and turn about, if that's how it's going to be.'

'Yeah, go on,' he said, 'I'll get in the drinks.'

While Jayde and I danced, I saw him speak briefly to Toby at the bar. The music improved; she moved well, showing a good sense of rhythm, but we did not dance close. When we rejoined Jake there were only three drinks on the table.

'I take it Toby's found other interests,' I said.

'You're all right with us,' Jake answered, 'don't bother about him. What do you think of the place?'

'Never been anywhere like this before, I'll give it that. Not many people in, though.'

'Quiet night. Seen anything you like?'

'Do I fancy anyone here, you mean? Not really.'

Halfway through the beer Jake had bought for me I began to feel extraordinarily tired. The Jays tried to get me up to dance again, but my leg muscles would not work properly and I sank back into the seat. They sounded odd, as though they were talking to me from a long distance away, and I could not make out what they were saying.

A little later Toby came over, lifted my head up, leaned over me and said in my ear, 'Ben, mate, you're all in. Jayde and Jake are going to take you back to the flat now, I've got a couple of things to do. You like Jake, don't you? He likes you. So does Jayde. Just go back with them, they'll see you're okay. I'll catch up with you later.'

My recollection of what happened after that is unclear. They must have walked me out of the club and pushed me into a taxi. Toby must have given them the keys to his flat, for I remember going in and Jayde wiping my face clean of make-up. They put me to bed, and got in with me. They did not force themselves on me, I lacked the will to refuse what they wanted me to do. It was as though the conscious, thinking, normal me was suspended and only a kind of physical, sex-toy version of me remained. I was dimly aware that I had been drugged, and this chemically modified 'me' responded to what was demanded of it, shifting from one position to another, and thrusting this way or that as required.

The next morning I woke alone in Toby's bed. My private parts were tender, leaving no question that sex had taken place. My Dracula teeth were missing. A hangover, like the after-effects of being hit hard on the head, seared my brain. A message on my mobile phone from Toby said he would be out for the day until late. The effort of reading his few words made my head pound. Finding my clothes and dressing made me feel nauseous. Recovering from that night took me all day.

Except for leaving the message on my phone, Toby did not contact me again, nor I him. Jake, however, sent me a couple of friendly messages, which I ignored. Then he rang me at work a couple of days later. Jeremy was in the shop, making it difficult for to me tell him how disgusted I was with him, and with Jayde. What I truly wanted was for the excruciating memory of being in bed with them in Toby's flat to fade as quickly as possible. He was determined to meet me, and intending to let him know my feelings I agreed to meet him the next day at lunchtime. It was a sunny day and we took sandwiches to the park nearby. He must have noticed my stern expression, for straight away he said, 'I get the feeling you're not too happy.'

'You're right about that.'

'Why not? Because Toby's went off and left you with us?' He waited for my response, but getting only a hostile glare said, 'Do you think he saves himself for you?'

'No, it's so easy for him to get anyone he wants. I did think of him as my boyfriend, even so.'

'He's the same as he's always been. Okay, let's say he's your boyfriend, but other than that he's the same old Toby, he goes with anyone he fancies. Ask yourself what's so special about him? He's got the looks, but what else? You know that he's screwing your flatmate?'

Those words 'he's screwing your flatmate' were like a smack in the face. I had assumed that he was picking other guys up, but not that he had seen Dale again. Trying, but failing, to hide my incredulity, I said, 'You seem to know a lot about it.'

'I'm in the flat upstairs. I've seen them together. Toby hasn't exactly been hiding what's going on, except from you. He plays games, he's showing off, proving he can get anyone to do whatever he wants. He boasted to me you didn't have a clue about him and Dale. He was the one who suggested Jayde and I give you a threesome to bring you out of yourself more. You acted as if you were enjoying it all right. We certainly did.'

We sat in silence for more than a minute. He shuffled his feet and sighed. 'Oh fuck. That isn't what I wanted to say to you at all. You must think I'm as big a shit as Toby is. The thing is Ben, I really do like you. I've never seriously gone for guys before. Toby and I tried it once, but it did nothing for me, it was going through the motions… an effort, probably, for him too. Once with a kid at school… I slept over at his house, we played around. Kids fool around with their mates a bit, don't they? With you it's completely different. You've got to me, really got to me.

Understand what I'm saying?'

Jake was not unattractive, and he could be good company, but I had never thought of him as someone to sleep with. To me he and Jayde were a straight couple. Some people, for all sorts of reasons, you do not think of in a sexual kind of way. Did he assume that, simply because he fancied me, I ought to have sex with him? I had never done anything to encourage him.

'Sorry, this is too much for me. Half an hour ago my impression was that Toby was my boyfriend, to some extent anyway, Dale was my flatmate, and you and Jayde were a fun-loving straight couple who never knew when to say no. Now you tell me none of it is true. Jayde is your girlfriend, your partner… isn't she?'

'Wise up, Ben. Lots of people have open relationships. Think about what I said. It would be different with me, not like it is with Toby. I've got respect for you. You'd be someone special. We could have fun together, the two of us. Why not? Everyone else does.'

Who the hell was he to tell me how to live my life? Despite being angry, and dazed by what he had said about Toby and Dale, for him to say he fancied me was flattering. But what was he after? To have me as a bit of gay fun on the side while he continued with Jayde as before, neither of us ever to feel jealous or possessive? He evidently had no inkling of anything being wrong with what they had done to me the other night. Anyway, I wanted someone who cared about me, who would be there when life got tough. I said, 'You think I'm likely to want a relationship, after you doped me in that fetish club and did what you did?'

'We were helping you get rid of your inhibitions.'

'That's not how I see it.'

'We gave you a good time. All right, you're not happy about it now, so obviously we went too far. Give it a few more days.

You might see it differently. How will you find out what you like if you never try anything new?'

'What I try or don't try is not up to you. Until the other night I *was* beginning to think of you as a friend.'

We walked in silence back to the park gates, parting with barely another word. I dreaded facing Dale. Jake would hardly have made up the story about Toby and him. Given the ease with which the Jays and Toby hopped into bed with anyone they fancied, to be jealous would be silly, but how could Dale have let me talk of Toby as my boyfriend, and have said nothing about what they were up to?

That evening, when I got back to the flat, Dale was in the kitchen peeling vegetables. 'Can we talk?' I asked.

He turned to face me. 'What's wrong?'

'You don't know?'

'Toby?'

'Toby and you.'

'Okay, okay, you're right to be... I'm not going to lie to you. Let's go and sit in the lounge. It might help if we had a drink.'

He poured two large vodkas and we sat facing each other. 'So,' I said, surprised by my own self-control, 'you've been seeing Toby.'

'I have to admit it's true. I'm sorry. You must think I'm a total bastard. This is going to sound like a load of excuses, but what happened is... do you remember that first night when I saw you at the bar with him at the Give and Take? I hadn't slept with anyone for nearly a year, and had been building myself up to do something about it, and there he was, a terrific-looking guy coming on to me. I grabbed the chance and, well, picked him up, or let him pick me up, whichever. I should have known better, he's not... I didn't contact him again, and when you told me you were keen on him, and you wanted him to be your boyfriend, I thought, well, good luck, hope things work out for you, I'll stay out of the way.

'Unfortunately, I'd given him my number that first night, and one day he rang me, saying he had to see me about something. I thought he must want to talk to me about how things were with you. He asked me not to tell you we were meeting. When we met he had nothing much to say, but he came on to me again. I can't really claim that he forced me into it. I should have said no, but... I was in the wrong. He was so hard to resist.

'Afterwards I felt guilty. Next time he rang I said no. The thing is he wouldn't let it go, he threatened to drop you, and to upset everything by telling you about his second time with me. So I agreed to see him again, and said nothing to you.' He took a gulp from his glass, reached over to the one I was holding, and pushed it up to my lips to make me drink too. 'I should have stood up to him. Perhaps I didn't have the courage. The better part of me was hoping he would get tired of me, and then the problem would solve itself.'

My anger towards him had pretty well drained away. I said calmly, 'Even so you should have told me. You lied to me and helped him make a bloody idiot out of me.'

'How did you find out?'

'Jake knew. He told me. Can you imagine what hearing it from him was like?'

'I knew whatever I said it would sound like excuses. Toby's so attractive, he makes you feel... It was physical, nothing more. Please, Ben, don't hate me for it. The dishonesty is over now. Whatever you think of me, please believe I'd never intentionally do anything to hurt you. You know I think the world of you.'

How could I believe anything he said ever again? Having owned up and said he was sorry, he rubbed his hand up and down my thigh. Did he really think that would get him anywhere? He looked utterly miserable, the way he had the first time we met when I turned down sharing the flat with him. He had been in the wrong, but he had said he was sorry. What good would having a go at him do? What he needed was someone to comfort him. I did, too.

Seven

My circuitous route into Dale's arms had been like one of those yarns about a stranger in town who goes tramping down street after street, eventually to find the place he sought was round the corner a few yards from where he started. Having at last crossed into the territory of physical love, I felt that everything between us was right, exactly as it ought to be. From that first night together, it was to be the two of us against the world.

The next day, just after one, he rang me at the bookshop. His voice was so soft and deep that it made me long to touch him. 'You all right?' he asked.

'I'm in a daze. Jeremy's noticed. He saw me gazing out of the window, sneaked up and startled me by slamming one of the big encyclopaedias shut behind my head.'

'I'm as bad. In the staff restaurant, I went up to the counter but couldn't face eating anything. All I had was a cup of tea.'

'You can't not eat.'

'I'll recover.'

Later, Jeremy called me into the little office at the back of the shop to help him with some figure work, and I explained the cause of my dreamy abstraction. 'You, Dale, ah… I see! Good.

Steady, dependable type. I'm pleased, hope it all works out for you. You must both come over for a meal at my place, Sunday after next if you're free. Actually, Ben, there is something I have to tell you, another development with the business.'

'Oh?'

'Well, development might not be quite the right word, it's not going to affect you all that much. You know that empty shop a couple of doors down that used to be a funeral parlour? Well, someone I know has taken it. As a matter of fact, in a way, you are partly responsible. Remember those astrology books Dale's aunt had? I contacted an old friend who is fascinated by the paranormal, to see if she might be interested. She told me she had been thinking of setting up a little business, a psychic shop or something of that sort. When I mentioned the old funeral parlour, she decided to come and see it. She has wasted no time, she's taking possession next week. She'll be on her own at first, most of the time anyway, and she's hoping we will be able to cover for her if she has to slip out somewhere during shop hours.'

'A psychic shop? Does that mean making appointments for people to have their fortunes told?'

'No, not fortune telling... well, possibly, I'm not sure. More likely Alicia will sell things. Books, crystal balls, magic potions, I don't know, whatever nonsense that kind of shop sells.'

'Sounds a bit eccentric.'

'Now don't pull a face. It's a matter of business. If a customer came in here wanting a book about racehorses or famous casinos, I would try to find it for him even though I think gambling is a waste of time, effort and money. We may not think much of astrology and crystal ball gazing, but if others attach importance to it, who are we to sneer? Actually, Alicia is quite an expert in all things Egyptian. She's been engaged as a professional... been on archaeological digs in the desert sands, can translate the hieroglyphics. Anyway, wouldn't be a great problem to keep an eye on her shop for half an hour or so if she has to pop out, would it?'

'Well, if she's a friend of yours obviously... but we are trying to build up the business here.'

'She will reciprocate when she's settled in, I'm sure. Should make it possible for me to show you more of the book trade, take you along to some of the book auctions, that sort of thing.'

'Oh, good.'

'We mustn't be over-critical of paranormal fancies,' he coaxed. 'Ask yourself how rational and logical a lot of our own trade is? We make sales to collectors desperate to get their hands on books on arcane subjects of no importance or relevance to the world we live in. Think of the Victorian good housekeeping guides. Aren't they merely curiosities from a bygone age? Are we entitled to sniff at the items a psychic shop sells? Alicia's a good sort. Outspoken, but a good sort.'

Whether she was a good sort or not, what would wags like Smiles at the Give and Take say if they found out about me helping in a psychic shop?

The appearance of a sign saying 'Hatshepsut's Pavilion' above the old funeral parlour's window warned me that Jeremy's friend Alicia was about to manifest herself. She was a woman in her forties with large brown eyes and shortish hair, fawn but tinted to a darker shade of brown in places – or it might have been the other way around. When Jeremy introduced us, she gripped my right hand firmly in both of hers for so long I wondered if she meant to keep it. I said, 'Unusual name you've given your new shop?'

'It's Egyptian. Everyone has heard of Cleopatra and Nefertiti.

Well, Hatshepsut was the only female Egyptian pharaoh, from an earlier period, a highly successful woman, well regarded as a ruler, and she ought to be better known. Glad you asked. Has Jeremy mentioned the possibility of giving me a hand?'

'He has mentioned minding the shop for five minutes if you have to pop out anywhere.'

Jeremy nodded.

'Well, that would be a help, but I've got boxes full of books on astrology and other occult subjects. Jeremy says you're an ace at organizing stock. Loads of stuff is being delivered over the next couple of days. Be a change for you from the worm-eaten old tomes Jeremy fills his shelves with. What do you say? Are you up for it?'

Jeremy showed no reaction on hearing his valuable rare books described as worm-eaten old tomes. Offended for him, I said defensively, 'Jeremy buys things that his business sense tells him are in demand. What do you mean, am I up for it? I've got a boyfriend.'

'I was not referring to your sex life. Are you willing to give me a hand with my stock?'

Jeremy said, 'I did tell Alicia we would find space in the basement for her books while the shopfitters are in at Hatshepsut's. If you have time, she would appreciate it if you would go through what she has.'

Wanting to sound unenthusiastic without actually refusing, I said, 'No problem, though I'm not familiar with the subject area.'

Alicia's boxes of books were too heavy for me to manage on my own, and Jeremy was gasping for air after helping me manoeuvre one of them down to his basement. I got him a chair and took the rest of her books down by myself in manageable quantities. Most had come from a bookshop in Hay-on-Wye that had closed, and luckily the owner had compiled a list in alphabetical order, everything from Astrology to Zend-Avesta. They were a mix of second-hand books and new ones that had been published years ago and had not sold. Checking the market value on the internet and updating the prices, some of which were still in pounds, shillings and pence, took me hours.

The shopfitters needed only a week to install shelves and furnishings for the new psychic emporium. After they had left, Alicia invited us in to see how it was progressing. Wind chimes suspended above the door tinkled ethereally as we entered. Shelves and glass display cases had been positioned so as to create all sorts of nooks and crannies, good for encouraging people to linger and inspect the curiosities on sale, but the hidden corners increased the risk of pilfering. 'Have you thought of getting a closed circuit TV system,' I asked, 'to discourage the kleptomaniacs?'

'You're very cynical,' she said. 'Don't you think people who are interested in the occult will be above that sort of thing?'

'I'd have thought the opposite. You're not relying on extra-sensory perception to find them out, are you?'

It was meant as a joke, but she said seriously, 'To be truthful with you, I'm not at all gifted myself. Not that I haven't tried, but...' she shook her head. 'Oh dear. *You've* sensed something though, haven't you? Don't say there's a jinx, please. After all, the place used to be a funeral parlour.' I did not know how to respond to this. She turned to Jeremy. 'He's not keeping anything from me, is he?'

'Ben wasn't hinting at anything being wrong, Alicia. It's his sense of humour. You'll get used to him.'

'Well, let's hope so. It would be really useful if he could keep shop for me when I go to my Egyptology meetings on Wednesday afternoons.'

'What do you say, Ben?' Jeremy asked.

The hour helping out now and again had suddenly lengthened to half a day every week. Thinking quickly I reminded Jeremy he often went to a book fair on Wednesdays.

'He's right, Alicia. They're about once a month.'

'Sorry,' she said. 'I asked you round to see the shop, not to twist your arm. One or two of my friends might help out if I'm stuck. Let's leave it for now. How about a glass of wine and some nibbles, as a little thank you for your help so far?'

She had only two chairs, so I cleared a space on the counter to sit on. Above my head hung a mobile with little ceramic tiles in the shapes of stars and planets. A shapeless black thing in one of the crates attracted Jeremy's eye. 'What have you got over there, Alicia?' he asked.

'My Cleopatra headdress!' She lifted out an Egyptian-style wig and positioned it on her head, the long black hair hanging down over her shoulders. 'What do you think?' Jeremy and I laughed, and she said with mock annoyance, 'Not meant to be funny. You might show a little respect, especially you, Jeremy. Ben is still young, he can be forgiven.'

Actually Jeremy himself had come in that day dressed rather like an overgrown schoolboy in a royal blue blazer with gold braiding; the pair of them made the place look like a fancy dress shop. At the centre of Alicia's headdress was a cobra's head, possibly stuffed, but certainly dead. I gave in to the temptation to hold out one of her Garibaldi biscuits towards it, and asked, 'Does it eat squashed flies?'

Patting the sides of the headdress she said, 'Isis, help me. Protect me from these heretics.'

On the way back to the bookshop Jeremy said, 'She's not so bad you know. Heart's in the right place. Half a day for a little while, Ben, to help her get started. We could take turns.'

'Wonder what her Egyptology meetings are like. Probably

people sitting around a table, pretending to sharpen razor blades by putting them under a plastic pyramid.'

'You're wrong about that. She is recognised as an expert on the hieroglyphics of a certain period. It's not like you to be grumpy.'

'No, it's not. Sorry. Maybe it's sorting out at all those books of hers in the basement. Soon have them finished, anyway.' Working half a day a week in her psychic shop was a bit of an imposition, but not bad enough to risk Jeremy's good opinion.

'Anyway,' Jeremy said, 'you know she's one of us.'

'What, Alicia's a shirt-lifter?'

'You know perfectly well what I mean. She's a lesbian.'

Hatshepsut's Pavilion opened six weeks before Christmas, a good kick-off time for any business selling what, to my mind, were trinkets and novelties. Alicia crammed the place with an amazing variety of stuff: porcelain phrenology heads, palmistry hands, peculiar-shaped candles, supposedly Egyptian artefacts, large sparkling crystals – a thousand oddities cluttered her shelves, the more expensive safely locked in a display case. The shop had bright sales areas under spotlights, and shadowy nooks where the intrepid might try on tribal face-masks or handle totemic figurines. In one corner rubber vampire bats and big hairy spiders hung from imitation webs.

The first time I went in for a stint of minding her shop it appeared to be deserted until, after a couple of minutes, the cobra's head became visible above an ornate screen. 'Ah, I sense a presence,' she called out in a wavering voice from her hiding place, 'Have you come from afar?'

'I've come from Jeremy's bookshop.'

'Oh it's you, Ben. In good time too. Lucky, I'll be able to do your horoscope before I go. I've just installed a new software package that's been highly recommended. Come and sit down.'

'Afraid I'm just not into that sort of thing.'

'Help me try it out. It won't take long. Fortune telling by computer instead of astrological charts, you must admit it has a funny side to it. I need the exact latitude and longitude of where you were born, and the date and the exact time.'

'You're not serious. I was born in Southend in the early hours.'

'Isis preserve us!' she said. 'Early hours? You might have had more consideration for your poor mother. How do you expect me to produce your horoscope if you can't give the map reference and exact time?'

'I don't expect anything. Doing my horoscope was your idea. Forget it.'

'I've spent hours trying to get to grips with this damn thing. You might try to be a bit more co-operative. Oh never mind, I'd better be on my way.' She took off the Cleopatra headdress and placed it on one of the phrenology heads.

'You don't wear that to the Egyptology meetings, then?'

'Heavens no. They're all much too serious. And passers-by in the street might think me a bit weird. You're not smirking at me, are you?'

'As if I would.'

'Don't think that's the last you've heard of the astrology system. I can understand you not sharing my fascination with the cusp of Venus, but you might try to show a modicum of interest in Uranus. One thing does come over very clearly, all the same. Someone you know will be front page news before the week is out.

What was going on in her head for her to say someone I knew would be in the news? Surely she had broken a basic rule in the fortune-telling game: never make a prediction definite enough for events to prove you wrong. I couldn't help blurting out 'It is highly unlikely that anyone I know will be front page news.'

'Willing to bet on it?' She harassed me into betting a fiver, grinding down my resistance with the argument that a refusal would imply I did not believe what I was saying myself.

'By the way, if any customers do come in you'll find that some of the stock still needs price tags. I've left a price list on the shelf under the till. Help yourself to tea or coffee, and you'll find plenty of biscuits. I'm hoping to be back at about half-past four. If you do need to go out, put up the 'Back in five minutes' sign, lock the door and don't forget to take the key. It's in the till under the ten pound notes. You've got my mobile number?'

Left alone in the shop, I switched her computer on again, thinking of checking my e-mails. She had set up password protection, and on the off-chance I typed in 'Cleopatra'. The log-in screen disappeared and a message in large red letters scrolled across: *Ben, if that's you trying to guess my password, try Nefertiti.* She had clearly predicted, or anticipated, that I would try to use the machine after she left. Worried she might have set further traps for me, I gave up and tied price labels on some necklaces and amulets instead to pass the time.

Next I rang Dale to relieve the tedium, but could only leave a message as he was at a meeting. When he called back he pretended to be a sheikh wanting to buy love potions to stimulate the sexual appetites of his wives. 'Hi Dale,' I said. 'Alicia probably has some love potions in stock somewhere. You should see for yourself all the weird stuff she has.'

'Much as I would like to drop in for five minutes, I've just come out of a meeting and a load of urgent stuff is waiting on my desk. Means I'll be late getting home again.'

The next day he came into the bookshop. The hospital owed

him lots of time and he had taken a couple of hours off to see Hatshepsut's Pavilion for himself. We hugged and kissed, and over tea and some of Jeremy's biscuits he showed me his newspaper. At the bottom right of the front page, under the heading *Double Celebration for British Writer*, was a paragraph that read *Champagne Corks were already popping for Loyd Larcher on publication of the omnibus edition of his novels, when The Bookseller's Guild announced he was to receive its lifetime achievement award. A Guild spokesman said 'Nobody in contemporary fiction can touch him for range and variety.'*

'Oh no.'

'What do you mean, "Oh no?"'

'Yesterday Alicia bet me five pounds that someone I knew would be front page news.'

'She's must be cheating. She's been tipped off.'

'How could she know he would be on the front page?'

'Jeremy might have heard somehow and told her.'

However she learned that the story would be on page one, she had tricked me out of five pounds. When we went in to see her I showed her the paper and said, 'You win. You've caught me out somehow. Loyd is someone I know, and the story about him did make the front page.'

'Loyd Larcher? Can't stand the man. How did he get himself onto page one? Let me see.' She read the paragraph and said, 'Still, I've won our little bet, haven't I? Thank you, Isis, thank you,' she said, clasping her hands together and gazing upwards, though the object that hung from the ceiling above her head was not Isis but a plastic vampire bat.

'Thought your predictions came from astrology, not from Isis. Anyway here's the five pounds.'

'I wasn't thinking about that silly old coot Larcher. This is what the bet was about.' She pulled the current month's edition of the magazine *Psychic News* from its plastic wrapper. On the front page was a small photograph of Alicia herself under the heading: 'Egyptologist opens new London venture', and inside was a half page article about Hatshepsut's Pavilion. 'I don't want your bloody five pounds,' she said, picking up the note and slapping it down in front of me. 'I was joking. Did you really think I was trying to rob you? What I would really like is someone to give me a hand with the astrology system.'

To my great surprise, Dale volunteered: 'I'll have a go, if you like, though frankly I think astrology is a lot of twaddle.'

He discovered how to change the settings so that the nearest large town or city could be entered instead of the map grid reference, and made the time of day that someone was born an optional entry. As an experiment we generated a horoscope for Loyd Larcher, entering a date of birth that would make his present age a hundred-and-two. With a lot of trial and error we worked through until we generated a ten-page horoscope, including an impressive coloured chart of stars and planets.

'It is a clever package,' Dale said, 'ingenious. I'd better leave you to try it out and go back to work.'

'Surely you want to see what the stars hold for you?' Alicia suggested.

He smiled wryly and put on his coat. 'Maybe another time.'

'Well, let me give you something from the shop. Has anything caught your eye? How about one of these?' She unlocked the display case and took out a turquoise glass pyramid, inside which could be seen another smaller, pyramid in glass of a lighter hue. 'Would this go nicely on your desk at work?'

'It might go missing. You don't need to give me anything, really.'

'But I want to. Do take it, you'll find somewhere for it.'

As the weather cooled towards Christmas, Jeremy came into work wearing one of those winter coats with thick, padded horizontal bands of fabric like motorbike tyres going all the way round. These insulating layers increased his girth, and on his way to the little back office he had to squeeze between shelves of children's books on one side and encyclopaedias on the other. The fabric squeaked loudly as it rubbed against the spines. Thinking that if he became wedged in the gap I would have to climb over him to fetch the office scissors and cut him loose from his clothing, I suggested that he remove his outer covering before he entered the bottleneck. He went into a huff at first, but could not resist examining the spines of the books for signs of damage, and then said, 'I suppose I'll have to do as I'm told.'

He had been out of spirits the day before because Loyd Larcher was hesitant about coming to his little Christmas party. The veteran author had another engagement, and doubted if it would be over in time. Dale and I, Alicia, her girlfriend Muriel, and a few of Jeremy's business contacts were expected, but Loyd's presence would have made the event special.

I cleared some space in the shop and put up folding chairs and a trestle table for snacks and bottles of wine before going home for an early dinner. When I returned with Dale, Jeremy had put on a big sweater with broad brown and yellow horizontal stripes. Judging he was in far too amiable a mood to take offence, Dale said, 'I know who you're meant to be, Jeremy, you're Mr Bumble the beadle from *Oliver Twist*.'

'I expect any minute Ben is going to tell me I'm always bumbling around,' Jeremy replied.

About twelve people, in all, attended. Dale struck up a conversation with Alicia about alternative medicine, and soon we were exchanging opinions about acupuncture, hypnosis, herbal remedies, vitamin pills, and how to choose from the hundreds of different remedies and tonics available.

We enjoyed a couple of hours chatting, eating and drinking. Then Alicia asked me if, when I was left alone in the bookshop, I ever noticed anything odd, such as strange noises, tricks of the light, or peculiar smells.

'Oh no, not really,' I said. 'Jeremy's customers aren't as decrepit as that.'

'You know what I'm getting at. These shops have been here for more than a hundred years, had different owners, survived bombing during the Second World War. Traces of the past remain behind, some are visible like that old-fashioned bell on the shop door, but others cannot be detected so easily.'

Then Jeremy suggested she bring out an Ouija board she had recently acquired. He added, 'This is a traditional time of year for ghosts, so perhaps we should... by way of a little entertainment...'

Most of Jeremy's guests decided the time had come to leave, and I whispered to Dale that we might do the same, but he said, 'It's okay, let's indulge him, if we go hardly anyone will be left.'

Alicia, her girlfriend, Jeremy, Dale and I were the only ones to stay on. We sat in a circle around the Ouija board, an ornate affair with the letters of the alphabet in Gothic script. We were all to place our fingers in grooves on a special hexagonal glass dish with a lighted candle in its centre. Jeremy switched off the lights. The flickering candlelight made our faces appear mysterious, conspiratorial. At first the glass dish in the centre remained immobile. We all waited. I turned my head and caught Dale's eye. He was smiling faintly, probably thinking how silly we all were. Then the glass dish began to glide slowly across the board. We audibly drew breath. Was one of us pushing it? It came to a halt above the letter M. We all pronounced 'M', our voices somehow achieving unison and harmony. Next the dish moved off to the letter A, and as we all said 'A' it moved off to R, followed by L. A cold blast of air suddenly blew out the candle, and at the same moment we heard books thudding onto the floor.

Jeremy turned the lights on again. 'Oh blast,' he said, 'must have caught the bookshelf somehow when I reached out for my glass of wine. Sorry everyone. Help me put them back, would you Ben?' Among the books I picked up was Dickens' *A Christmas Carol*. It had fallen open at the page in which the phantom first appears. Jeremy took it from me and read out the description of Marley's ghost.

When I sat down again Alicia fixed me with a questioning gaze. 'Are you quite sure, Ben, that you have never noticed anything *otherworldly* when you have been on your own in the shop?'

'Oh, come on Alicia,' said Jeremy, 'don't overdo it. Let's have another try. See if the spirit world has a message for us.'

Dale put his hand over mine under the table. 'I can feel a freezing draught coming from somewhere,' he said.

'Must be from the window at the back of the shop, can't have put the latch down properly,' Jeremy answered. This was an improbable explanation; that window had not been opened since I had been working there. Once again we settled around the Ouija board in the flickering candlelight. Again, after initial hesitation, the glass glided across the board, and we intoned the letters at which it stopped, 'M, A, R, L, E, Y. Marley!' Suddenly we heard a determined rapping at the shop door. Behind the blind, a dark figure was silhouetted by the glow of the street lights. The latch clicked. 'Who's there?' cried Jeremy in alarm. The door opened wide and the temperature in the shop plummeted. A ghastly apparition, weighed down by chains, floated into the room. As it crossed the floor it left an eerie greenish-brown powdery trail behind it. I shrank back, afraid that some of this deathly deposit might rub off on me. Dale clasped my hand.

I could not take my eyes from the spectre. In the meagre light of the candle I begin to make out its features, which were, I began to realize, uncannily like those of Loyd Larcher. The mouth opened, and it spoke in what was unmistakeably his plummy voice: 'Terribly sorry, Jeremy, may have dropped a bit of a clanger.' He rattled his chains. 'Could have sworn you said this evening was to be fancy dress.'

Jeremy put on the lights. He, Alicia and Loyd grinned widely, all three obviously in on the joke, their teeth shining like rows of tombstones on a moonlit night. They must, though, have been a little disappointed that more of Jeremy's guests had not stayed on for Loyd's performance. Of course I had not really thought, in my rational mind, that a ghost had been conjured up by the Ouija board, but for a while my heart had been thumping all the same.

Eight

My help in Hatshepsut's Pavilion soon amounted to much more than minding the shop occasionally while Alicia nipped out. She rang, or came into the bookshop, several times a day to ask about local advertising or wanting an opinion on potential new items of stock. Once she showed me a couple of parchment scrolls, one illuminated with Egyptian hieroglyphics, and the other with the early Germanic script known as runes. They cost about a pound each wholesale, and she thought they might sell for double that – a one hundred per cent profit!

Deciding which of thousands of items on the market might be profitable, from aromatherapy candles to complex psychometric charts, must have been perplexing. As she always put up with my teasing about crystal ball gazing being akin to navel gazing, or that reading tea leaves could have no advantage over reading coffee grouts or the scum someone left behind in a bath, now that she had asked a sensible question I said, 'Maybe the hieroglyphics are worth two pounds as they're so attractive and colourful, but the runes are are not that striking, are they? They're basically a series of black lines that sometimes cross one another.'

'Runes are supposed to be psychographic,' she said, using a word that was obviously psychobabble. 'Still, you may be right. Perhaps I'll put them in at one-fifty and see how they do. Ah!' she sighed, 'The sales rep was a very attractive and persuasive woman.'

When I told Jeremy about the parchments, he remembered an old black and white film, *Night of the Demon*, in which the villain contrived to plant a runic script carrying a curse on his victims. At nightfall a monstrous fiend would appear and savage them. The only chance of salvation was to pass the runes on. Whoever held them as daylight faded would then become the fiend's prey.

At home after work I found a runes parchment in my bag that Alicia must somehow have planted there. I showed them to Dale. 'Guess where these came from!'

'Alicia? What are they?'

'Runes. Here,' I said, trying to pass them on to him.

'Prunes? No, I'm fine in that department at the moment, thanks all the same.'

'I said runes, not prunes. They're an old Teutonic script. Did you ever see that film…'

'Oh yes, ages ago on TV, it's coming back to me now. The villain passed them on to his victims, who would see them waft away on a sudden breeze, before being attacked by a monster. So you're trying to bring me to a horrible violent death are you?'

'Only to save myself. I wouldn't inflict anything like that on you unless it was in a really good cause.'

'That's your excuse, is it? Fine boyfriend you are.'

In the evening, we took the runes with us to the Give and Take. A terrific hunk stood at the bar wearing a denim shirt and a pair of low-cut jeans. As a little prank, Dale asked me for the runes, and casually meandered up to him. I followed. Pulling the parchment from his pocket, Dale said to me, 'What do you make of this. Any idea what it could be?'

'Some of your fan mail?'

'Ha-ha.' He caught the eye of the Adonis in denim and asked him. 'Have you ever seen anything like these?' The guy smiled and took the scroll from him. After he made a few wild guesses, we explained about the old horror film and the curse of the runes. Smiles half heard what we were saying and came over.

'Well, that isn't like any sort of music I've ever seen.'

'What makes you think they're a kind of music?'

'You were talking about tunes.'

'Not tunes, runes.' Soon a little group of us at the bar were passing the runes to one another, slipping them down each other's shirt fronts, and pretending to be terrified of being left holding them when the bar closed. After a while the conversation moved on, and I forgot about them until, getting into bed, I saw the parchment sticking out from under my pillow.

Dale, who had been watching me, said 'Did you think you'd got away with trying to pass the curse on to me? And what you don't know is that actually I am the demon from the film, and I'm taking vengeance on you right now.' He grabbed me, pushed me down and sat on my chest. It was not too difficult to topple him over sideways. We wrestled for a while, the bedding and the two of us sliding down to the floor, until we tired of the struggle, relaxed our grip on each other, caressed and made love.

The following afternoon I went to serve in Hatshepsut's Pavilion so that Alicia could go to her Egyptology meeting. 'I wonder,' she said, taking off her Cleopatra headdress, 'what this would look like on you.'

'Wonder all you like, it's not going to happen, especially now you've given the cobra's head those green glass eyes.'

'Spoilsport. Where's your sense of fun? I spent hours renovating that wig. It was a moth-eaten old thing I found in a theatrical costumier's store. You have to admit it does make an impression on customers in the shop.'

'You're right about that,' I said, not saying what kind of impression I thought it made.

'Oh... nice of you to say so, Ben. Must admit I did wonder if the beady green eyes were going a bit too far. Well, see you later.'

I was trying to decide how to amuse myself during my solitary hours in her shop, when a friend from the Give and Take came in.

'Oh, hi Ben, got any of those runes?'

'Well, yes, in that box over on your left. They gave us a good laugh last night, didn't they.'

'One-fifty each, okay,' he said, picking up three parchments. 'They were fantastic at breaking the ice with that new guy, you know, the dream in denim. Starting up a conversation for the first time with someone you really fancy is always tough going. Everyone uses the same tacky old chat-up lines. How many times have you heard "I thought it was totally dead in here until you came in?" The runes were a great opener. A couple of the other lads want to have a go, too.'

During the next few days a stream of customers for runes came in. Learning how well the parchments were selling, Jeremy put in an urgent order for some for the bookshop. He had not had them on display for long when, of all people, Toby appeared.

'Been a long time,' he said. 'Don't worry, it's only your runes I'm after. How are you doing?'

'They're one pound fifty.'

'Everyone is larking around with them in the club. I'll take a couple. You're looking good.'

I took his money but said nothing.

'Not still pissed off with me, are you?'

'Sometimes it's best to move on. I have.' I handed him the runes. 'Watch out for the demon.'

'Demon, what d'you mean?'

I wanted to keep our conversation brief and said, 'Oh... nothing.'

'If that's how you feel,' he said tersely, and left.

For a short while, in trendy pubs and clubs, going up to people and trying to pass runes on to them became a craze. I asked Alicia why, with so many parchments being passed around, no attacks by the fiend had been in the news.

She countered by asking, 'Did you think there would be?'

'No, but, I suppose the whole thing started with runes being passed on to you by a sales rep. What this means is that one bit of the occult has been proved to be nonsense. You are still here, not assailed by the fiend, despite having dozens of runes parchments in your possession at nightfall, and none of your customers has been attacked either.'

'But they're only *fake* runes. You don't think I would risk creating mayhem by selling *genuine* runes to anyone who happens to walk into the shop, do you?'

'What? Have you got genuine runes in a box under the counter for special customers? Someone should report you to Trading Standards, selling fake runes.'

'Don't be so mean. Actually, you and Dale might be interested in a new line that's coming in on Monday. Little polished pebbles in sets of six, each with a rune inscribed on it. According to the leaflet, you can tell people's fortunes by the order in which they come out of the bag. You can also slip them into someone's pocket to summon the demon, or throw them all up into the air and try to catch them. You could take a set, show them around,

103

see if they catch on.'

'Thanks for the offer, but maybe we have had enough runes for now.'

My view of the paranormal was as sceptical as ever, but Hatshepsut's Pavilion had provided more entertainment and hilarity in the weeks since it opened than all my months of work in the bookshop. The next little adventure started with the sale of a tin of biscuits, Nefertiti's Nubian Assortment. Each nibble was in its own paper wrapper, and had a message on the inside saying that the omens for love were very strong, or that good fortune lay ahead, or giving some other groundless prediction. A smartly dressed woman who grinned all the time approached the till carrying one of the tins, evidently wanting to impress with her constant display of teeth. She must have been very fond of snacks, for I saw a few crumbs from an earlier treat on the lapel of her coat.

When she had gone I noticed some flyers for Alicia's so-called personal astrology service on the shelf under the counter. At the bottom of the page were the words *Ask Alicia or Ben for your personal consultation*. She had included my name without asking me. I tackled her about the leaflets when she returned from her meeting.

'I thought you'd be pleased,' she said. 'A male customer might be happier to talk to another man, especially if he is hoping for the more personal subjects to be included. He might tell you a few juicy bits about himself.'

'I'm not interested in some weirdo's juicy bits. People will think I'm setting myself up as a fortune teller. If anyone at the Give and Take sees one of these I'll be a laughing stock.'

'You're so difficult sometimes.' She sighed and put on her Cleopatra headdress, now even more ridiculous as she had replaced the green-eyed cobra's head with a grotesque plastic spider. My irritation evaporated as I suppressed the urge to laugh. She said, 'I put your name in as an acknowledgement of all the help you're giving me in the shop. Actually, since you've raised the subject, I do sometimes sense that you might be gifted. Now don't pull a face. I always envy the gifted. I'm not myself, you see, except that I think maybe I'm good at spotting those who are.'

'Alicia, please tell me you won't invite people to contact me to arrange horoscopes, fortune telling, or anything else of that kind?'

'All right, if you must be so fussy. At least your boyfriend doesn't have a closed mind. He's agreed to come in on Thursday to help me add some new material to the reports on the astrology system.'

Dale did not believe in the stars any more than I did. He had probably agreed to help because he found it hard to say no. I went back to the bookshop to see if any orders had come in via the internet. Half an hour later she burst in, clearly overwrought. She was still wearing the Cleopatra headdress, the eyes of the plastic tarantula now glowing intermittently, presumably battery powered.

'Ben, you haven't sold any of the crystal scarab beetles lately, have you?'

They were probably the most expensive items not to be locked away in a glass case. 'No. The rune parchments were still going well, but nobody bought scarab beetles.'

'Three or four of them are missing.'

'My only sale, other than the runes, was one tin of Nefertiti's Nubian Assortment.'

'The last time I checked the beetles was a week ago. My fault. We can't watch everyone a hundred per cent of the time. It would be easy for anyone to slip a couple into a bag or their pocket.'

Unable to think of any comforting words, I offered to make her a cup of tea.

'Thanks, but I'd better go back and open up again.'

'Jeremy's gone out, but I could come round a bit later when he's back, maybe in half an hour?'

When I went round she was sitting behind the screen at the back, looking forlorn. I sat opposite her. 'You could put the scarab beetles in the lockable display case.'

'Yes, but it's what the theft says about people in general. You begin to lose faith.'

'Not everyone is trying to steal, are they? We'll just have to keep an eye out for anything suspicious. In a shop you have to accept some losses.'

She said, 'You did once suggest putting in security cameras, didn't you? Things have not got as bad as that yet. Let's talk about something else. You're good with words, aren't you. Ever thought about ghost writing?'

'Don't you have to be dead first?'

'Very funny. You're determined never to take anything I say seriously.'

'I take shoplifting seriously. You see the funny side of some of this stuff yourself sometimes.'

'Well, some of it… plastic vampire bats and spiders are just for amusement… people mainly buy them to give to their kids. The fascination, though, is in trying to get some insight into the unknown, or unexplained. There is uncertainty all around us. Even with ancient Egypt, despite all the artefacts and records we have, that world is mysterious to us. For instance, we don't know why the pyramids at Giza were built to the particular size that they are, or why they are in the configuration of the stars in

Orion's belt, or why pyramid building was abandoned for underground tombs. All the unknowns in our world are worrying in one sense, but they also give us hope.'

In order to help with Alicia's astrology system, Dale took off a few more of the hours that the hospital owed him. Her idea was to add some optional paragraphs to the standard reports for people who were trying to lose weight. This extra guidance was to slot in with all the usual guff about Jupiter coming into your birth-house and Mercury going into retrograde. He had been with her for nearly an hour when she rang to ask me to go over.

Dale had found, in the software package, a way of doing what she wanted, but having adapted a couple of sentences from a booklet on dieting, they were stuck for ideas. All they had put in was: *Planetary alignments may make comfort foods particularly tempting, but remember, efforts to lose weight can so easily be undone. Be firm of purpose.* The second was: *Your ruling planet is in your birth sign. This may help with concerns about weight. You may find a gradual reduction in calorie intake over a longer period more successful than a short drastic diet.*

'People write whole books about dieting. I thought this would be easy,' Alicia moaned. 'Most of the hospital's booklet is too clinical, too medical. The wording is wrong for a horoscope. You're never lost for words. Any ideas?'

'Well, let me see. How about: *Cut down on sugary drinks while Saturn is in Uranus.*'

'Is that dietary advice, or lewdness?'

'Bit of both. How about: *The influence of the moon makes this a good month for round continental cheeses;* or you could say: *as Taurus is your star sign avoid beef sausages;* and for Pisces, *Shellfish may help stimulate new interests.*'

'Oh for heaven's sake, why can't you be serious?' she said.

'That was just a bit of mental limbering up. I thought it might help free up our creative side. Dale calls it brainstorming.'

As we were talking, I noticed that the woman who had bought a tin of Nefertiti's Nubian Assortment from me a few days before had come in again, and was browsing the stock intently. She decided on another tin of biscuits and walked over to the till. Alicia got up to serve her. Something, maybe the woman's stance, maybe her forced grin, or the memory of the crumbs on her coat, made me suspicious. I ran across, and insisting on making sure the contents were complete, grabbed the tin and removed the lid. The inner transparent wrapper had been opened, two of the biscuits were missing, and in their place were four scarab beetles.

Alicia's face became fierce with hurt and anger. The spider's eyes of her headdress glowed intensely red. She took the scarab beetles from the box and held them out on her palm in front of the now terrified customer. 'Well, we could make this a matter for the police. Otherwise, these four crystal scarabs will cost you twenty-five pounds each, on top of the price of the biscuits. Will you be paying in cash or by credit card?' Her tone would have frightened off the runes demon.

The woman paid by credit card, her hands shaking, and hurried from the shop. Alicia turned to me. 'See, I told you,' she said.

Surely, I thought, she was not about to say she had suspected the woman of stealing all along. 'Told me what?'

'You know very well! Exactly what made you go and open the biscuit tin?'

'Oh, I'm not sure, there was something about the woman, the way she…'

'You *knew*, didn't you, you just *knew*. I was right. You are gifted!' she said, wagging her finger at me.

I shook my head. Dale came over and stood beside me, smiling mischievously. 'You must admit she has a point. You definitely are gifted,' he said, touching me in a very private place, the shop's counter preventing Alicia from seeing what he was doing.

Perhaps the most curious line Alicia decided to stock was bio-thaumaturgical hats. She came bustling into the bookshop one day, her face flushed under the Cleopatra headdress, the spider's eyes red but not glowing. 'Tell me what you think of these hats,' she asked. In the brochure of the Natural Clairvoyance Company she showed me pictures of three wide-brimmed hats decorated with plants. Attractive female models tilted their heads coquettishly under luxurious flowers and leaves.

The blurb claimed amazing benefits. One hat was said to have magical herbs to bring healing qualities, another to have a selection of meadow flowers that would help the wearer regain contact with nature; and the third was a 'miracle of germination' special that would awaken psychic powers or boost fertility. Alicia obviously wanted me to say they were wonderful. To avoid her question I said, 'I'm afraid, Alicia, they wouldn't suit me at all.'

'Isis give me patience. It's all right for you. You know that you're gifted. You may deny it, but you don't fool me. Try to imagine how I feel, being in the business but completely bereft of any sort of psychic ability. Anyway, let's not get into that. What I'm asking you is – do you think the hats would be a good line for the shop?'

This notion that I was in some unspecified way gifted, based on me twigging who had stolen her scarab beetles, was an embarrassment. She had begun whispering to customers in Hatshepsut's Pavilion, 'That's Ben; by the way, he's gifted, you know.' She ignored my denials because, she insisted, my actions had given me away. She said she understood my reluctance to talk about my powers, because psychics tend to be distracted a lot of the time, a weakness easily exploited by the unscrupulous. Thinking this to be another of her harmless fancies, I did not make a fuss about it. Only a few days earlier she had given Dale and me necklaces with a long central bead enamelled in rainbow colours – a discreet and attractive way of letting people know we were gay. Now she smiled at me, hoping for an encouraging comment about the Natural Clairvoyance Company's bio-thaumaturgical hats.

'You could order one of each, they should look impressive in the window at least. Why not? See if they sell.'

She smiled. 'Do you really think I should, Ben? You're not just saying so?'

'Yes. You'll try them on as well, won't you, to see if they suit you?'

Obviously pleased to be told what she wanted to hear, she said: 'Now you're in a sensible mood, please give a bit more thought to the ghost writing; I've asked you about it before. Now don't just dismiss it offhand like you did last time. Tell me you'll think about it.'

I smiled but did not answer, hoping that shortly some other notion would displace the subject from her mind. Later that day I met Dale in the Give and Take and mentioned to him that Alicia had spoken of ghost writing again, thinking she wanted me to attempt spiritual contact with someone like Oscar Wilde. He said, 'You're confusing ghost writing with spirit writing.'

'What?'

'People who think the spirit of Charles Dickens is using them as a human agent to write a new novel. That's spirit writing. Or you sometimes hear of automatic writing, though I'm not sure exactly what that's supposed to be. Ghost writing is where a book, usually an autobiography, comes out in a celebrity's name, but it was really been written by someone else who isn't mentioned.'

'Is it? Of course, now you've said that... yes, you're right... how stupid of me.'

'Could turn out to be interesting. Maybe she wants you to write her family history.'

'I'm not sure if I want to get to know her as well as all that.'

Soon after this, Toby appeared at the bar, the first time I had seen him since he came into the bookshop to buy runes. He must have spotted us, but avoided looking our way. Smiles stayed at the other end of the bar, deliberately making him wait. A few minutes later two strangers came in, clearly there to meet Toby. Smiles beamed at us to get our attention, stuck his tongue out and moved his index finger from side to side under his chin in a throat-cutting gesture, then relented and went to serve them. The group did not stay long, perhaps ten minutes, and after they left Smiles picked something up from the floor near where they had been standing. He brought it over to us. 'Your ex said he was just back from Amsterdam. He dropped this. It's a packet of cannabis seeds.' He left them on our table, and we carried on talking. When we left, for no real reason, I took them with me.

When the bio-thaumaturgical hats, decorated with artificial flowers and leaves, arrived, Alicia cleared everything else out of her shop window. Displayed on porcelain phrenology heads they were certainly eye-catching. According to the instruction sheet from the Natural Clairvoyance Company, for them to be fully effective the imitation herbage supplied had to be replaced with living plants. She asked me to help set up the 'miracle of germination' model, which came with a tubular propagation unit that fitted all the way around the wide brim, rather like a miniature rainwater gutter with a transparent plastic cover. The special growing medium was ready-sown with 'inspirational' seeds, including wood anemone to attract spirits of the forest with their psychic powers, enchanter's nightshade to help with spells and charms, and red clover to improve fertility.

Toby's cannabis seeds were still in my pocket, and when she was distracted briefly by a phone call I opened the envelope and dropped several into the compost. She turned her head suddenly and almost saw me. To engage her mind on something else I suggested we plant the other two hats with mustard and cress so that, should the psychic benefits prove elusive, at least we would have something green to put in our sandwiches.

'Why can't you ever be serious?'

'Well, I seriously mind the shop while you go off to Egyptology meetings.'

'Yes. But then you always make silly remarks if I mention ghost writing, and now you're doing the same about the hats, even though you said earlier that they were worth getting.'

'Okay, what was it you had in mind about ghost writing? I'll be serious.'

'Are you really going to listen at long last? This concerns someone very famous, very much in the public eye. Everything to do with him has to be treated with secrecy. I am not sure if I should even tell you his name.'

'If you want me to listen you'll have to tell me what this is all about. What kind of person are we talking about, a politician, a TV personality?'

'Promise me you won't let this go any further? All right, he's a rock and roll star, one of the biggest: Rick Schwagger of The Rocking Boulders. A long time ago when he was going through a particularly difficult time, he came to me for advice. We are still in touch... a couple of times a year at least.'

Could it really be that Alicia, who was about to remove her Cleopatra headdress and put on a newly planted miracle of germination bio-thaumaturgical hat, was in contact with such a world-renowned star of rock and roll? 'You're telling me you know Rick Schwagger?'

'Shh. Keep your voice down. Years ago he needed guidance on dealing with a sect claiming to be a revival of an old Egyptian religion. The Oracles of Aten, they called themselves. In the nineteen-sixties strange hippie cults were springing up everywhere. You probably remember seeing some copies of a book called *Oracles of Aten* among the stock you took down to Jeremy's basement. Their leader was hoping to lure Schwagger's group in the same way as that bogus maharishi got his hooks into the Beatles. They claimed their beliefs harked back to the period when Nefertiti's husband, the pharaoh Akhenaten, turned away from the religion of Isis and the other traditional gods, and set up a new capital city for himself in the Nile delta. The modern sect lasted only a year or so.

'Rick Schwagger has been trying to find someone to help him write his autobiography for years. Part of the problem is, he blows hot and cold about it. Everything would depend on whether he took to you or not. Are you interested enough for me to mention your name?'

Simply to meet Rick Schwagger would be fantastic, maybe the most significant event in my whole life. Putting cannabis seeds into the brim of Alicia's new hat now seemed a very silly thing to have done. What if she found out, and the prank made her think me too unreliable? Still, I could hardly go digging around in the brim in the hope of finding them again. And they would probably not come up.

Nine

The three copies of the book *Oracles of Aten*, currently stored in Jeremy's basement, were proof that Alicia's story about the sect was not entirely fanciful, however imaginative her general interest in the occult might be. Could she, for instance, really believe in astrology? Dale asked her once why, since the constellations and planets were clearly visible in the night sky, no one had successfully predicted the winning numbers of the national lottery from them. Her answer was that the stars might be useful for forecasting general trends or bringing out people's inner natures, but they might not be suitable for pinpointing specific items of data. Did she, though, really believe that something that did not work with straightforward questions would be effective with highly complex ones?

Yet, after the dodgy sect had been wound up, her twice a year contact with Rick Schwagger might have been only very brief phone calls or e-mails. Even if he still wanted help, it might only be with checking dates and sorting out old papers, not actual 'ghost' writing, for which other people, Loyd Larcher for instance, were likely to be much better suited. Not that I would be sniffy about even routine work for such a famous rock and roll celebrity.

She e-mailed him about updating his horoscope, adding that if he still wanted help with his autobiography, she knew someone who might be suitable. Inevitably she mentioned that I was 'gifted'.

A reply came the next day, commissioning the horoscope update, and asking for more information about me. Within a week I received an e-mail asking for a short meeting.

I was collected from Fulrose Court by car a few evenings later, having left work early, showered, and put on my coolest clothes. Bang on time the door bell rang. I opened it to find a middle-aged man with a shaven head who said, 'Hello, you Ben? All ready to go?' I followed him down to a limousine. He opened a rear door for me, said everyone called him 'The Handyman', and invited me to help myself to drinks from the little bar fitted behind the front seats. Worried that alcohol, combined with anxiety, might dull my brain when I saw the man himself, I chose a small bottle of orange juice. The Handyman must have been watching in the mirror, for he said, 'You're not a boozer, then?'

'I do drink alcohol. It's a bit early.'

'Excuse me for asking, but are you working? Alicia said you helped out in her shop sometimes.'

'Yes. But I work mostly in the bookshop a few doors along.'

'Bookshop? Sounds okay. Last one we tried for Rick's book was full of crap. Turned out to be a journalist wanting to dig up smut on the lads. Caused us no amount of trouble. Had to teach him a lesson.'

Worried, I said: 'I hope we're not starting off with the idea that I'll need to be taught a lesson?'

'Don't take it like that. If you're straight with me, I'll see you're okay. You have to understand people are trying it on with the lads all the time. My job is to keep shit stirrers away. If you're

115

genuine you've got nothing to worry about. What do you sell in the bookshop? Porn?'

'No, it isn't bloody porn. We sell antiquarian books.'

'Got you going, have I? I'd better not call it a second-hand bookshop, then. Look, I've got nothing against you. For all I know you're a diamond. Relax, forget I said anything. Sit back and have your drink. I'll put some music on.'

I could see very little through the car's tinted windows, and he would not tell me where we were headed 'on account of security'. The opening guitar riff of The Rocking Boulders' early song *Striped Candy* came through the speakers behind me, followed by the voice of the young-sounding Schwagger:

> *Striped candy, it's a part of the scene,*
> *Striped candy, I lick it real clean,*
> *Striped candy, makes me feel randy,*
> *Striped candy, you know what I mean.*

Half an hour later we turned off the road into a short drive. We left the car and walked to the entrance of a large villa, the front door ornamented by art nouveau glass panels. The Handyman ushered me up to a first-floor parlour, where I saw waiting for me the The Rocking Boulders' lead guitarist, Heath Prityards. He was on his own, sitting on a long sofa, blowing his nose loudly and at length.

'I dunno, you're supposed to have come off everything, but you're still doing a lot of snorting,' The Handyman said disrespectfully.

'Very funny, Handyman,' Heath said, not appearing to mind the jibe. 'So,' he asked, nodding in my direction, 'this him, the one with the sixth sense? Least he don't look too much of a freak.' This remark came from a man whose wizened face was even more lined and haggard than in recent press photographs, and whose hair sprouted from his customary head scarf like the bristles of a severely battered paint brush.

'You've got about an hour,' said The Handyman, leaving us together.

I sat down and refused Heath's offer of a drink. Next he offered a smoke, and when I turned that down he lit up a cigarette for himself. Then he asked if I wanted to try some of his prescribed medication, all the 'stuff', he said, his minders would let him have these days, although one of his 'tabs' could, he promised, give me a bit of a buzz.

'Thanks, but I'm fine, really.'

'Suit yourself. What d'you want to do then? Go through some of our old photographs?'

'Yes, that would be great.'

He pulled out one of perhaps a dozen enormous photograph albums. 'Sit beside me over here so I can show you.'

With the album spread across our laps, he turned page after page of pictures from the nineteen-sixties, the faces of the adolescent group appearing astonishingly innocent. Some were of the band on stage, some showed them relaxing indoors, but the most striking were outdoor shots. They had a rawness to them. 'Wow,' I said, 'plenty to choose from here for an autobiography. When will Rick be joining us?

'Sorry mate, he's still in Saint Tropez. He's left a voice mail for you though.' Heath handed me a phone.

I was awed to hear one of the music world's most famous voices speak to me personally. 'Came down here on a quick trip but have got a bit sucked in so, you know, thought I'd leave you a quick message to say, you know, basically, got to be quick, thing is, me and Teef go far back, way far back, so he should be able to clear up any queries you've got. Hope to have a quick word

117

with you some other time. Quick bye for now.'

I handed the phone back to Heath and said, 'It sounded like he called you "Teef".'

'He calls me that, on account of me having buck teeth when I was a kid.' He pointed to his incisors, as though I might not know where his buck teeth had been. He added, '*I* sometimes call *him* Quick.'

'Quick?'

'Because when he talks, every third word you hear is "quick". Don't put that in the book, will you? He don't like other people knowing about the nickname, thinks Quick Schwagger might be misinterpreted.'

I laughed.

'What's so funny?' he asked.

'Haven't heard him called Quick Schwagger before. What actually is it that he wants me to do?'

The question surprised him, and he stared at me open mouthed.

'What I mean is, does it make sense for me to start researching his early years, family history, school days and so on? In the phone message he said you would know…'

'Like to help, but I have to admit taking so much stuff over the years has more or less blown my brains out. Quick and I did go to school together, but I don't really remember that far back.'

'You can't have lost it to that extent. You still play on stage in concerts.'

'My fingers still seem to remember what to do, unless it's the sound technicians playing it all back from recordings. An army of people are hidden away backstage who take care of everything. I strut about up front, *that* I can still do, but I don't really know what's going on, tell you the truth. Don't put that in the book though, will you. Quick wouldn't like it.'

'Well, in that case, I'd better wait until I can talk to Quick, I mean Rick, himself.'

'That won't help you much. He can't concentrate for long… round about fifteen seconds. Not because of the drugs. He thinks he takes a load of stuff, but he doesn't really. Thing is he gets pissed on half a pint of beer; a couple of tokes of a spliff and he's away with the fairies, no offence to you like, you being a bender.'

Alicia must have mentioned that I was gay. He had been friendly until then, but the word 'bender' is a put-down. I said, 'Yes, I'm gay. Can you tell me what help is actually wanted from me with the book?'

'Not for me to tell you something like that, is it? What I was saying about Quick was… well… let him near any coke, soon as a couple of specks have gone up his nostrils he'll be straight out of the door, stopping women in the street and asking them to swap clothes with him. He thinks he's taking genuine stuff big time, but what The Handyman does, is let him have a small shandy or half a tab of something and the rest is all vitamins and sugar pills. You need to understand, when you do see him, you mustn't give him anything that's too strong, in fact best not give him anything at all.'

He was surely having me on, so I said, 'The photographs are great. Is there anything else, personal papers or diaries, that I could see?'

'No. The idea is for you to do it by reading the tarot cards, shaking round the old juju beads, or whatever it is you use.'

'Very funny, but we've only got an hour; we need to be practical. To do research, I'll need to have access to personal papers, or interview people.'

'Oh no, Quick won't want you to go round asking people about him. They might say all sorts of things he wouldn't like.

You mustn't tell him you was thinking of doing that. He can get nasty if he don't get his own way. Alicia told him you was gifted.'

'She thinks I know things intuitively, but…'

'That's better. I'll tell Quick you'll find out intuitively what to put in the book. He'll like that.' A gong, the dinner signal, rang downstairs, bringing our meeting to an end. 'Thank God the food's ready,' Teef said. 'You don't half get desperate for your nosh when they won't let you have any decent gear. Nice to have met you. Try and smuggle a few tabs past The Handyman for me if you come again. He'll take you back home now.'

'Why do you call him that, "The Handyman"?'

'It's his nickname. His real name is Andy Handman, and he's handy to have around, so we call him The Handyman. Get it? He does loads of jobs for us, not just ferrying people about in the car.'

On the way home The Handyman asked me whether Teef had offered me any of his pills. I said evasively, 'I don't do drugs.'

'Proper Goody Two Shoes, aren't you? Didn't come on to you, did he, you being a bender? You never know, these days a gay boy might get him going. You're not bad looking.'

'Why should it matter to you if he did fancy me?'

'Well, I make anything to do with the lads my business. Teef doesn't really have sex any more, not as we know it. Do him good to have a bit of fun with someone. He used to be mad for the girls, but he hasn't made a play for anyone for years. I've taken high class chicks up to the room for him to try to get him interested, but it's no use, waste of money, he's not like he was in the old days. Having you might have been a bit of novelty for him.'

'Well he didn't. You're making a lot out of me being gay.'

'Oh, you're well known for it, mate. That and the fortune telling.'

120

My hour with Teef, memorable though it had been, was not what anyone would call an interview. Surely he had been joking when he said information for the book was to come through tarot cards or juju beads. Ought I to take anything he or The Handyman had said seriously? Perhaps they had been expecting to enjoy a good laugh at some clairvoyant type who would go swooning around the room detecting supposed concentrations of psychic energy and having to be revived with smelling salts.

When I reported back to Alicia, infuriatingly she asked, 'Well, Heath's suggestions are not a surprise to me. Why can't you use your gifts to help you?'

'I am not psychic. A biography is a life story. It needs facts, not fancies.'

'You're so stubborn. If you're to get anywhere in life you'll have to come to terms with having special powers. You're in a state of denial. Do you want the high point of your career to be having a cup of tea with Jeremy? Can't you try to open your mind to wider possibilities a little bit?'

This was unkind to Jeremy, who had helped her so much to set up her shop. He always spoke well of her, and defended her against my charge that she made money out of hocus-pocus. Even Dale did not understand how I felt about my meeting with Heath. He said, 'You're a lucky bastard. First you get to meet Loyd Larcher, now it's Heath Prityards. People pay hard-earned cash to go to concerts to see him far away on stage, and treasure the memory of being one of the crowd. You get driven to his home and spend time on your own with him. What more do you want? So far the best thing that's happened to me all week has been finding a firm that might offer a few hundred pounds to buy some of the old laundry equipment from the hospital.'

Almost a week passed without any further word from The

Rocking Boulders. Thinking over the exchanges with The Handyman, and Heath's reluctance or inability to tell me anything useful, they might well have given up on me. I was thinking about sending an e-mail to ask how things stood, when The Handyman rang to say he would collect me again that very evening. In the car he resurrected my hopes, saying that Teef was really keen to see me. 'He's started calling you "Bendy" – on account of you being a bender. It's almost like old times, Teef coming up with a nickname like that. Rick's away again, though.'

'You didn't think I might be offended by being called "Bendy"'?

'No, being given a pet name by the lads is a great privilege. Can't say I was exactly thrilled about being called The Handyman, makes me sound like I do odd jobs, but you get used to it. Think of it as a step towards being accepted. Lots more steps to go, mind. Anyway it's best not to complain. If you do they'll call you something really nasty, like rat-face or bollock-chops.' When we pulled up outside the villa he said he wanted to search me for drugs.

'If that's how it's going to be, you can take me back home right now.'

'Come on Bendy,' he said, 'You ought to like having a man pat you down and put his hands in the pockets of your jeans. You mystics are a bloody touchy lot. What worries me is Teef getting hold of something that would harm him. Checking people out is part of my job. I'm not accusing you. Alicia's recommended you, and Quick's got a lot of confidence in her from ages ago when she helped him out. Will you promise me, word of honour, that you're clean?'

'Yes. Even if I was into drugs, which I'm not, do you think I would risk causing Teef to have a relapse?'

'Okay then. Don't get so pissed off. You have to understand

being suspicious is part of my job. I've got nothing against you. Shake hands with me, come on.' He grasped my hand, pulled me towards him and patted me on the back before ushering me up to Teef's room.

'Bendy, my old mate,' said the Boulders' guitarist, 'nice of you to come over! He's in good shape, isn't he, Handyman?'

'He's fine. What would you say, Teef? Do you think he's a cute one?'

Teef was non-committal. 'Expect all the other gay boys think so.'

'You bet they do. You enjoy yourselves. I'll come back when it's time for dinner.'

'The Handyman must have taken a shine to you, asking me if I think you're cute. This is rock and roll you know, it is allowed, if you and him wanted to have a bit of…'

'I've got a boyfriend.'

'Up to you. He's married anyway. How's it going with Quick's autobiography?'

'I've nothing to go on, have I? No one has told me properly what I'm supposed to do. I could spend days researching stuff, only for Quick to say it's not what he wants. Lots of issues we've not even talked about, like whether the book should be a couple of hundred pages or a thousand, when it's supposed to come out, and the money side of things. No one has made any proper arrangements.'

He nodded, thought for a moment and said, 'Can't all that be sorted out after? P'raps you need something to get you in the mood. If the book's not coming to you yet, we'll have to be careful what we say to Quick, don't want him turning nasty. He's left a message for you, by the way.' He handed me the phone.

'Allo there Bendy,' the voicemail began. 'Just a quick call. Teef's give me a quick, you know, appraisal like, and says he thinks you could be the right man to do the book. Sorry, but have to be quick, got a plane to catch, quick trip to Rio for a quick couple of days, you know, lot of partying to catch up with, so quick bye for now.'

'Understand why I call him Quick, can't you,' said Teef. 'Do you think touching some of his belongings would help you with the book?'

I shrugged. 'How is that going to help?'

'It might give you some ideas. It's all right, you can trust me, I know you guys can't turn the mojo on and off, it's not like something that comes out of a tap. If I try and help you get the 'fluence going, maybe you can help me with my problem. I'll show you some of his things.' He opened a cupboard and pulled out an assortment of stuff including a feather boa, some cricket pads and a pair of maracas. 'Try having a shake with these,' he said. 'With his attention span they're about the only instrument he's ever been able to play. See if they get that old sixth sense of yours tuned in.'

Fooling around with a few of Quick's belongings was hardly likely to help, but the opportunity to play with the very maracas that those famous hands had held so often was too good to turn down. 'They're big, aren't they?' I said, picking them up.

'Be careful with them, won't you. They're easily damaged. He's very fussy about anyone touching his private bits and pieces.'

'Don't worry, I'll be gentle with them. Wouldn't want to do anything to hurt the most valuable maracas in the world.' I took one in each hand, shook them back and forth gingerly, and listened to the contents swishing about inside. Urging me on, Teef picked up a guitar and strummed a few chords. I tried different ways of shaking the maracas, rotating them beside each other in opposite directions, holding them in one hand and smacking them gently against my free arm and so on – they were easy to play. Having a go with them was terrific, and somehow touching things so personal to Quick did make me feel, in a way, that I was getting closer to him. After a few minutes Teef stopped playing, and I rested them on my lap. He grinned impudently and said, 'Thought I'd better stop. You was getting a bit carried away, wasn't you, Bendy? Began to worry you might be over-exciting yourself. Mustn't go too far. Remember we didn't have Quick's permission to play with his maracas. Promise you will never tell anyone about our little session, not even The Handyman? Quick might turn nasty if he ever found out.'

'I won't say a word, don't worry.'

'Have you ever heard of drugs being hidden inside maracas and smuggled through customs?'

'It must have been tried.'

'Watch this,' he said, unscrewing the handle of one of them to show me it was hollow inside. The dinner gong sounded downstairs.

'Oh fuck,' he said, and quickly returned the maracas and other oddments to the cupboard before The Handyman appeared to take me back home.

In the car he asked, 'How'd it go, Bendy? Anything to report?'

'We got on all right.'

'Sex?'

'No,' I said, smiling at the way he always turned our conversations to drugs or sex.

'You know I can see you sitting there in the mirror. You've got a sweet little smile on you. I could park, nip round the back and give you a quick one if you like.'

'Thanks, but I've got a boyfriend.'

'What's that got to do with it?'

125

'Everything. Look, about the autobiography, is anyone going to tell me properly what it is I'm supposed to be doing?'

'Writing it, of course, what else do you want me to tell you? Quick'll be wanting to see something before long. Soon as you're indoors, if I was you I'd get shuffling those tarot cards. He's dying to have his book come out. We don't want him turning nasty.'

Hatshepsut's Pavilion was usually ready to welcome the world before nine o'clock. On Monday at ten I noticed that Alicia had not yet opened up. She was always bright and sparkling first thing, difficult for someone like me who needs time for the brain cells to warm up. When Jeremy arrived at the bookshop a little later he was in an agitated state, his face flushed, his hair messed up, one shirt sleeve down and the other rolled halfway up. 'Thank heavens you're here,' he said. 'Something awful has happened. I don't know what on earth to do.'

The last time he had been like this was when he had dropped his breakfast egg on the floor and, as he tried to clean up, spread the goo everywhere. I got him to sit down while I made him tea, took the steaming mug in, and sat opposite him. 'Now, tell me all about it.'

'There's no way of breaking this to you gently. The fact of the matter is…' – he took a deep breath – 'Alicia's hat has been taken into police custody.'

'What did you say? Her hat?'

'Yes. You remember, that wonderful bio-thaumaturgical hat, the *miracle of germination* one that you helped her plant up.'

'Is Alicia all right?'

'She's taken it very badly. And it had to happen during one of her country weekends with her girlfriend, Muriel. I'm so upset for her. I think I may have to lie down.'

Afraid that Toby's cannabis seeds in the brim had resulted in the police charging Alicia with possession of an illegal substance, I held back a feeling of panic. Could my little joke have caused such a disaster? What if sniffer bloodhounds, excited by the scent of the weed, had leapt through the air, grabbed the hat in their teeth, and knocked poor Alicia to the ground? Concealing my own fears I reassured Jeremy until he was calm enough to go into the little office to do some work on the accounts, a task that might distract him from worrying about Alicia.

We heard nothing more until midday when she rang to say she was in the shop and had opened up. Jeremy took his sandwiches over and kept her company over lunch, and I went in during the afternoon to see how she was, ready if necessary to admit responsibility for the drugs in her hat. For the first time in months she was not wearing headgear of any kind. Actually her hair was rather nice, sort of sandy coloured and fluffy. Cautiously I told her I was sorry to hear of her bad news.

'What bad news?' she asked.

'About the police and your hat.'

'Oh that. Well, I suppose Myrtle and I were asking for trouble.'

'Myrtle? I thought your girlfriend was called Muriel.'

'Yes, Muriel is her name really. My pet name for her is Myrtle – rather sweet, don't you think? You're showing off, aren't you? You've never heard me call her Muriel, I never do, but you just knew it without needing to be told, didn't you?'

'Did I? No, of course I didn't. Jeremy always refers to her as Muriel.'

'Not when he talks to me he doesn't. Is he all right? He was a bit shaky when he came over for lunch. He's a worrier. Well, of course, no need to tell you that. Can I ask you something? Do you know everything that's going to happen in advance? I mean, did you set off for work this morning thinking oh dear, Alicia will be late opening up and Jeremy is going to be in an awful tizzy, I'll have to calm him down?'

'Please don't start going on about me being "gifted". Tell me about the hat.'

'You're so stubborn… in denial as usual. Anyway, where was I? Oh yes, the hat. The trouble started when Myrtle and I were driving to her cottage in Hay-on-Wye. We usually stop off at this pretentious tea shop full of posh old biddies. It's one of those snooty places where the staff dress up as maids from days of yore. We thought we'd give all those wilting petunias in their Sunday best a jolt, so we strode in, argued about which table to sit at, and banged the chairs about before plonking ourselves down. Then we complained about lack of choice on the menu, and when our order arrived we said it was barely enough to sustain a budgerigar. We slurped our tea, talked loudly, then pretended to have a row. You know the sort of thing, I don't suppose it's much compared with what you and Dale get up to when you go out. Well, the looks of indignation from all around almost curdled our milk. We were really pleased with ourselves. The manageress actually came over and asked us to leave. We got up, protesting vociferously, and said it was no good her hanging around expecting a tip.

'Unfortunately in the excitement I left the hat behind, and the vindictive cow of a manageress noticed some strange leaves among the seedlings in the brim. She called the police and said she thought they were cannabis. Half an hour later, on the road, we were pulled over. Myrtle is now terrified I'm turning into a drug fiend.'

'Doesn't she mind you calling her Myrtle?'

'Mind? Why on earth should she? You do say the strangest things sometimes, even if you are gifted.'

'What happened next about the hat?'

'It's still at the police station. God knows what they're doing to it. I suppose the firm that made it could have accidentally put some hemp seeds in the compost. It's hardly my fault if they did. Anyway, the leaves didn't look much like hemp to me. Myrtle is quite a plantswoman, she would have spotted hemp leaves, I'm sure. No, it's just the thought of that snooty manageress causing us trouble that riles me. In a way I wish they were cannabis. Imagine what a laugh the court case would be... newspaper headlines screaming *Psychic shopkeeper grows drugs in her hat*. If only we had thought of putting some in when we planted it up! You could have spoken in my defence in court and said you saw someone sneak something into the brim while we were on a bus.'

'You haven't been wearing that hat on a bus?'

'No, silly, as if I'd risk damaging it on a crowded bus. What is up with you today? Is anything wrong?'

Her attitude made it difficult to decide whether to confess to planting the cannabis seeds or to keep quiet. Luckily, a few days later she learned the suspect leaves had turned out not to be cannabis after all. The police had sent the hat to the botanical gardens at Kew, where they were identified as a common wild flower, cinquefoil. Finally I showed her Toby's seed packet and confessed to what I had done. She was very good about it and joked, 'I suppose you were getting your own back for those runes I planted on you.' By the time the hat was returned all the leaves had shrivelled. Alicia, though, may have been more worried by the incident than she made out, for she never wore the hat again.

Ten

Now that Dale and I were boyfriends, you might think that we would have lost interest in his erotic computer game. It was not designed for two to play at the same time, but we hit on a way of using it together.

One of us would set up situations in which the other had to overcome various challenges. We each created on-screen personae for ourselves, 'avatars' in the jargon of the game. Lots of scenarios could be generated by choosing from the options included with the software. It being an erotic computer game, events always ended with sexual coupling. When, one Sunday, he had to go in to work, he left a new scenario for me to explore. After a couple of hours cleaning the flat, I broke off to see what he had come up with. My avatar was a youthful Latino with broad shoulders and slim hips. Dale had dressed him in a leotard and placed him on the low end of a see-saw, surrounded by a troupe of acrobats. A member of the troupe climbed onto a platform, and when I clicked on him he jumped down onto the high end of the see-saw, flinging my avatar up into the air. He somersaulted on his way down again. When he landed the impact launched the man on the other end into flight, and he returned to his previous position on the platform.

This sequence could be repeated again and again; the challenge was to find how to progress to the next step. A third acrobat held the end of a trapeze, and by trial and error clicking all over the screen I found he could be made to grab the outstretched arms of my avatar, and carry him across to a trampoline, where the on-screen version of me bounced up and down performing mid-air acrobatics.

Meanwhile Dale's avatar, created using a terrific photograph of him in the shorts and singlet he used for rowing, appeared and stood on the low end of the see-saw. He could similarly be transported up into the air and over to the trampoline. The other acrobats had then to be removed from the scene by sending them up to the trapeze and swinging them beyond the edge of the screen, leaving only the two of us. Our pleasure at bouncing up and down together became obvious — well, in an erotic computer game, you can guess how the situation developed.

Since in real life we cuddled up to each other in bed every night, fooling around with on-screen versions of ourselves might be thought a bit unnecessary, but it was fun. Anyway, this made it my turn to devise a scenario for Dale. I clicked on the *Historical scenes* menu and chose *Ancient Egypt*, dressed his avatar in a loincloth, and had him climb up the side of a huge pyramid, pausing now and again to reposition his minimal clothing whenever it slipped slightly out of place. When his on-screen self reached the pyramid's top, he would tumble down the other side and have to climb back up again. This would continue until the real-life Dale clicked on a protruding stone to trigger a trap door, making him fall down into the pyramid.

Two Nubian guards then appeared, dressed in long white flowing robes, translucent enough to reveal their handsome slender forms. They chased Dale's avatar through the pyramid's narrow passages. He turned this way and that, but they were never far behind. His only escape was to risk a drop of about six feet into a large chamber cluttered with grave goods. By dragging and dropping with the mouse he could be made to jump down and land on the lid of a sarcophagus.

The Nubians ran off to find a rope ladder. To escape from them again, he had to be made to jump off the sarcophagus. The lid then slid open. Guess who, apparently mummified but about to spring back into life, was waiting in the casket? It was of course my avatar, in full pharaoh's regalia – the crown, false beard and so on, and to make sure he knew who it was really, I wrote *Pharaoh Ben IV* on the sarcophagus in fancy snake-like lettering. Dale's avatar climbed in with me, the lid of the sarcophagus closed gently over us, and as Dale and I engaged with each other, the whole stone casket shuddered. When the Nubian guards saw it moving, they fled in terror. After they had gone the front panel fell off, revealing the two of us in the kind of action you might expect at the end of the game.

Fun as this was, Sunday dinner had to be prepared, and while peeling the vegetables my thoughts wandered back to Teef, and how peculiar our meeting had been. He had been very friendly, but since I had no intention of supplying him with drugs, my next visit could well be my last. So far, except for the photograph albums, he had given me nothing of any use for Rick Schwagger's book.

My hopes that Rick's 'auto'biography might be my big chance in life were increasingly like pipe dreams. Why had I not been able to make more of the opening? If Dale had been given the chance instead of me, he would surely have planned everything out by now, or decided the idea was impractical and moved on. He would not be dithering as I was.

When he returned from work he was worn out. Dinner was

in the oven and the smell of roasting food drifted appetizingly into the hall. I gave him a drink and encouraged him to watch TV until it was time to eat. When we ate he said, 'You're very quiet.'

'Sorry. I've been thinking about Rick Schwagger and his so-called autobiography. I don't want to worry you about it. You've done a day's work already.'

'What makes you think you'd be worrying me? The weird situations you get yourself into are part of your attraction… they can't be coincidence entirely… must be something about you. How could you get them to believe you were going to write a book using psychic powers you haven't got?'

'So what's the answer then? Give up the whole idea? Tell them it was all a misunderstanding?'

'How about having a "brainstorming" session with Jeremy, where we all throw in ideas and you follow up the best ones? We may or may not find a way forward, but at least we'd have tried. Better ask Alicia as well. We don't want her to feel left out, though since she started all this you being psychic nonsense, heaven knows what she'll come up with.'

We arranged to get together in the little office at the back of Jeremy's shop; Dale sat on a pile of encyclopaedias as there were only three chairs. Alicia wore an outsize beige trilby, not for her an outlandish piece of headgear, but it reminded me of the episode with the bio-thaumaturgical hat and made me feel guilty all over again.

Dale took charge and asked me to summarise the situation with the 'auto'biography. I said a little about meeting Teef at the villa. Alicia interrupted, saying: 'I've found the answer: low frequency energy fields. They're very big in the States now. They're being written about all the time in magazines and on the web. I saw a report from the Minnesota Mystics only last week. Basically what happens is that everybody emits lots of energy every single moment in a range of wavelengths, you can feel it, that unmistakable 'buzz' you sometimes find at a party. Naturally the energy fades over time, but residues always linger on in low-frequency energy fields, and these traces can be picked up by sensitives like Ben.' She stopped abruptly and sat up very straight, waiting for an enthusiastic response.

None of us knew what to say. At last Dale spoke calmly and moderately. 'Thank you for the thought you've given to the problem, but how exactly could these energy fields help to write a book?'

'Isn't it obvious? Throughout his life Rick Schwagger has been emitting energies, a whole spectrum of frequencies, and given the kind of person he is, they will have streamed out from him with great gusto. Residues of his emanations, reflecting all his thoughts, experiences and emotions, still linger in low-frequency energy fields, so someone gifted like Ben has only to tune in to them, and hey presto, he will have a fully detailed record of every incident and experience Schwagger has ever known, big or small. The only problem will be sifting through such a vast quantity of knowledge to pick out the most suitable events for his book.'

Jeremy diplomatically raised a finger to ask for our attention. 'In a situation like this all ideas are worth an airing,' he said, 'and low-frequency energy fields are certainly not something I would have thought of, but I have a more mundane suggestion to make. It might be worth consulting my old friend Loyd. You probably know that he's been busy recently promoting the omnibus edition of his novels, but that is not taking up so much of his time now. He has a huge range of knowledge and experience to draw on. He knows as much as anyone does about writing books. At any rate, Ben, it would do no harm if you made contact again.'

Alicia protested volubly, calling Loyd an 'old fool', but as three of us thought this worthwhile Dale added *consult Loyd Larcher* to the list of ideas, under *Alicia's emanations*. He then made his own suggestion, unfortunately the very thing I was going to propose myself. 'What about press and magazine cuttings?' he said. The Rocking Boulders' more notorious escapades were widely reported in the papers.'

'Oh yes,' Jeremy agreed. 'Good thinking. You have to watch out though, some of the stories may not be reliable. And ploughing through news reports can take forever. I remember once, before you joined us Ben... He rambled on and on about a customer who came into the shop asking for a book he had seen a review of, but his memory of the title and author were vague. Hours of searching the internet were needed to track it down. By the time Jeremy finished this reminiscence, my mind had wandered off the meeting and back to the villa, and how odd it was that Teef, who played electric guitar, should be summoned to dinner by the sound of a old-fashioned gong.

'Did you have any suggestions, Ben?' Dale asked.

'Erm... oh... erm... how about researching records of births, marriages, deaths, and old census information? Maybe I could trace Rick's relatives and unearth enough for a chapter on his family background.'

Mention of searching official records set Jeremy off on another tale about how he had traced the history of all the shops in the parade back to the early twentieth century. When he paused for breath Alicia said impatiently, 'Local history is all very interesting, but we are supposed to be helping Ben with the 'auto'biography. Here you are, Ben, this should help you to tune in,' she said, and produced from her bag a funny little metal bar with a sort of zigzag electrical spark shape at one end, and an odd, rounded nodule at the other.

'What is it?'

'It's an antenna for detecting low-frequency energy fields. You need to take it somewhere as quiet as possible, free of interference from current goings on, preferably places where Rick himself has been.' Not wanting to appear ungrateful, I put the antenna in my pocket, intending to drop it into a drawer at Fulrose Court and forget about it.

Jeremy's suggestion of talking to Loyd was the best thing to come out of our meeting. When I rang him he invited me to go round to his flat, where he welcomed me with a vigorous handshake. 'Dear, dear boy! Good of you to come! How've you been? Afraid I've had to endure one of those wretched periods when the commercial side, the selling of books, had priority. My publisher ordered me to be available to reviewers, TV presenters and similarly tiresome people. So good that has all quietened down and I am able to see friends again. Jeremy said you were having a spot of trouble. Let me offer you something to drink before you tell me about it.'

I asked for coffee, thinking this would be quick, but he was in the kitchen for ten minutes, and returned with a silver tray coffee pot, bone china milk jug, cups and saucers. I explained about Rick Schwagger's 'auto'biography and the difficulty of getting started. He exclaimed: 'Amazing! Uncanny! How on earth did you know?'

'Sorry, not with you…'

'It was years and years ago, of course, before my literary career took off. I did the odd spell of what's now called supply teaching. For a couple of weeks I stood in for Schwagger's form master, who was ill – having a knife removed from his back, I shouldn't wonder. I hardly ever think of those long-gone days

136

when starting out as a writer was such a struggle. Somehow you must have picked up on it. Perhaps you are psychic. Of course it could be a fluke, pure coincidence, but the fact is here you are, asking me about an ex-pupil. Afraid I can't tell you much, though. My impression of the lad was that he was bright, but had a terribly short attention span. Even then something about his voice commanded attention in an irritating, rasping sort of way. Deputy headmaster had a poor opinion of him. Something to do with a cricket match with a neighbouring school. Their pads had been tampered with, pins or spikes or something worked into the lining. Schwagger was the main suspect but nothing was ever proven.'

'Really? You actually taught Rick Schwagger at school? You're not joking? Do you remember the Boulders' guitarist, Heath Prityards, who went there as well?'

'The experience was not the high point of my life. Can't bring Prityards to mind, I'm afraid.' He went on to tell me everything he could remember of Rick and the school, and I jotted down a couple of pages of notes. I mentioned Alicia's mistaken belief that I was 'gifted', and showed him the antenna, still in my pocket, that was supposed to help me detect low-frequency energy fields.

'Afraid she has it in for me. Years ago at some do of Jeremy's I launched into a demolition of the French writer Simone de Beauvoir, among other things referring to her as Simone de Boudoir, without realizing she was Alicia's great feminist idol. By the way, you know her real name is Alice Hatchette, don't you? She always indulged in a fascination with silly hats. I say, I couldn't borrow that antenna thing for a minute, could I?'

'Surely *you* don't believe in low-frequency energy fields?'

'Well, no, though just what did make you decide to consult me about Schwagger, eh? But my reason for asking is entirely down to earth, or to be precise, a couple of floors above ground, where we ourselves are at this very moment. The other day the key broke off in the lock of the balcony door, and that little implement might just serve to winkle out the remains.'

Loyd scratched around in the lock, and after a minute or so the end of the broken key fell to the floor. 'You see, Ben, you should never underestimate the value of the paranormal,' he said, smiling. 'You came to ask my advice on this book about Rick Schwagger. Obviously you are going to want some help. I need to give it a little thought. My publisher keeps what he refers to as "the Loyd Larcher brand" under tight control, so my involvement would have to be unofficial, but I'll do what I can.'

When I told Dale of my visit to Loyd, he was not at all surprised to hear Alicia's real name. He already knew it, having seen it on an envelope in the shop one day. 'I didn't need to be "gifted" to find that out,' he said wryly.

Loyd had given me my first usable material for Rick's 'auto'biography, but I left out the part about him having sabotaged a rival team's cricket pads, thinking he would not want it included. Given my lack of progress during two visits to The Rocking Boulders' villa, the pages of notes were a real achievement. Until then my folder contained only peripheral papers – the print-outs of the e-mails that preceded my first meeting with The Handyman and Teef – and the suggestions from the brainstorming session in the bookshop. To this, surely, could be added what Alicia knew of Rick's involvement with the Oracles of Aten. I resolved also to read the sect's book and note anything of use.

Most important, I was able to report my progress to The Handyman and Teef. For my third trip to the villa, I was collected from home as before, and ushered up to the first-floor sitting room, where The Handyman left me alone with Teef. He was preoccupied with counting some white oval tablets, presumably part of his prescribed medication, which he had laid out in an evenly spaced row on the table. At first he did not respond to my news about Loyd having taught Rick at school, but said, 'Ah yeah, Quick's book. Great to see you, Bendy. You brought me any gear?'

He grimaced at my excuses. 'We've got to think of something, Bendy. Me being stuck here with nothing but the pills the doctor gives me and the odd shot of Jack Daniel's, and that's if I'm lucky, for someone who's been used all his life to taking everything he could swallow, shove up his nose, or shoot into his veins, it is real purgatory. You could get hold of a couple of lines of coke or a few pills for me, course you could, no trouble, especially you being a bender. The gay clubs are swamped with stuff, more than even I could dream of. Remember the maracas I showed you last time? It would be too risky to let you take Quick's away with you, but a friend of mine has managed to smuggle in another pair for me.'

He went to check the landing outside in case anyone might be listening, then pulled a leather holdall containing the maracas from under an armchair. The highly polished surfaces were flawless, but with a wink he unscrewed the handles, which were hollow inside. Then pressing and twisting the tops with the palm of his hand, he unscrewed the upper section, revealing two more hidden compartments. 'See Bendy, you can hide enough stuff in them to keep me happy for a whole week. I don't want to cause you hassle. Just get what you can for me, hide it in the maracas and bring them back next time. What we'll do is this. We'll practise a few numbers together, and when The Handyman comes back we'll tell him you're learning to play them; then when you leave, you just pick them up; all natural like, act easy and, er, nonchalant, don't overdo it mind, and take them home with you. Before you come to see me again, take yourself down to a club and get whatever you can, especially a few grams of coke. I can't give you cash now, they make it difficult for me to get my hands on ready money, but I'll definitely be able to pay you next time you come.'

I tried to divert him by asking, since he had been to the same school as Rick, if he remembered Loyd.

'Oh yes, you were saying earlier. You've actually made contact with some geezer who taught Quick and me? How did you find out about him? He might have taught us, but with my memory...' He shook his head, 'Not that I doubt what you say. Shows you must be psychic after all. Waiting for so long without hearing of any progress, Quick and me were beginning to think you was a lot of whistle but no tune. He'll be really chuffed when I tell him.'

'Coincidence, that's all it was...'

'Yeah, yeah, if you say so, Bendy. The genuine ones have to play it down, don't they, too worried about people taking advantage. You can trust me, I won't spread it around. Obviously you have to be careful who knows about the old sixth sense. You don't want to be plagued with punters trying to get you to tell them which horse is going to win the Cheltenham Gold Cup. Anyway, better get started with the music. Remember? We want The Handyman to find us playing when he comes in.'

Even though my role was merely to shake the maracas as instructed by vigorous nods of Teef's head while he played guitar, and even though he had only suggested it as part of a scheme to get some 'gear', I happily did as he asked. How strange that Teef, with his enormous fortune from records and concert tours, with millions of devoted fans, was so much in The Handyman's control. After almost fifteen minutes we reached a rhythmic climax. Then the dinner gong sounded downstairs, and as on my earlier visits The Handyman appeared at the door. 'Ho, ho, ho,' he said, 'what have we here?'

'Nothing,' Teef said. 'We were just making music together.' He took the maracas from me, put them in the holdall, and dropped it in my lap.

The Handyman's expression softened and he said jokingly, 'Was that what it was? I'll give you a tip. Next time you're thinking of playing together, try taking your clothes off first.' We gave his attempt at humour a stony response. He shrugged and said, 'All serious tonight, are we? All right, but a bit of fun wouldn't do you no harm, Teef. He's a nice-looking boy… anyway, suit yourself… time to go, Bendy.'

I took the holdall with me, only realizing on the way to the car this would encourage Teef to think they would be packed with 'gear' the next time he saw them.

Rather than having me sit in the back of the car, The Handyman opened the front passenger door and gestured for me to get in. He slowed down and glanced across at me quizzically as the car passed a very dark area under trees by the gate, but I kept my eyes ahead. He edged us forward and turned onto the main road. 'Your visits have gone all right so far, Bendy. We don't want anything to happen that might spoil it all, do we?'

'Why should anything?' I said, turning towards him. He returned my stare. 'No phone message from Quick this time though,' I added, trying not to sound guilty.

'You keep in your mind that I'm watching out for signs of any goings-on that Quick wouldn't approve of.' His tone was flat, matter-of-fact. 'Actually, it is possible you might get to meet him. He is in London. Got his eye on a woman he met at some posh party. Lady-in-waiting at the Palace, he says. Got to be extra careful whenever he's about, we don't want him turning nasty.

141

And don't go expecting anything much to develop with Teef. Remember, he doesn't really have sex any more, not as you and I know it.'

'I do have a boyfriend.' I reminded him. 'Can't imagine Quick with a lady-in-waiting. Not becoming respectable, is he?'

'He doesn't know the meaning of the word. What I've heard is, every now and again one of them in the big house fancies a bit of rough. Expect that's the reason.'

He pulled up outside Fulrose Court and turned towards me again. In the same flat voice he said, 'Give us a kiss, Bendy.'

'What?

'Go on, why not? Before you go, give us a kiss.'

What harm could there be in a kiss? The request was a big improvement on his offer last time, to give me a 'quick one' in the back of the car. He had not turned off the engine, so he was probably just being friendly. I leaned forward and gently touched my lips on his. He pulled me to him, hugged me tightly and pushed his tongue into my mouth. After perhaps half a minute he let me go.

'You excite me, you know. I'm a happily married man, but you excite me.'

'I don't play around, well, not these days. Dale… my boyfriend… we really want things to work out for us. It's not because I don't like you, but my partner is in and he's waiting for me.'

'Okay, if that's how it is. No hard feelings. Let me know if you change your mind.' He shrugged and turned away. I got out of the car and said goodbye.

To give myself time to think, when the lift doors closed I did not immediately push the button for the sixth floor. Might refusing The Handyman a second time have harmed my chances of at last meeting Rick Schwagger? Casual sex might well be a

142

sort of entry ticket to their world. Yet, Dale was more important to me than anything or anyone else, even more important than the chance of working on Quick's 'auto'biography.

Eleven

The next time he took me to The Rocking Boulders' villa, The Handyman promised that Rick Schwagger himself would be there. I was nervous already because the compartments in the maracas remained empty of drugs. How Rick, with his reputation for turning nasty, would react to me was even more of a worry.

Perhaps being on edge made me want to talk, for on the way I complained about the difficulty of finding information for the 'auto'biography. For once, The Handyman was sympathetic. 'Tell you the truth,' he said, 'I never thought much of all that mumbo jumbo about astrology, tarot cards and juju beads. You were worth encouraging, not because of all that mystic twaddle, but because you cheer Teef up, and that's not easy these days. Trouble is, we can't tell Quick that, he's sold on the idea of you being psychic. When you meet him, particularly this being the first time, try not to say anything that might aggravate him. Thing to remember is that he has a very short attention span, so if you can keep chatting about a subject for maybe a minute, sometimes half a minute will do, by the time you stop, his mind will have wandered off. Doesn't guarantee he won't meander back to it, but if he does you just bluff him again till he's thinking of something else.

'In this business you have to find your way round dozens of obstacles to survive. Trying to work out what to do can make your head hurt. Doing the book, and keeping Quick and Teef happy at the same time, is not going to be easy. A good thing to mention to Quick is money, like who is going to get what percentage. Anything that might lead to a big wad of notes will have a magic effect on his powers of concentration. The thought of earning yet more cash to add to his millions will occupy him for, ooh, might be as long as two whole minutes. If you've got a few pages of notes to show him, that should keep him happy for now, but be very careful what you say to him. If he shows any sign of turning nasty, do a runner. Don't let him get between you and the door. You're not on your own, I'll try to keep things steady.'

'What do you mean by him "turning nasty"? Does he get violent?'

'Not sure if you would call it violent exactly … Well, it is in a way. He's developed a ruthless streak. Bullying, you might call it. Or assault. Highly unlikely you'll come in for aggravation. I'm good at calming him down, but be on your guard just in case.'

His manner was calm and relaxed, despite giving this sphinx-like warning. When we arrived at the villa, quiet determination had replaced my earlier trepidation. If Quick took an instant dislike to me and kicked me out, I would be disappointed, but he was not about to decide my fate. Life with Dale and work at the bookshop would carry on as before. With luck, other opportunities would come along.

The Handyman pointed at the holdall. 'You don't usually bring anything with you. What you got in there?'

'Maracas.'

'Teef's not trying to pull the old trick of filling maracas with dope, is he? You'd better let me see.'

I took them out of the bag and said, 'The handles are hollow and you can unscrew them; there are hidden compartments at the top too. They're empty. He did ask me to fill them with gear. I said no, but he wouldn't let it go. It was useless him asking me, I've never gone in for drugs. I picked them up without thinking when I left the villa last time. You can open them up and see for yourself, if you want.'

He shook his head. 'I believe you, but see what I mean about needing to be careful? You've built Teef's hopes up now. Always tell me about problems like that, I know how to handle things.' He shook his head and sighed. 'So you've "never gone in for drugs." There seem to be a lot of things you aren't into, things we normally take for granted in this game.'

Before we entered the villa, we looked at each other, eye to eye, for a few moments. He appeared to be waiting for me to say or do something, so I walked towards him and put a friendly arm round his shoulders. He hugged me briefly and then let me go. 'All right,' he said, 'I'll make sure you're okay. Teef does find it hard to go without his gear, but the medics say another binge will probably kill him. He can't stop himself once he starts… if you'd seen the terrible states he's been in. Tell you what, here's a few miniature bottles of Jack Daniel's. I always have some handy in case he gets desperate. Say you managed to sneak them past me. That should soften his disappointment. Even his booze is rationed these days.'

Gratefully I put the little bottles of Teef's favourite spirit into the holdall. Previously the house had been quiet when we arrived, but now the sound of one of The Rocking Boulders' hits, *Black Treacle*, a number one in the nineteen-seventies, drifted into the hall:

146

Black treacle, she gave it to me,
Black treacle, how good it can be,
Black treacle, if you look you can see,
Black treacle, she put her hand on my knee.

This was obviously a recording, not Quick and Teef upstairs playing live. Not having heard the song for ages, I had forgotten how catchy it was. The raunchy vocal was brilliantly matched by Teef's edgy guitar riff. My pulse quickened as we approached the door to the upstairs lounge. The music stopped and I could hear one of the most famous voices in rock and roll say: 'Er, well, you know, to be quick, right, you know as well as I do like, well, right, quick, what I mean to say is, you know...'

Timidly I hung back, not wanting to interrupt Quick's flow of ideas, but The Handyman grabbed my arm and pulled me into the room. Sitting, legs crossed, in the middle of the floor, was Rick Schwagger. He got up as we went in. Though he and Teef were the same age, in stark contrast to the Boulders' guitarist, the skin on his face was smooth and unblemished.

'Screw me, is this him?' he said, gesturing in my direction. 'I was expecting some ink-spot type with thick glasses.' He swivelled round to face Teef. 'Take a quick shufti at this one, he looks a bloody sight better than you do, Teef. It's time you got yourself a quick lift,' he said, patting his own deceptively youthful cheeks.

'Nah,' Teef replied, 'my fans are used to me like I am. Snip and tuck's not really my style, Quick.'

'Your style, Teef? Right. Give us a quick clue about what sort of style that might be? A style much loved by old age pensioners? Right. Come on, give me a quick answer. Is that what they are, your fans, these weirdos you give a quick mention to whenever I see you? Are they a bunch of pensioners, zombies and necrophiliacs? Let's ask my friends The Handyman and Bendy here what they think? Give us a quick opinion of this fan base Teef's always so keen to talk about.'

Instinctively I defended Teef: 'I'm sure all kinds of people are fans of Teef.'

The Handyman, who was standing behind Quick, looked at me in alarm. He shook his head and waved discreetly with his palm open, warning me to change tack. Quick stiffened and glared at me, then slowly and melodramatically stood up, put his hands on his hips, and pursed his lips.

'No one told me you was a lippy one,' he said. 'What you have to understand, Mister Bendy, is that when you come here, *I'm* the one with the lips. Maybe,' he continued, turning towards The Handyman, 'trying on those special cricket pads of mine for a minute or two would help Mister Bendy understand better how things are done.'

'Aw, Quick,' said The Handyman, 'no cause to go getting out the pads. I'd hate to see you and Bendy get off to a bad start. You know how long it's took to find someone to write your 'auto'biography. He's brought a couple of pages of notes he's made... he's managed to contact someone who remembers you from school. Show him what you've brought, Bendy.'

Quick snatched the notes from me, and while he glanced at them The Handyman mouthed the word 'percentages' at me. After about half a minute Quick gazed up at the ceiling, and Teef gave me a further hint by moving his hand in front of his mouth to encourage me to speak.

'Can I just ask how you see the percentages from the book working out?' I asked.

Quick lowered his eyes, and then glanced around as though searching the room to identify who had spoken, before setting

148

his gaze on me. 'Who was it mentioned percentages? Was it you, Mister Bendy? That's better. This is something we need to come to an understanding about. If books are anything like music, we'll have to be quick off the mark or the middlemen will take most of the bread. Quick as a flash they are. So the author needs to make f'in' sure he maximises his return. We need a regular agent who'll get us a good deal, not some quick mover who grabs all the cash. Anyone got any ideas? If you have, quick, let's hear 'em.'

I thought Quick must have meant me when he used the word 'author', but he continued: 'Of course that's fine for me, me being the author of my 'auto'biography. What you get paid, Bendy, for using your psychic 'fluences and making the marks on paper, is something you'll have to sort out for yourself. I don't want it coming out of my share. Shouldn't be too hard for you, having your magic crystals, potions and all that sort of crap to work with. P'raps you can come to some arrangement with the publisher for your cut. You're lucky having the old sixth sense. Suppose it saves you from needing to work hard for a living like I have to.'

'That's not fair, Quick,' Teef said. 'If Bendy's writing the book, he's the one who should have the author's share.'

Quick glanced around the room, again pretending not to know who had spoken. 'My ears must be going funny; for a minute I thought I heard Teef express an opinion. Of course he can't have. He knows perfectly well that when it's down to him an' me, I'm the one who does the vocals. Well, glad to have met you Bendy. I'll leave you to sort out contracts and all that. The Handyman will take care of my interests. Got to be going... just time for a quick spruce up then off to a party in Mayfair. Don't suppose you get invited to many parties in Mayfair, do you Teef? No? Thought not. See you all some time... unless, Bendy, you've got any other quick questions?'

'I was wondering when might you be able to spare some time to tell me be a bit of your life story, since essentially that is what I'm supposed to be writing.'

'Busy over the next few months. Anyway, the whole point of getting you in was that you're supposed to be gifted, so you could find everything out from your Ouija board or whatever, without taking my time up with a bloody interrogation. Probably see you next when the book's finished. Want it done quick, mind. Understand?'

With that he left the room, followed by The Handyman. Teef got up and went to the door to make sure they were out of earshot, then asked me, in a half-whisper, 'Bendy, did you bring me any gear?'

'Really sorry, Teef, but The Handyman is so suspicious. He wanted to search the holdall, and as soon as he saw the maracas he knew what they were for. I did sneak these in for you though.' I gave him the miniature bottles of Jack Daniel's.

'Oh Bendy, terrific, you're a real good mate. He took them over to the sideboard, where a quart size, but almost empty, Jack Daniel's bottle stood on a tray. He opened the miniatures in turn and emptied the contents into it. Then, so as not to waste the tiniest drop, he filled the miniatures with mineral water and replaced the tops. 'I think you've earned yourself another little music lesson. Forget the maracas, lot of good they did. This time, since we're mates now, you can have a go on one of my favourite guitars.'

How different he was from Quick. Despite all his years of rock stardom, Teef was never arrogant or rude. He had me sit beside him on the sofa, where he placed his valuable instrument, a Fender guitar, in my hands. 'Be careful with it, Bendy. I've always taken good care of it, like a proper musician should.

Don't understand performers who show off by mistreating their kit. Quality equipment deserves respect.' Teef carefully positioned the fingers of my left hand on the neck of his instrument. 'Now, try a few strokes lower down with your right hand. Gently now. That's nice, isn't it, Bendy?'

'Oh yes, Teef.'

'Good, now try another position,' he said, and rearranged my fingers. 'Use the plectrum, a bit firmer now with the right hand, follow my rhythm, one... two... three... four... See? We're making music together now, you and me, aren't we Bendy?'

Regrettably, shortly after we had found our rhythm, the dinner gong sounded downstairs and we had to break off. How sweet of him to teach a novice like me a little basic strumming. He looked disappointed when The Handyman came in and said, 'Come on Teef, dinner time. I don't want to have to tell Quick what you and Bendy have been getting up to. You know he wouldn't like it.'

'There's nothing to tell. All I was doing was showing Bendy my guitar. Where's the harm in that?'

'It's what you might be leading up to. I'll say a couple of things. First of all, we've somehow found ourselves a gay bloke whose got a boyfriend, doesn't play around or do drugs. No, Teef, it's true, I'm not joking. Second, you remember, if anything is going on, you might as well own up. I'll find out anyway, you can be sure of it.'

'What, have you got something against me making a bit of music with a mate? So, that's the first point and the second, what about the third?'

'They'll have to do you. There's no third.'

'Well, you should have one. Rounds things off better when there's a third.'

The Handyman smiled. 'Does you good having a session with

Bendy, doesn't it? Sharpens you up. Come on you,' he said, glancing towards me and jerking his head towards the door.

Reluctantly I obeyed. On the way home The Handyman again had me sit next to him in the passenger seat of the car. 'Well, you finally got to meet Quick. Had me worried, standing up for Teef against him like you did. Always been a lot of rivalry between them. Never *ever* interfere in their quarrels. Best advice I can give you is this. If Quick actually gets as far as bringing the cricket pads out, pick up your coat and bag and make a run for it. Typical of him to want to keep all the cash. I have been wondering, has anyone paid you for what you've done so far?'

'What is there to pay me for? The book is still nowhere.'

'You worry too much. We'll think of a way round it. Better have this,' he said, throwing a thick envelope onto my lap. 'You know that Quick goes off his head on a little drop of beer or half a tab of anything, so we buy pills and capsules in the health food shop and pretend they're the real stuff. Well, I can't hand over what's supposed to be a couple of weeks' supply of hard drugs and say that'll be fifteen pounds eighty-five, can I? So I put in for the street price for the real thing. You might as well have the proceeds this time. You deserve something, your visits to Teef really have done him good.'

I lifted the flap of the envelope and saw a wad of twenty pound notes. 'I don't know if I should take this.'

'Who's going to be the one in trouble if any questions are asked? All you have to say is I gave you some cash for the work you've done so far. For fuck's sake, Bendy, you've got no idea, have you? This is nothing compared to what goes on when they're on tour. Far more money than that goes down as hospitality expenses, no one asks for details. In a second-hand bookshop everything might be counted down to the last penny, but not if you're working with The Rocking Boulders.

'Now Quick has accepted you for doing his 'auto'biography, I need to talk to various people who handle the business side. By the way, you might like to know you're the fourth one we've tried for the book. None of the others got this far. The first bloke was up to no good, he was hiding a little digital recorder. I could see him fiddling about with it in his pocket. As soon as the sneaky bastard got back in the car I searched him, found it and wiped everything. The next one turned up with his pockets full of pills... he didn't get as far as the villa. The last one kept turning the conversation to what went on off-stage when the boys were touring. Turned out to be a newspaper hack. Quick would have had the cricket pads on him if I hadn't chucked him out first. Anyway, most people come off a lot worse from their first run in with Quick than you did. Leave it to me to fix things up. Take that money and sleep well tonight, you and that boyfriend of yours.'

Alicia was delighted to hear that I had at last met Rick. She attributed my progress, limited as it was, to the influence of her current fad, low-frequency energy fields. She had read, on the California Clairvoyants' website, that they could be used to cure chronic illness, and researchers had discovered that the fields not only acted as a store of past events, but could also influence the present and future. It all made sense, she argued, because what is happening now, and what will happen in the future, all depend on what has happened already in the past. While she was telling me this, my eyes kept straying to the new adornments she had added to her current favourite hat, the beige trilby: a pair of imitation humming birds on springy wires. The slightest movement of her head set them into iridescent oscillation.

Eventually she let me turn our conversation to Rick's contacts with the Oracles of Aten in the nineteen-sixties. I wrote down every scrap of information she could remember, and borrowed a copy of the cult's book. This was more like a historical novel set in ancient Egypt than a religious tract. The style was contrived: deliberately flouting the rules of grammar, full of words that were nonsensical or inappropriate, with a sprinkling of weird pseudo-biblical phrases, and the plot, about intrigue in the pharaoh's entourage, was very routine. Here is a typical extract:

Verily, the Pharaoh lustfully ebonyed his royalty beard, as he strolled roundly cornering the pillars of temple erection. In the many journeyings and desert traverses of the Pharaoh's son Aken, laden as he and his followers were by countless manifold trappings of most-high status, his purpose being the viewing of the many eclectically dedicated monuments, which includeth pyramids, lotus-pilloried temples, squarely rising occult obelisks, carved and painted entrances conveyancing the order of all things in the upper and lower kingdoms from the most High Priestess of Isis to the lowliest animal tethered to the service of the most wretched slave, from the heights of the much labouringly-hewn cliffs of Aswan to the smallest grain of desert sand, all that Aken's eyes had beholden could not still the stirring in his royal breast of a restless yearning which drove him ever outwardly onwards in his quest for knowledge and consort with his worshipful people.

Reading it was like wading through congealed porridge. Twenty pages of this mind-bending prose made me want to fling the book on the floor and stamp on it. Maybe it was written like that to put the sect's adherents off studying it, so that those in charge could make up any rules they wanted without being challenged.

Dale and I decided to call another meeting to work out how to make better progress with Rick's book. Jeremy contacted Loyd and asked him to join us, even though Alicia had not forgiven his attack on her idol Simone de Boudoir.

Otherwise life at Fulrose Court and in the shops continued as before. Routine tasks like keying in details of Jeremy's latest acquisitions for the internet shop were reassuringly simple, in contrast to the unpredictability of everything to do with The Rocking Boulders. We now had over a thousand books listed online, and the profit from internet sales was enough to cover half my wages.

One day, while updating the list, I heard the shop doorbell ring and had to break off in mid-entry. Jayde, of my old neighbours the Jays, was approaching the counter. 'Hello, you're looking well, Ben,' she said. She wore a skirt, something I had never before seen her in before. She smiled in an obviously forced way.

'Thanks. You too. How are things?' I asked.

'Can I talk to you?'

'Yes, of course. What about?'

'Not here. Somewhere private. What time are you going for lunch?'

Half an hour later we bought sandwiches and took them to the little park about five minutes walk away, where we found a bench near a deep border of daffodils. Following a few casual remarks, punctuated by awkward silences, she said, 'There's something I've got to tell you. I'm having a baby.'

'Are you? Congratulations,' I said, surprised.

'The thing is, I think you're the father.'

'What?'

'Don't try coming over all innocent.'

'There's something I'm not quite following here. I'm gay, remember?'

'No, like, you remember. Don't try pretending you don't know what happened. That won't work with me. Before Christmas Jake and me brought you back from that fetish club we all went to. When we got to Toby's flat you wanted to go to bed straight away. Me and Jake got in with you and gave you a

155

really nice time. It's no good saying you can't remember.'

She obviously meant the night they had drugged me and I ended up with that awful hangover. 'I was completely out of it that night, and not because of anything I did to myself. Someone doped me, on purpose. You could say anything about that night. How could I deny it?'

'You knew what you were doing. You enjoyed yourself all right. You had me, and you had Jake too, you couldn't get enough of us. You've turned him queer, you cunt, he's as bad as you and Toby now.'

'Thanks a lot. Talking of Jake, isn't the baby likely to be his?'

'It can't be. He's had a vasectomy.'

My private parts had been tender the next morning; so I must have had sex with someone, but that did not prove her baby was mine. Was she after money? For a few minutes we sat in silence. She obviously wanted to make trouble. I kept cool and asked, 'Does Jake know?'

'Never mind about him. You and your boyfriend are doing all right aren't you? You're both working. You've got to do what's right by the baby. I don't want to drag you through the courts, but I will if I have to.'

DNA tests could show whether the child was mine, but until the truth was known I would have to be careful what I said. For all I knew she might be going to half a dozen other potential fathers and saying the same thing. She was not at all like she used to be, interested only in having a good time. 'What do you expect me to say?' I asked.

Having no ready answer, after another lengthy pause she said, 'You'll be hearing from my solicitors. Count on it.'

I was worried and upset, but determined not to show it. I shrugged, got up, threw my half-eaten sandwich in the bin, and walked away.

Twelve

Dale listened closely to my account of Jayde's accusation. He then, of course, had to know the full details of that wretched night when the Jays had shagged me in Toby's flat. He must have wondered how anyone could stumble their way into such a daft situation. However he did not criticize, but shook his head, and uttered a long 'H-u- u- u -mph' sound. Then he said quietly. 'Her whole story sounds like bullshit. That one night was the only time when you might, just possibly, have impregnated her?'

'Yes.'

'The odds must be against it. And Jake may have had a vasectomy, but you've told me that the Jays had an open relationship, so any of her other bedmates could be the lucky man. It sounds like a story made up to screw money out of you.'

'Can she really be that evil? I suppose it's possible, but if what she says is true the thought of having to pay up every week until the child grows up is very worrying. What happened that night wasn't my fault. They spiked my drink.'

'You can't prove that. Let's forget about being tricked by Jayde and her being after your money for a minute... suppose she is pregnant and the child is yours... in your heart, would you be pleased, or sorry?'

'Having a child by Jayde? What do you think?'

'Well, you're not going to have one by me, are you? Try seeing it from another perspective. Wouldn't the child be lucky to have a kind and sensitive man like you for a father?'

'You're joking. I'm like a sodding child myself half the time.'

'Is that seeing it from another perspective?'

I turned the question back on him. 'What about you, would you like to have a child?'

'For lots of people the children are what they live for. Having kids is their big achievement in life. It's not an easy decision for us to make, having no mum and two gay dads might be difficult for a kid, and this situation with Jayde is not a good context for thinking about it. We've never talked about what you and I want in life, though, have we? Not that I'm unhappy with the way we are, but what are the long term possibilities, not only whether kids might be part of what we do, but what about having HIV tests so we could stop using condoms if we both want to be faithful? Or should we think about a civil partnership? We would both need to be completely sure to make that kind of commitment. Even then, there is the risk that responsibilities and constraints might take the fun out of what we've got. We might be happier as we are.'

Anything that would bring us closer together sounded good, but how long would we last? Expecting too much too soon could invite calamity. I said, 'I haven't been with anyone else since we got together.'

'Nor me.'

'Does anyone at work ask, you know, if you're with anyone?'

'Yes, a few times. I've been saying I'm spoken for. If they're interested, I tell them about you.'

Maybe that was enough commitment-making for one day. We

fell silent for a minute or two. Then, no longer serious, he said, 'So you haven't been with anyone, but I hope you won't mind me asking… have you had any offers?'

This was a leading question. If I said yes, lots, it would sound like I had been deliberately leading people on. If I said no, then it would sound like my faithfulness was a result of lack of opportunity. I said, 'A couple of people looked like they might be interested. Has anyone been after you?'

'Not a soul. Guess I'd better try to hang on to you.'

A letter from The Rocking Boulders' management company arrived the next day. It commissioned me *to provide professional services pursuant to the completion of an autobiography of Rick Schwagger.* Further instructions were to be given by Andy Handman, who was authorized to supervise and give guidance on all aspects of the undertaking. A cheque for one hundred pounds was enclosed as a retainer. Any further fees and expenses were to be agreed in advance with Mr Handman.

The letter did not say that Rick's life story was expected somehow to coalesce in my mind out of the ether, but neither did it suggest any more practical way forward. Whilst I liked The Handyman and his earthy outlook, he was an odd choice to give supervision and guidance on putting together a biography. I showed the letter to Jeremy, who studied it for a minute or two, then asked, 'The retainer, they enclosed a cheque?'

'Yes.'

I took it from the envelope and held it out for him to see. He said, 'Good, you still have it. Hold on to it. Until you accept money, you've not committed yourself to anything. It gives us time to think.' He read the letter again and smiled ruefully. 'I've liked having you here in the shop, but it's your future that counts. I won't try to hold you back. Have to say I'm not a fan of The

Rocking Boulders' music. Jazz has always appealed to me more. I could once sing one or two of the old standards, a passable rendition, and given the chance I used to do so at parties. All a long while ago, of course.'

'I was hoping somehow to fit this in as well as working for you. The Rocking Boulders are so unpredictable, and they still think that the book can somehow be written through extra-sensory perception. I'll never be able to write it all on my own. You write all sorts of stuff, business letters and so on, so does Dale. I know you're busy, but is there any chance of you helping me out?'

'Would The Rocking Boulders accept me being involved?'

'Would they have to know?'

'*Professional services* are what this letter requires of you. I suppose that might allow calling on others for help. This book project for Rick Schwagger has a surreal quality that appeals to me. We did talk about holding another meeting, but we haven't fixed a date yet. I have mentioned it to Loyd, and he says he'll come along, though like me he's not sure how Alicia will react to him being there. I hope she's not going to harp on about low-frequency energy fields all the time. If you give me some dates when you and Dale are free, I'll speak to Alicia and Loyd.'

We set the meeting up for Tuesday in the following week.

The Sunday before we met, newspaper headlines announced that Rick Schwagger was to receive a knighthood. He was the sole rock star to be honoured among a motley group of celebrities, including a stand-up comic, an ex-pole-vaulter, a horse breeder and a pastry chef. None of the others were to receive anything as elevated as a knighthood. On Monday evening The Handyman collected me and took me to The Rocking Boulders' villa. 'We should find Quick at home again. Best not to say anything about the palace or his gong,' he said.

'Why not?'

'The newspapers have been making a lot of it, especially since no hint of it leaked out earlier, but they've not sniffed out any scandal so far. I've heard a story that's going round about what really happened. If I tell you, don't drop me in the shit by repeating it to anyone, especially not Quick, will you?'

'No, of course not.'

'This is supposed to have come from an equerry, via a stable boy at the palace. Word is Quick got off with a lady-in-waiting at a party he went to in Belgravia. She invited him into Buck House and up to her room. Silly cow let him have half a bottle of champagne. As you know he can't cope with drink. Well, after a bit of hanky-panky with the high-class bird, Quick staggers off into the State Rooms and falls asleep on a sofa. Cleaner sees him, thinks he must be one of the family's hangers-on having a nap, and covers him up with the ceremonial cloak that what's-her-name wears when she dishes out the gongs. The cleaner wasn't to know he'd had half a bottle of champagne and would be out of it for hours. Anyway after a while *herself* comes in, and, well, you can imagine, her equerry reaches out for her togs, but… no bloody ceremonial cloak on the hook. They say she's getting forgetful, and one of the corgis has been trained to sniff about and find any clobber she's mislaid, so the dog runs round, finds the cloak with Quick lying underneath it, gives his leg a sharp nip, he lets out a scream, and the corgi runs off with the cloak back to her in charge.

'She goes over to Quick and asks what the fuck he's doing there, but her main worry is he'll make a stink about being bitten by the dog. So, to avoid giving the tabloids another scandal to bash the royals with, they decide to add Quick's name to the honours list and pretend he'd been missed off the press notice by accident. Don't let on to anyone about this. It's a story that's going round, it might all be bollocks.'

'Okay, Ma'am's the word.'

'What's that, Bendy?'

'It was a joke. Since we're talking about her in charge, I said Ma'am's the word, not Mum's the word.'

'Don't think I'm with you.'

This was the man who was to give me guidance on writing Quick's 'auto'biography. 'Forget it.'

At the villa, going into the upstairs sitting room, I said cheerfully, 'Hi Quick, hi Teef.'

Quick responded in an offended tone, 'I think a quick apology is in order here. You're not keeping up with the news, Bendy. Surely you must have heard. I am now *Sir* Quick, if you don't mind.'

Teef said, 'Don't overdo it, Quick.'

'Was that *Mister* Teef *esquire* who just spoke? Should a mere common guitar plucker be talking to a knighted person without first asking permission? Give us a quick opinion, *Mister* Handyman and *Mister* Bendy?' He glared at each of us in turn, but we said nothing. He pulled a face. 'What's the matter with you lot?' he asked. 'You should know me well enough to know when I'm joking. I only accepted the bloody gong because some well-past-their-best-days so-called bloody rock and rollers have been going around pretending they're better than me. Anyway, reason I've hung about here is to ask you, Bendy, when you will be giving me a quick dekko at my autobiography? You've been working on it for at least a couple of weeks now. It must be more or less finished.'

'Now you *are* having a joke. If you give me a regular half-hour slot to talk to you a couple of times a week, I could make progress. It needn't even be face to face. We could talk over the phone.'

'Don't start that again. I've already told you I'm too busy, and that the book has to be done quick. That was the whole point of bringing in a psychic. You're sure psychic is what you are, not psychotic?' He said this with a sneer, though he may have intended it to be funny.

The Handyman intervened. 'That's not nice, a psychotic's someone who's mentally disturbed. Bendy's all right, I've checked him out. If you give him a rough time and he walks off, don't expect me to go searching for somebody else.'

'All right, all right. Don't start ganging up on me. Actually, you could say having a sixth sense is being mentally disturbed, in a way. It can't be natural, can it? What you need to understand, Bendy, is this: Teef, The Handyman, and Alicia have all assured me you're the right man to do my autobiog. The public has been begging for a proper book about me for years, so I am requesting politely that you get your pen out quick and start making marks on paper. Quick as you can. Got it? Especially now the palace has given me some well-deserved official recognition. And I don't want no funny made-up stories being put in it neither. A bit of respect is due, so no more of the old sideways glances and quick snide remarks behind my back. Well, I can't hang about. Been invited to stay at a stately home for a quick few days hunting. Don't suppose you get many invitations to the hunt, do you Teef? No? Thought not. Of course, now I'm Sir Rick Schwagger, expect I'll be invited to all the high class social gatherings. Good thing about the nobs, if the weather's bad you can go indoors where they have the servants and plenty of rooms for having a good time in. Well, tally-ho, as we say in the country.'

He left, followed by The Handyman. Quick's knighthood must have driven ideas of drugs from Teef's mind. He did not, as before, ask if I had brought him any gear, but joked that a gong was probably not a bad thing to give Quick, since it was one of the few instruments he might be able to play.

'Couldn't he learn the drums?' I asked.

'One drum. He might be able to learn to play *one* of the drums. Well, nobody's good at everything. My voice is lousy, but all the same I have a go at singing once in a while. Do you know our fourth big hit, *Maple Syrup*? How about if you try playing the guitar chords while I do the vocal? Just for a laugh, neither of us would win any prizes.'

Minutes later I was sitting in front of a music stand holding one of Teef's very own Fender guitars and studying fingering diagrams for the chords. I struggled to press down the strings and fluffed at least half the notes, while he gently beat out a rhythm on the table and sang gruffly:

> *Maple syrup, don't you be coy,*
> *Maple syrup, be a good boy,*
> *Maple s'rup, from my fav'rite toy,*
> *Maple syrup, fill me with joy.'*

Thankfully, no one was around to hear the agonized racket we made. The effort needed for me to reconfigure my fingers for each new chord demanded all my concentration, and my stopping and starting spoiled the flow. Teef had to wait for me before he could continue, his voice almost as awful as my guitar. After the first verse he asked, 'Has it ever occurred to you that it's a gay song? The singer, Quick, a bloke obviously, has smeared syrup over his favourite toy, we know what that means, and is asking a boy to be good and fill him with joy. Don't go getting any ideas though, Quick and me both go for the birds, not the lads, but if you actually listen to the words themselves, it is a gay

164

song.'

I always feel uneasy when a straight man decides to make a point of the fact that he is not gay. Is he implying that being hetero makes him better than me? As for the song being gay, surely different people interpret lyrics in different ways according their own predilections. Anyway, my fingertips were becoming sore from pressing the metal strings down hard on the fretboard. When The Handyman returned, I was not unhappy that the session had come to an end.

When Alicia, joined Jeremy, Dale, Loyd and me at the bookshop, she set entirely the wrong mood for a business meeting by wearing the beige trilby with darting humming birds fixed to wires. She had added a couple of imitation gladioli, positioned so that the birds kept dipping their beaks into the centres of the flowers. Struggling not to laugh, I began the meeting by passing round the letter hiring my services for Quick's book, and reminded everyone that squeezing any usable information about his life story from him or his side-kick Teef was not possible. Quick had also ruled out talking to anyone else who knew him. Save for the very helpful information Alicia and Loyd had given me about the Oracles of Aten and Rick's school days, the only other sources suggested were old newspaper reports and public records of births and deaths.

'But Ben,' Alicia interrupted, 'I've already found the answer for you. Those wonderful low-frequency energy fields that hold residues of all our experiences. All those preserved trace memories are just waiting for you to tap into them. Surely you've been able to use your powers to access them by now?'

Loyd saw me struggling to reply and tried to help. 'I'm sure Ben has been using his "powers", as you call them, in so far as he can. But my guess is that today he is hoping for some rather more down-to-earth suggestions. How best to locate relevant newspaper cuttings, for instance. You find researchers who undertake that kind of work, for a fee, naturally.'

Alicia was not deterred. 'Well, you can't get more down to earth than low-frequency energy fields. Experiments have shown that they hug the ground and will even follow the curvature of the earth! I was reading about the latest discoveries on the Philadephia Psychics website only the other day. The Professor Emeritus of Physics at the University of Pottsville was asking if anyone could get their hands on a klystron, and if so would they contact him urgently. He says that before transistors were invented, klystrons were a special type of electronic valve.' As Alicia was speaking, I started to imagine I could hear a faint sound emanating from her hat.

'Sorry Alicia,' Jeremy said. 'Did you say professor of physics or professor of psychics?'

Alicia glared impatiently at him. 'Physics, Jeremy, I said physics! Given the number of physics professors there are in the world, some of them must be psychic, I dare say. Psychic professors of physics? I wonder.' The noise coming from her direction, a humming sound, was getting louder.

Loyd weighed in again, but now in a dangerously patronizing tone: 'My dear Alicia,' he said, 'you may be interested to hear that I worked on radar systems during the Second World War, and I happen to know that the klystron valve is used for high-frequency circuits. Not low, not even medium, but high. Very high in fact.'

Hoping to divert them from an argument about the klystron valve, Dale asked, 'Alicia, is that humming sound coming from your hat?'

She glanced briefly at him, but turned swiftly back to Loyd, setting the humming birds whizzing ever more energetically in and out of the flowers. 'Surely, *my dear Loyd*,' she said, 'you're not claiming to know more about low-frequency energy fields than a professor of physics? Physics, in case you didn't catch the word again, Jeremy, not psychics, although I'm sure a professor of psychics would know as much, if not more, about the new and exciting developments in the subject.'

Loyd said: 'You said professor emeritus, didn't you? That is retired professor is it not? Of where did you say? Pottsville? I've heard of the world famous Massachusetts Institute of Technology, but never of the University of Pottsville. Are you sure he's not some crank inventing fancy-sounding titles for himself?'

The humming from Alicia's hat became ominous, and when she threw back her head the birds darted to and fro alarmingly. I kept trying to appeal for a return to the topic of Quick's book, but they talked over me. Dale put his hand over mine, pursed his lips and tilted his head slightly in a silent appeal to remain calm.

Alicia delivered her counterblast. 'What a talented man you must be, Loyd, not only a veteran author, but an expert on low- and high-energy physics too, and with an encyclopaedic knowledge of American universities. An ordinary woman like me can never hope to compete! I'll leave you to provide Ben with the answer to all his worries, since nothing I have to say is appreciated.' She stood abruptly, causing one of the humming birds to dip down so low it became lodged under the brim of her hat. She ignored this mishap and strode out, slamming the door.

Jeremy remonstrated with Loyd. 'However impractical her ideas may be, she was intending to help.'

'And so was I! Did you want the whole meeting hijacked by a lot of arrant nonsense?'

The following discussion, without Alicia, was rational, but not

167

much use. We talked about possible sources of press cuttings about Quick and The Rocking Boulders, but the task sounded as though it would be awfully slow and tedious, and there was no guarantee that the articles would be reliable. We soon ran out of ideas and the meeting petered out with feeble promises to give the subject more thought.

On our way home Dale said, 'Not much help, were we Ben? Alicia must have been drinking some of those magic potions she has in the shop.'

'The whole thing is more and more like a pipe dream, isn't it? Maybe I will have to turn it down. I can send the Boulders' cheque back. Alicia and Loyd are an explosive mixture. How the hell did her hat make that humming noise?'

'She must have fitted some sort of novelty sound-effect box into it. You can get burglar alarms that sound like dogs barking, and clocks that reproduce birdsong, so someone could have brought out a gadget that makes a humming sound. You know how much she likes making a show, it's all part of the business she's in. More than likely she is now congratulating herself on a successful performance.'

'Successful? From her point of view, maybe. No one else's. She can't have felt too clever when that humming bird got stuck under the brim.'

'If only we had caught that on video. Don't give up on the book yet. We can surely come up with something better than low-frequency energy fields, or hunting for old press cuttings. The meeting was a disappointment, but let's talk about it in a day or two, just you and me. Try to persuade The Handyman you need a lot more time. See what he says.'

That evening Alicia and Loyd both rang, full of apologies. Jeremy had contacted each of them to complain that their row had ruined the meeting. He had persuaded them that we should get together again, and made them promise to keep their personal animosity in check.

After dinner Dale and I went for a drink at the Give and Take. Smiles was chatting to a saxophonist from the Gay Symphony Orchestra who liked jazz as well as classical music, and he and Dale were soon engrossed in conversation. Smiles and I did not know enough about serious music to join in, and I began talking to him about Alicia having got to know Rick Schwagger when he was involved with the Oracles of Aten. I was about to mention my visits to The Rocking Boulders' villa when Dale, overhearing me, grabbed my arm, dug his fingertips into my flesh and said, 'Nothing has actually happened yet, has it Ben? This story of Alicia's, if she was being serious, happened yonks ago, and she only made a few offhand remarks. Anything else, at the moment, is all speculation, not to say wishful thinking.'

How could I have been so stupid as to chatter about The Rocking Boulders to Smiles? Good friend though he was, one of the reasons for the bar's success was that he always had lots of gossip to pass on. 'Er… well… um… speculation, yes, you're right there.'

On the way home I said to Dale, 'God, what have I done, prattling on to Smiles about Rick Schwagger and the Oracles of Aten.'

'Did you mention the 'auto'biography?'

'No, I don't think so.'

'We must be more careful. We'll have to hope Smiles doesn't make a big thing out of what you said, and The Rocking Boulders don't suspect that any stories they hear have come from you.'

Thirteen

Now that Quick had engaged me for his 'auto'biography, The Handyman's attitude swung between enthusiasm because his own standing would benefit if the book was a success, and worry that he would be blamed if it was not. Up to now he had been called on as a chauffeur or as a troubleshooter when physical toughness, or the threat of it, was needed. Now he was expected to provide quite different services he was struggling.

He had no experience of books, publishing, or management. So far his only contribution was a fallback plan to minimize the effects of failure. This was to tell Quick that worrying about the book was making me ill; a week or so later he would say that I had had a nervous breakdown and gone into therapy. Having nervous breakdowns and going into therapy is common in the rock and roll business, and the story would, he said, not be questioned.

Disappointed by his low expectations, I told him that Loyd had agreed to help me put the book together.

He was unimpressed. 'The bloke who taught Quick and Teef at school? How old is he, for god's sake?'

I mentioned that the next meeting was to be at Fulrose

Court, and that Dale would be there, along with Alicia and Jeremy. 'You should come too,' I said. 'You are supposed to be providing me with supervision and guidance.'

He became less negative. 'Always wondered what kind of person your boyfriend is. Okay, I will come to your meeting, but I might have to leave early. It's not how we normally do things, having meetings.'

On the morning before the get-together, Alicia came into work wearing her beige trilby. She had stripped it of its humming birds and gladioli, and in their place had fixed a dozen or more ceramic bees that bounced up and down on the end of wires. Any slight move of her head excited them into motion. Struggling not to laugh I asked, 'You didn't happen to pass a tree with a swarm of bees in it on your way here, did you?'

'Well, I might have done. Why, is there something on my hat? Bees? Well, don't worry, they're not aggressive.'

'Aren't you worried that people will cross to the other side of the road when they see you coming?'

'Of course not, new fashions have to start somewhere; it's not as though I'm doing anything eccentric. I am planning to install a few miniature jars of honey inside. If someone says something particularly nice to me I will take one out and present them with it. Millinery is nothing unless it's imaginative. Don't worry about the meeting at your place, I've been told not to wear it for that. Jeremy has given me instructions on how to behave. I am not to speak except in response to specific questions. Even then, under no circumstances am I to address Loyd directly, or to mention low-frequency energy fields. Pity, because the Tulsa Telepaths have achieved amazing results using them for telekinesis... that is to say, making objects move by paranormal means... but then I don't need to tell you that, do I? You know what I'm going to say before I've said it anyway... don't you?'

'If I am to know what you're going to say in advance, you do actually have to say it, otherwise, all I can predict is the opposite, that you won't say it, though I might be able to predict that you are going to say something else instead.'

'Sorry, of course I didn't realize... being gifted must make life so complicated... I'm not surprised you're so reluctant to talk about it. One thing though,' she burbled on, 'some novelty pens, a new line, came in. There would be no harm in me giving some out as a sort of goodwill present, would there? They're magical realism pens, with pictures of the Mexican winged serpent and other mythical beasts.'

The Handyman was the first to arrive at Fulrose Court for the meeting. 'So this is the love nest, is it? Not bad for a couple of blokes,' he said. He shook Dale's hand vigorously, and later whispered to me, 'You've done all right there, I'll give you that.'

'Yes, he's fantastic, isn't he.'

Jeremy arrived next, followed by Alicia and Loyd. The two protagonists said hello politely, but otherwise avoided speaking to each other. Dale handed out an agenda he had drawn up headed *Autobiography Project, Third Meeting*. The topics listed were: Sources of information; Structure of the book; Writing it; Illustrations; Working arrangements; and, finally, Remuneration. After allowing us fifteen seconds to read the list he said, 'Right, I spent a couple of hours in the library yesterday and came away with these.' He picked up his bag and took out nearly a dozen books. 'They are unofficial biographies of Quick and Teef, and a couple on the history of the band. What I suggest is that Ben draws from them everything that might be useful, and writes the facts out in plain simple English in his own words. If he finds gaps we may have to research other sources, but there ought to be enough here to give us most of Rick Schwagger's life story.

Since this is going to be an official autobiography, we could do with some personal in-depth stuff that has not already been published. We may have to do some real, proper research to find that, but it can be slotted in as and when.

'Call what I am suggesting information gathering, or call it plagiarism,' he continued, 'call it what you like, but material has to come from somewhere, and this is a way to start. Even gossip can be worked in if it's interesting enough, if the source is given, with comments about reliability.'

Loyd immediately backed him up, saying that biographers always drew extensively on earlier written material, and that autobiographies in particular were often so selective and one-sided that they came close to being works of fiction. He thought it essential to agree a timetable, as even for a professional writer, a biography was at least a year's work. A quicker and safer approach might be for each of us to undertake a section of the book. Five of us, not counting The Handyman, might stand a chance of completing it in six months, working part time. Since Loyd himself had known Rick Schwagger briefly at school, he might be the best person to tackle the early years, up to the time The Rocking Boulders began performing in pubs and clubs. Alicia, if she was willing, could pick up from there, and go on to the Oracles of Aten stage and the release of the group's second album. Jeremy could tackle from then to the end of the nineteen-seventies, Dale could do the 'eighties, and I could bring the story up to the present day. When we had all researched our periods, we would get together to review what we had, and agree on any further research needed to fill gaps. I would then go through and put everything into a consistent style, and Loyd would take on the final editing and polishing before the material was submitted to the company acting for The Rocking Boulders. Whatever fees were due for the ghost writing could be split up among us according to the hours of work put in.

Quick's expectation of receiving the author's share of any profits, was a worry, but Loyd persuaded The Handyman that he should ask the Boulder's management to pay an agreed fee for our work. Who took what share of any profits would not then be our concern.

Dale pointed out that the library books were on loan for only three weeks, but thought that with renewals and a bit of planning we should all be able to have our turn at reading them.

I asked The Handyman, who had said nothing so far, what he thought. 'Sitting here, listening to you all taking this book so serious, if anyone has a chance of succeeding with it, maybe you do. You have to realize you are walking into a world that is ninety-nine per cent crazy. I'll give you an example. A few years ago the lads wanted to do another concert tour. A team of people spent months on it, working it all out, identifying possible venues, designing a new stage set, and... a thousand things had to be done, costing god knows how much. Then Quick and Teef fell out over using a new arrangement for one of the songs. Neither of them would give in, and once they'd started arguing they disagreed about lots of other little niggles too. The concert tour plans, the whole thing, ended up being dumped. That is typical. Rick has been wanting to publish his life story for years and years, but suppose someone at a party tells him books are out of date now, that everyone these days is doing video clips of their lives and putting them on the internet. They might only be saying it to take the piss, but he might go against the book idea altogether.' He stopped and glanced around at us.

'I can see from your faces you're taking no notice. So, if you've convinced yourselves this is something you want to do, you'll all have to sign confidentiality agreements. I have to say this to you; the lads are known for hitting back hard at anyone

174

who is disloyal.'

Remembering what I had blurted out about the Oracles of Aten in the Give and Take a week earlier, I crossed my fingers. Jeremy said, 'You're right, there are obstacles and there are risks, but we can't give up now. This is a real chance for Ben, and you yourself admit that we might be the best people to bring off this exercise. Alicia, how do you feel about handling the period up to the second album?'

'No problem at all. I'm flattered to be asked. If you don't mind a moment's diversion, I've brought along some special pens that have just come in... magical realism pens ... I'll pass them around, if you'd like one, please take one. You never know, they might help to inspire us.'

Everyone, including Loyd, accepted one of her novelty pens, while Dale shared out the books he had borrowed. When Alicia, Jeremy and Loyd had gone, The Handyman said, 'Suppose I'd better be going,' several times without making any move towards the door. Thinking a hug might help him on his way, I opened my arms in invitation. He clasped me tightly, then when we separated he looked over at Dale. I tilted my head to ask him to do the same. While they hugged I noticed The Handyman rubbing my boyfriend's lower spine with his right hand.

After he had gone I said, 'He seems to like you.'

'He's a straight man wanting to dabble. There's no harm in a hug, but that's as much as he'll get from me.'

We had to make time to write the 'auto'biography while continuing our usual work much as before. As if that were not enough, Alicia decided to install a palmistry system on her computer, and asked Dale to help. Clients for this service were to put their right hand on the glass plate of a scanner; the resulting image was matched up automatically with one of thousands of

175

images that came with the software. The corresponding standard 'reading' was brought up on the computer screen, to be adapted by Alicia with any bits of personal information she had obtained while chatting to the client. An introductory paragraph claimed the reading was *derived from the centuries-old wisdom of mystics enhanced by the power of proven modern technology*. The dark blue cover of the resulting booklets bore the words *Personal Palm Consultation* and the customer's name in fancy lettering.

Dale probably found that a little time spent in Hatshepsut's Pavilion was light relief from the never-ending troubles with the hospital laundry. Alicia's own attitude was a paradox. Mostly she treated palmistry, astrology, fortune telling and all the rest as good fun, but from time to time would act as though one of these examples of extrasensory perception, low-frequency energy fields being her current favourite, deserved to be taken seriously.

She wanted the palmistry system to be working in time for a 'Psychic Fayre' at the local church hall. When she and Dale were ready to test it, they called me in to the shop to have my palm scanned. The printer must have jammed as he was tidying away some pieces of crumpled, ink-spattered paper. 'Playing up?' I asked.

'It's the paper. In order to save trees Alicia insists on using the backs of old letters and odd bits of paper that have been shoved through the letter box. They get stuck.'

'Not all that often,' she said. 'I hate to waste anything. Right, Ben, put your hand on the scanner. I wonder what your palm will reveal about you.'

I did as she asked, saying, 'You know all about me already. How about instead of reading palms, we bring the whole thing up to date by having people sit on the scanner with their pants down? You hear of people doing it on office photocopiers. I bet there aren't many fortune-telling services that use people's bottoms. You could start a new trend.'

'Isis preserve us. Do you have to ridicule everything? Anyway, what you propose may be all very well for you and Dale, with your little gay men's bottoms, but for lots of people my scanner wouldn't be big enough to obtain the full image. Then there's the matter of privacy. We would have to set up a cubicle. Besides, who would want to show their friends a booklet with an image of their bottom in it? The idea is totally impractical. Where's your common sense? Do you realize you are mocking something that, according to historical records, was being practised in China in three thousand BC, and,' she said, picking up a leaflet that came with the software, 'even the psychiatrist Jung wrote: *Hands, whose shape and functioning are intimately connected with the psyche, might provide revealing and therefore interpretable expressions of psychical peculiarity of human character.*' She nodded emphatically as she read this, sending the bees on her beige trilby into wild excitement. If any of them were to come off their wires they would ricochet around the room like bullets.

Dale said. 'Come on, Ben, give it a chance. Let's try to be positive. If you could manage to get Rick Schwagger's palm print, you could put something in the book about it... a few paragraphs comparing what his palm reading says with how he is in real life. We could include the image of his palm as an illustration. With a bit of imagination it would make a nice little section of several pages. He's keen on the paranormal, so he would probably go along with the idea. We are supposed to be putting in original material about him, remember?'

'And how are we going to obtain his palm print? Wrap plasticine around the handles of his maracas, and peel it off with the imprint when he puts them down?'

'Or,' Dale proposed, 'how about wet plaster? You could tell

177

him all the big stars are leaving their hand prints in plaster for posterity.'

Not to be left out, Alicia said, 'How about leaving a bottle of cooking oil in the kitchen with some of the contents smeared on the outside. You could ask him to pass it to you. You'd have to be careful to preserve his hand print intact. I'm sure Dale would be able to find a way of scanning it in.'

'Oh yes,' I said, 'Rick and I often pass bottles of cooking oil to each other in the kitchen.'

'Seriously,' Dale said, 'why not ask him for his palm print? Tell him it would help you write his book – after all, he believes you are using psychic powers for it. Suggest to him that The Rocking Boulders' fan club might be interested in putting it up on their website. The club might also have some ideas about original material for the book.'

The upshot of this suggestion was that The Handyman arranged to bring Quick and Teef to visit the Psychic Fayre at the local church hall, a Gothic building originally built as a school. Above the entrance, inscribed in stone, were the joyless words *Bring thy children unto me that I may teach them the ways of the Lord*. In defiance of this Victorian adage, inside the hall were more than forty stalls offering tarot reading, crystal healing, numerology predictions, more tarot reading, astrology, books on parapsychology, tarot reading again – about one out of four stalls sold tarot cards or books about them, or offered on-the-spot card readings.

Alicia had finished setting up and was sitting beneath a banner with the outline of a human hand in glittering sequins. Six major lines of the palm were labelled in gold: life; heart; head; Apollo; Saturn; and Mercury. The computer, scanner and printer were at one end of the stall, surrounded by screens decorated with palm prints in pastel colours. I stared thoughtfully at the banner with its intersecting palm lines and, when Alicia looked up to greet me, said, 'Oh, it's just like a sketch of the tube train lines around King's Cross and Euston.'

A loud female voice came from behind me. 'What are you trying to do? Put people off?' I could feel the breath that carried the words on my neck, and turned to find Muriel, or Myrtle to use Alicia's pet name for her girlfriend, standing behind me, wearing a tweed suit. She was holding a large marmalade cat that began to purr loudly.

'You've met Myrtle before, haven't you?' Alicia said.

'The name's Muriel actually.' I smiled at Myrtle/Muriel, who continued, 'Myrtle is a little pet name Alicia has for me.'

To suggest that Boadicea or Dragon might be more appropriate would have been far too rude, if not likely to provoke assault. Alicia said, 'Myrtle, or Muriel as I suppose I should call her since we are at a public event, is going to give psychic readings through the medium of Phoebe, her cat.'

'Oh,' I said, 'that explains it. Seeing the moggy I thought the fayre had been double booked with a cat show.'

'Very funny,' Muriel/Myrtle said dismissively. She and the cat fixed me with eyes that commanded obedience. 'As a reward for that remark you can be my first victim. Come along. Since, according to Alicia, you are "gifted", I will be particularly interested in your impression of the performance Phoebe and I have devised.'

'You shouldn't call telling someone's fortune *"a performance"*, Muriel,' Alicia reproved.

'I was speaking figuratively.'

Quick and Teef had yet to arrive, so I followed Myrtle and Phoebe behind one of Alicia's screens. We sat down at a table covered with a black fibrous cloth, surrounded by silhouette images of cats, the eyes painted green.

'Not cat's fur, is it?' I asked, stroking the tablecloth tentatively.

'Don't get excited, it's artificial. Now I want you to take Phoebe from me,' she said, handing me the docile moggy. 'Stroke her head gently, and when she looks into your eyes, look back into hers.'

I took Phoebe as bidden and gazed into the rich amber of her eyes. She was so plump that holding her made my arm ache. She resumed purring, and after a few minutes Myrtle reached across and took her back. The two of them gazed lovingly at each other.

'Oh yes, you've made a very strong impression,' she said, toying with a holographic pendant at her bosom, the colours changing as she fiddled with it. 'Phoebe is telling me that you are the sensitive type. You must take care not to be easily offended by what people say. Though they may be abrasive at times, they usually don't mean to insult you. Remember, when someone says something amiss it will usually be through ignorance or lack of understanding rather than malice. You're artistic. Don't be put off by early disappointments, you must keep trying. And you have someone who is very close to you – a relationship with another man who is very important in your life. Phoebe senses you are one of those special gay men who is truly suited to a long-term loving relationship. But you must be careful. Being male, you are of course hampered by your essentially self-centred nature, lack of interpersonal skills and poor emotional development. You must make every effort to moderate these innate flaws in your character. The philandering male within you, and the attentions of others who lack your loyal and faithful nature, could easily lead to ruin. You have been fortunate to bond with one of those men who is an exception to the general rule, who is sincerely concerned for those around him. If only you could be more like him. Regrettably, like you, he has to struggle against his fundamentally oppressive and power-hungry masculine characteristics.' Perhaps judging that she had insulted me enough, she paused, smiled and asked, 'Well, Ben, how did I do?'

'You're quite sure you learned those things about me from Phoebe, not from Alicia? Anyway, the good things you said about Dale are right. You were convincing, you and Phoebe... though I'm not sure you are likely to get much repeat business from male clients if you're going to be so free with your ultra-feminist opinions.'

There was little prospect of changing her views about men in general, but not wanting to let her insults go completely I said, 'Dale is not at all oppressive or insensitive.' The steady gaze of Muriel and Phoebe, and the glimmer of light from the holographic pendant drew me on. 'Dale is someone who brightens up the room when he walks into it. The world is a better place when he is around.'

The words slipped out, expressing feelings that in the past had only ever half-formed in my mind. Because Myrtle and I did not know each other well, realizing that I had revealed some of my inner thoughts to her left me terribly embarrassed. Could Phoebe's warm, glowing eyes and the holographic pendant somehow have made me express feelings normally kept at the back of my mind? I looked down, afraid that my facial expression might give away even more.

Myrtle cleared her throat and spoke gently, 'Ah... to feel so about someone has to be a very good thing. Of course Alicia often talks to me of you, so we can be frank with each other.' She shifted in her chair, alarming Phoebe who rose up on her arm. 'Careful Phoebe, watch your claws on my best jacket.'

She stood and put Phoebe down on the chair. 'I'm a schoolteacher. It helps you understand the way people tick.

Fortune telling, what fun! You know, I think I could get to like you. Have to make allowances for you being a man of course. But tell me now… forget you are a friend of Alicia. Was my performance good enough to earn a fee from a willing punter?'

'To someone hoping for something to believe in, yes, it probably would.'

'You've got to the nub of it there. People always believe what they want to believe, and hear what they want to hear. Alicia has given me a few tips on playing the mystic's guessing game. One thing Phoebe did tell me though. You yourself are not really "gifted" at all, are you?'

I returned her steady gaze. 'Are you going to expose me as a fake? I wish you would. Alicia is the one who tells the world I have unspecified psychic powers.'

'Rob her of something that matters such a lot to her? She rates you highly, I'm not going to spoil it all. Phoebe and I know there are certain things we must keep to ourselves, don't we darling,' she said, picking up her cat again. 'All these theories about psychic phenomena, they are so very, very important to Alicia. She could never accept that all there is to life is the daily struggle to survive, followed by ultimate nothingness. We understand how she feels, we sympathize, don't we Phoebe?' The cat purred louder and louder. I was sure I could feel the floor boards resonating under my feet.

We left our hidden corner behind the screen to find Alicia stapling together a palmistry system booklet for an elderly woman, who watched her closely with sad, heavy eyes. Alicia took her hand and pecked her cheek, and watched her as she walked slowly away. Who would begrudge her any comfort the booklet might give?

Myrtle exclaimed loudly, 'They're here.' Quick, Teef and The Handyman had arrived and were coming towards us.

Bodyguards, two burly men in suits, followed a few yards behind.

You might expect the presence of such famous rock and roll stars to cause a commotion, but no one at the Psychic Fayre paid any attention to them. Rock stars were clearly unimportant alongside tarot cards and crystal balls. The group stopped at a stall with necklaces and bracelets of coloured quartz. Quick and Teef chose a couple of items each, and walked on, leaving The Handyman to pay. At another stall Teef bought a headscarf with white stars on a dark blue background. By the time they reached us, though, I could see that he was worried from the way his eyes darted nervously to and fro.

'Hi Alicia, hi Bendy,' said Quick, 'brought me best mate, Teef. He don't say a lot, he's gone a bit… you know.' He raised his right hand to his head and waggled his fingers vigorously to suggest mental confusion. Teef appeared not to notice. 'Anyway, got to be quick, dinner party in Sloane Square to go to. Not Teef, he'll have to go straight back home. You wouldn't take him to be with a lot of high-class people, not these days.'

'We're all ready for you,' Alicia said. She lifted the lid of the scanner, positioned Quick's right hand on the glass, covered it with a black cloth decorated with a floral pattern in gold thread, and began the scan. Teef stood beside me and whispered anxiously 'Bendy, won't hurt will it?'

'No, course not. Watch Quick being done, not hurting him, is it?'

'Yeah, but he doesn't feel much, he's not the same as us. Is it a laser? We've used them in the stage shows. One of the crew's eyesight got damaged. I suppose I'll have to go through with it. You'll stay with me, won't you?'

'Of course I will, but there's nothing to worry about. It's not a laser, it won't feel hot or anything like that, you can relax.'

When Quick's scan was complete and the quality of the

image checked on the computer screen, Alicia called out 'Next please,' as though she had a queue waiting. Teef, immobilized by terror, regarded me pleadingly. I took his arm and edged him forwards. He winced as Alicia positioned his hand on the glass.

I put my arm across his shoulders. 'It's okay Teef, all that happens is something a bit like a camera on the other side of the glass moves across and records the image of your hand. You won't even feel it.'

He closed his eyes as the ordeal began; beads of sweat ran down his face. 'Look at me,' I said. 'Come on, look at me.' He forced his eyes open. 'You're all right. You're fine. Honestly.' Fifteen seconds later the process was complete and Alicia lifted the cloth from his hand. He uttered a long 'Ooooh' of relief, then inspected his palm for damage. 'Is it all right?' I asked.

'Yes, it hasn't even touched me. I'm tougher than people think. It's fine. Thanks for staying with me, Bendy, I get a bit paranoid sometimes.'

'We all do. Do you want to go back to the car now?'

'Yes please.'

He clutched my arm as we made our way down the hall. We passed Quick, who was talking to a young black woman selling aromatic candles. 'Tell you what darling, if you're free later this week we could get together for a nice little candlelight evening, just you and me. How about it?'

She must have had no idea who she was talking to, for she answered, 'How about it? I think you should pick on someone your own age.'

Teef and I continued out to the car, and after he had settled inside I turned round to see Quick heading our way with a bag full of outsize candles.

'Here, get rid of these for me, will you Bendy? Not used to going to this much trouble to get myself a date. Hope she's worth it!'

Back at Fulrose Court I showed Dale the candles, and we decided to keep one that smelled of sandalwood and give the others to Alicia. She smiled knowingly when, passing them to her, I intentionally described them as 'automatic', not 'aromatic'. Smiling she made out a little sign saying *Automatic Candles*. They all sold over the next week or two, but not one purchaser asked what it was about them that was supposed to be 'automatic'.

The scanned images of Quick's and Teef's palms, printed boldly on expensive cream paper, were impressive. Below the palm prints Alicia added the words *Certified as a genuine copy of Rick Schwagger's/Heath Prityard's palm print, and issued under the auspices of The Rocking Boulders' official fan club.* They were advertised for sale with T-shirts and other merchandise on the club's internet shop, and within a week over a thousand were ordered.

As we were all so busy, Alicia called Myrtle in to help print another batch. As well as running off and laminating the palm prints, she helped out more generally in Hatshepsut's Pavilion. Her home was in Hay-on-Wye, over the Welsh border, where she worked as a part-time music teacher, but she regularly spent long weekends in London with Alicia. She was happy to take on all sorts of jobs, from shifting boxes of stuff around to helping with paperwork. It turned out that she and Jeremy had known each other for decades, having met in the Gay Liberation Front when they were in their twenties.

Fourteen

Meetings and conferences outside London sometimes took Dale away for a night or two. In mid-April his manager sent him up to Birmingham for three days on a training course about new employment contracts. The intention was that, when he returned, he should talk to groups of staff about new pay scales and terms of employment. A bit envious of these expenses-paid trips, I asked, 'And which plush hotel will you patronize this time?'

He smiled. 'If you feel like taking my place on this one, you're welcome. Pay scales and terms of employment are a grind. Expect half the group will nod off in the afternoons.'

He got up early to catch his train to Birmingham, and left me a note saying he had put a new game scenario on the computer for me. At home after work that evening, the first thing I did was to look at it. The game opened with my hunky Latino avatar, dressed in jeans and a white T-shirt with my name on it, walking on a sunny hillside holding a bunch of pink helium balloons. I clicked on the balloons to see if they would burst, but instead the funnel of a whirlwind appeared on the horizon, sped towards 'me' and whisked 'me' up into the air, trapping me in its spiral of dust and debris. Clicking on the balloons now made them explode one by one, but although the on-screen me would slip down towards the ground a little way as each one burst, a pair of eyes would appear at the top of the funnel and glance downwards, while the whirlwind spiralled round ever faster and drew me upwards again.

I was carried over some houses, spun dangerously around a church steeple, then whisked off to a field of rugby pitches where several matches were in progress. Seeing my avatar carried aloft from pitch to pitch, I clicked on the steeple, then on the rugby posts, but the on-screen me remained trapped, meandering round the sky. Then I clicked on a rugby scrum several times; it shoved itself a little in one direction, then back again. Then I clicked on the bottom of the whirlwind, and it came to a stop directly above the centre of the scrum. A ferocious cry came from the many-legged heaving mass. Hearing this, the funnel developed facial features, two eyes, eyebrows, a nose and a mouth – a face which contorted into a scream. The wind dropped me into the middle of the scrum, somersaulted and shot off back over the horizon. A series of lecherous grunts came from the players in whose midst my avatar had disappeared, as they threw my clothes up into the air.

Surely Dale was not going to leave me there being mauled by that lusty gang? The on-screen me, hidden by the heaving mass of muscle, was presumably struggling to get free, and frantically I clicked again and again at the spaces between the players' legs in the hope my avatar would come crawling through. Each click produced a cry for help.

The scene shifted to the woods at the end of the field, where Dale's avatar was sawing up a felled tree. Hearing my shouts, he cupped his hand to his ear, located their direction, and sped over to the scrum. He grabbed the players, one at a time, by the scruff of the neck and the back of the shorts and threw them across the pitch, quite an achievement since most of them were big powerful guys. The second rugger player to be hurled off landed on top of the first, and they began to caress and kiss one another, and so on until the whole lot had been paired off and were coupling all over the field.

Having rescued me, Dale helped me to my feet. I had retained my underpants, so obviously those ruffians had not despoiled me. We retrieved the rest of my clothes from the ground, and he led me into the woods, where we stopped by the felled tree. When I clicked on it he gestured to me to sit down. There was a red scratch on my forehead, which he patted tenderly, and then made instantaneously better with a kiss. One kiss led to another, and very soon we were, like the rugby players, in each others arms, only much more considerate and loving.

This was a delightful scenario, so I rang him to thank him, but he was too tired after a long day to talk for long. His inventive and well-wrought scenario would be difficult for me to match, and I did not want to be diverted for too long from Quick's book, but I resolved to to work up one for him before he returned.

On the second night he was away, I called in at the Give and Take for some company. There were perhaps half a dozen others in the bar. 'Quiet night.' I said, after ordering my drink from Smiles.

'There were plenty in earlier, including a few of the Gay Symphony Orchestra. They have a new violinist, he's really nice. Wouldn't mind a chance of vibrating with him some time. You on your own?'

'He's away. Work… a course in Birmingham.'

Smiles leaned forward and said confidentially, 'Sorry to have to tell you, but over there, in the far corner, sitting on his own, is someone you used to know. He's been in asking about you a couple of times. I tried to put him off by saying you hadn't been in much lately.'

In the mirror at the back of the bar I saw Toby's reflection. 'Oh god.'

'Well, you used to like him.'

'"Used to," you're right there. Not any more.'

'Well, not my business. Actually, there is something I wanted to ask you about, an idea I've had for the bar. You remember how those school disco nights used to pull in the crowds at that straight club in Hammersmith? Hundreds used to turn up, all wearing school uniform. You must have seen them.'

'Yes, there was a real craze for dressing up as school kids, and not only at Hammersmith. Pubs all over the place were having school disco nights.'

'Well, you know a while ago the owners of this place were talking about opening a new late night venue? They decided it was too risky. Now they want me to try some theme nights here, to bring more people in. I was thinking of a school disco night. Guys in sexy school uniforms, what do you think?'

'Generally the girls were better dressed, I thought the blokes were really scruffy. Still, could be worth giving it a try.'

'Would you dress up for it?'

'You couldn't make it a rugby kit night, could you?'

'Rugby kit… that's your thing at the moment, is it? Striped jerseys and tight little shorts? You and Dale are a bit skinny, but a few of the regulars in here might give you a tackle. I'll stick with the school discos for now though. We need more than one or two guys to dress up for it to be any good, which is why I'm asking you. Need to advertise a bit, here and there. What do you think?'

'Yes. I'm sure I could pick up some short trousers in a charity shop or somewhere, and I could borrow blazers from Jeremy.'

'There'd be a prize for best uniform, probably a bottle of wine.'

We were interrupted by Toby, who meandered up to the bar and stood beside me. 'Hi Ben, how are things?'

'Okay.'

Smiles said, 'We were just talking about trying a school disco night. Do you think it would bring people in?'

Toby smiled his easy, anything-goes smile and nodded. 'If you get any naughty boys in, I'll bend 'em over and give 'em a walloping.'

'That's not quite what I had in mind.'

'You sure?' Toby asked. The bar's phone rang and Smiles went to answer it. 'So,' Toby said to me, 'you're doing okay?'

I wanted to be rid of him, and responded with an offhand, 'I'm all right thanks.'

'The other night Smiles was saying you've become a big fan of The Rocking Boulders.'

Smiles would have to pass on to Toby, of all people, what I'd so stupidly blabbed to him. 'I like their stuff. I've read a few things about them lately. It's nothing much.' When we were boyfriends Toby had no interest in rock and roll. Why was he so keen to hear about the Boulders now?

'Your mate behind the bar said you know a friend of theirs.'

'Well… oh… it was some gossip I'd picked up. Second or third-hand stuff.'

'You've got me interested.'

'Why? Are you hoping to get a job as a roadie?'

'Very funny. Same old you. You always were one for a laugh,

190

weren't you?' He was not, though, going to give up easily. 'Seriously, I am interested. I heard they joined some funny sect, like the Prophecies of Arun or something? Maybe we could help each other. Me and Jayde are sharing the upstairs flat now that she and Jake have split. He's downstairs where you used to be. He's changed, the wanker says he wants to get a job, and he's decided he's gay. Tell us about this Egyptian thing The Rocking Boulders were into, and maybe I can get Jayde to be a bit more reasonable about this kid she's having, stop her saying it was all your fault.'

I had not told Smiles much about the Boulders, but clearly it was enough to have impressed Toby. What was he after?

I said, 'That's the deal is it? If I help you, the pair of you will make less trouble for me than you might otherwise? What about your part in all this? That night, when Jayde says I made her pregnant, I went to that club with you, expecting to go back home with you. If anyone is to blame it's you. In fact, you told me you were bisexual. Now you're living with her. Maybe you're the father, not me.'

'Now let's not get into a big scene here. I've come along to have a sensible chat, see if we can help each other. Understand what I'm saying? Jayde wants to have this kid, she doesn't want to get rid of it, that's the truth. She thinks you're its dad. If you help me, tell me about this prophecies thing and The Rocking Boulders, maybe I can persuade her to back off from pointing the finger at you.'

He must have thought she had worried me enough for this bit of blackmail to work. What did he want from me? To help him get in with the band's crowd so he could sell them some pills or some coke? If that was in his mind, he would probably believe almost anything I said. 'Well, since you're so interested, I did hear that in the nineteen-sixties they were interested in a sect

191

that was all to do with Egyptian mummies, pyramids, Cleopatra, and all that kind of stuff.'

He listened intently. 'Yeah,' he said, 'the bands back then all went in for religious shit, didn't they? It was a big thing with the Beatles and the other rock bands. So what happened about this sect? Are they still going?'

'I don't really know.' I hesitated.

'Come on, Ben. You can tell me. Were The Rocking Boulders, you know, into weird kinky religious ceremonies?'

I've never been good at lying, so I told him things that were nothing to do with the sect: that the Egyptian hieroglyphic symbol for life, the ankh, was like a cross but with a loop at the top; that when the ancient scribes wrote the names of the pharaohs they drew a line around the symbols called a cartouche; and that as well as the mummies of people that everyone knows about, mummies of cats had also been unearthed. He listened closely, but after ten or fifteen minutes my knowledge of ancient Egypt was running out. He still wanted more, so I risked an outlandish lie. If he caught me out, I could claim to have meant it as a joke. I said that most ancient cultures used to mummify their dead, and that the Australian Aborigines used to mummify budgerigars.

'Did they? Did they have budgies in Australia then? So when they made mummies out of animals, were they, like, hoping people would be able to have their pets with them after they died?'

Since he was so gullible, I grew bolder. 'No one really knows. You have to remember they built these enormous tombs, so they had to have lots and lots of things to put in them.'

'The Aborigines had tombs as well, did they?'

'Yes, but budgerigars may have been chosen because they're small. Or maybe the early Australians thought they were

192

intelligent, because they could teach them to talk.'

He appeared to be finding this last fib a bit hard to believe, so I changed the subject. 'Tell me, how did Jake take the news that his girlfriend was pregnant by someone else?'

'Oh, yeah, Jake. Well, he packed her in. You can't blame him. He knows it's not his. Funny him being gay, well, bisexual. Never owned up to it till now. Tell you what, since Dale's not here, how about we go somewhere quieter where you could tell me all about The Rocking Boulders? And, well, I haven't forgotten, you know, how things used to be with you and me.'

'What do you mean by that?'

'We had some good times together, before … you know.'

'I'm spoken for.'

'You sure? There are things that go together, bread and butter, salt and pepper. You and Dale are like salt and salt.'

Smiles had come back to our end of the bar and was pouring out a drink. '"Salt?"' I said. 'Doesn't sound like us. We're well matched, like vodka and tonic.'

Toby asked Smiles. 'Here, what was that Rocking Boulders sect you told me about the other day, the something of Arun, was it?'

'Oracles of Aten,' Smiles answered, to my annoyance remembering their name exactly. He nodded, in my direction and added, 'He'll tell you. He's read a book about them.'

Telling Toby all that rubbish about ancient Egypt and Aborigines might have been fun, but why had I not simply told him to f*** off? To change the subject I asked Smiles when the first school disco night was likely to be.

'In a couple of weeks, probably the Thursday. So, what do you say, can I count on you and Dale? I'll wear school uniform, so that would be three of us. I need at least a dozen, preferably more, to make it a success.'

'Yes, we'll get some school togs and show up.'

Somebody else I knew came up to the bar, and we recruited him for the school disco night. Toby hung around for a while, but we ignored him. He soon gave up his hopes of getting anything more out of me and left. I was pleased with my tale of mummified budgies, even if he might not have quite believed it.

At home again, too awake to go straight to bed, I started on a new game scenario for Dale. One anywhere near as good as the rugby game he had left for me would take hours, but I could set up the main features, leaving refinements to the layout and appearance to another time. Among the sports available was cycling, and I created three new avatars dressed in grey Lycra shorts and tops with swirls of blue and orange, who were to join Dale and me in a team. Our opponents had black shorts and yellow jerseys emblazoned with names like Nasty and Stinker.

I put in a naughty little feature that had them pull down their shorts if Dale clicked on their waistlines, giving a brief glimpse of white undies. Clicking on a bike anywhere near the pedals would make a rider mount. He would cycle to the starting line, where a marshal stood with a gun pointing upwards. When all the riders were present, clicking on the gun fired it and the race began, while half a dozen pigeons fell to the ground from the overhanging branches of a tree.

Left to themselves the two teams would continue racing along the lane indefinitely, one rider taking the lead for a minute or so and then falling back, the way cyclists do when racing in teams. The way to move on to the next stage was to drag and drop a sign with an arrow and the words *This Way,* leaving it in front of a side turning called *Lover's Lane.* Here half a dozen parked cars rocked gently to the rhythm of unseen sexual activity within. As a cyclist approached, a car door would open, an arm reach out, grab him, and haul him off his bike into the vehicle.

194

Clicking on a fallen bike made its rider emerge once more, pull up his shorts from around his ankles, remount and resume racing down the lane.

When all the cyclists were back in the saddle, they came to a sign saying *Men's Nude Bathing*. Ahead of them was a lake where a gang of about a dozen hard men were swimming. When they saw the cyclists, they emerged naked, blocked the road, grabbed the riders as they tried to pass, and dragged them into the water. This time, clicking on the bikes did not help, and the nude swimmers, holding their victims around the neck, took them to an island where they tied them to trees. My avatar poked his attacker in the eye with his bike pump and escaped. Clicking on the pump made my on-screen self draw water into it, and squirt any nude bathers who came near him in the eyes. After a couple of high pressure blasts they would run off. The on-screen me then set off to release Dale, who was tied upside down to a tree.

To defeat all the nude bathers, we had to release all the other cyclists and use the pumps as clubs and water guns. Then a rope ladder came down from the branch of a tree. Using 'drag and drop' Dale and I could be moved up into the tree house in the oak's branches, where we lay together on enormous cushions and made love. Well after midnight, I turned off the computer and went to bed.

On the day he returned from Birmingham, Dale arrived home before me. He was preparing dinner when I got in. Over the meal I told him about meeting Toby at the Give and Take, and said that my new scenario in the computer game would soon be ready for him. He was less talkative than usual, and would say hardly anything about his training course. Puzzled, I asked, 'Is there something wrong?'

'No, bit tired, these things can be draining.'

Maybe they could, but surely not to the point that they robbed him of speech. Did he think I had gone to the Give and Take to pick someone up?

I said, 'It's good to have you back. I did go out to the bar, but only stayed long enough for one drink. Anyway, when sodding Toby turned up that really put me off. Are you sure you're okay?'

'Yes, it's… I'd better tell you. Something happened on my last night in Birmingham. My head tells me it would be better to say nothing, but keeping quiet about it makes me feel guilty. This is really difficult. There was someone on the course who fancied me.'

I knew what was coming next. 'You went with him,' I said.

He nodded. 'I got chatting to these people from Leeds, a straight couple and this bloke on his own. They asked me to go for a meal, we had a certain amount to drink, and afterwards the guy who was on his own invited me into his room for a beer. I wasn't even thinking whether or not he might be gay. I could have said no, but I didn't want to be unfriendly. He started showing me some photographs of himself and some friends in a gay club in Leeds. Well, we fumbled around a bit, just hands, a bit of mutual you know what, nothing more. I should have said no thanks, there's someone waiting for me at home. I feel awful about it now. I'm sorry.'

So all it took was a trip away from home, a few drinks over a meal, and decent, honest, steady Dale was ready for a bit of fun with a stranger. I was jealous, but to show it would make things worse. In his place, in the same situation, what would I have done? Holding back my emotions I said, 'We've both been around. You don't have to apologize. When we go to the Give and Take we see men we fancy. It was going to happen, some time or other.'

'You say that, but you're really thinking that if you could go to the Give and Take and come back on your own, why couldn't I keep my hands to myself in Birmingham? When we talked about us being, well, together, a couple, we said we would tell everyone else we were spoken for. I let you down. I want to make it up to you, but I'm not sure how to.'

'Being away on a trip, things are always more likely to happen, aren't they? It's not like going down to a local bar. I'd better clear away.' My words were moderate, but I was also thinking you bastard, screwing around as if I meant zero to you. Why did he have to tell me about it? I would probably never have guessed. I collected up the dishes without looking at him. In the kitchen I asked myself how he, the one who was supposed to be sensible and reliable, could have had casual sex with some guy from Leeds on a poxy course in Birmingham? How could he cheat on me while I was devising a scenario on the computer game, rescuing him from that rapacious gang of nude swimmers?

Or had he cheated, really? We had talked of 'being spoken for', but was that the same as promising to be faithful? There were plenty of gay men who considered themselves to be in 'open' relationships who probably counted their casual pick-ups in thousands. Maybe Alicia's girlfriend was right about men, we were promiscuous by nature, users of pornography, clients of escorts, masseurs, and prostitutes, not capable of sustaining deep relationships. What was there for me to be surprised at? One-off sex with strangers was pretty standard behaviour on the gay scene. Being otherwise made me the oddity.

For the first time I was sorry when the last pot had been stowed away in its cupboard. I could hear the sound of the television in the lounge, but could not bear to sit down with him and pretend nothing had happened. I stepped into the room and said, 'I think I'll go through some of the stuff about Rick Schwagger again, in the spare room.'

He stood up and faced me. 'Give me a chance, please.'

'At this moment, I just want to do something on my own for a while.'

Miserable, he turned away and said, 'Okay, of course. I'll just watch TV for a half an hour or so and then turn in.'

In the spare room, which had been my room when we first shared the flat, I made some notes for the 'auto'biography. After a while I heard him go into the bathroom, then to 'our' bedroom. I carried on working for about half an hour until I began to feel tired. The spare bed was always made up, and I thought about spending the night there, not so much from a desire to punish him, but because even the thought of climbing into bed with him made me feel wretched.

Many of my personal things were still in the spare room. Among them was a book I had kept since I was a kid, *The Rubáiyát of Omar Khayyám,* a poem I had read in the past when times were tough. Some verses that I more or less knew by heart were about coming to terms with unhappiness in life, for instance:

> *The Moving Finger writes; and, having writ,*
> *Moves on: nor all thy Piety nor Wit,*
> *Shall lure it back to cancel half a Line,*
> *Nor all thy Tears wash out a Word of it.*

The third verse from last was surely written by someone who themselves had endured heartbreaking experiences:

> *Ah Love! could thou and I with Fate conspire,*
> *To grasp this sorry Scheme of Things entire,*
> *Would not we shatter it to bits – and then*
> *Re-mould it nearer to the Heart's Desire!*

Of course, Dale casually playing around with someone else had made me sad. Of course it hurt. He meant so much to me. At that very moment, though, was he lying in 'our' bed, feeling abandoned, wondering if I would ever go back in with him? I put the book down, and quietly walked through the darkness into our shared bedroom. The mound he made in the covers on his side of the bed, barely visible in the gloom, confirmed he was there. I undressed. Only after I had slipped in beside him did he tentatively move his hand across until it touched mine. I turned and reached out towards him. We held each other closely and clung to each other, remaining completely still, until we fell asleep.

Fifteen

Toby was not put off by the misleading information I gave him about the sect in the Give and Take. He strolled into the bookshop a couple of days later to ask for a copy of their book. He even claimed to have persuaded Jayde not to hassle me about the baby, at least until after it was born. Alicia's three copies were in store in Jeremy's basement, and reluctantly I went down for one, reassuring myself that it did not even mention The Rocking Boulders. Wading through all that turgid prose ought to stop him pestering me for a while. He took it from me and said thanks, but did not offer me any money, apparently expecting to get it for nothing. We usually reduced the price of books that had been in stock for a long time, and I asked him for half what had previously been pencilled in. He raised his eyebrows, but another customer was waiting and reluctantly he dug out his money and left.

Later I took the coins into Hatshepsut's Pavilion, telling Alicia that the customer was an ex-boyfriend. 'Well done,' she said, 'I had begun to think those books would be cluttering up the place up for ever. Actually, if any of my stuff is in Jeremy's way, I've got some space here now; one of the stallholders at the Psychic Fayre has taken a load of stock off my hands.' She continued: 'There's something else I've been meaning to ask you. What would you think of Myrtle coming in to help again, now the rest of us are busy researching material for Rick's book?'

'You're not going to fire me, are you?'

'No, don't be silly. Myrtle doesn't want a long term job.'

'Will she find out about Rick's book?'

'No, I don't think so. She's a music teacher and doesn't think much of The Rocking Boulders. If we happen to mention them in passing, she won't take much notice. Her taste is like Jeremy's, classical music and jazz. If she asks I can tell her we need her help because you're doing some work for Loyd for a month or two, sorting out papers for him.'

'She'll probably spend all her time telling me how useless men are. But... yes, why not ask her.'

'Odd you selling that book about the Oracles of Aten today, though. I've been making enquiries about them for my section of Rick's life story. I've tracked down a telephone number, in a town on the Sussex coast where the sect was based, for someone with the same name as their leader, though I can't be completely sure it's him until we've spoken. I'll try the number again this afternoon. If he's willing, I'll arrange to go down and have a chat one day when Myrtle is here to mind the shop.'

Rick's association with the Oracles of Aten was not covered in any of the books that Dale had borrowed from the library; more details were well worth hunting for. She thought it probable, for instance, that before the Boulders had split with the sect, they had worked out the story line of the rock opera together. Rick had once played her a tape recording of a couple of songs from it; sensitive and sophisticated, they were quite different from the band's usual stuff.

201

That evening I rang The Handyman to ask him about the abandoned rock opera. 'Oh that,' he said. 'You *have* been doing some digging, haven't you? Now you mention Egypt, I remember ages ago seeing some boards painted with pyramids and an oasis with palm trees. They might have been for an Egyptian stage set, I suppose. The basement and attic rooms in the villa are stuffed full of old studio tapes and god knows what else. You could spend forever searching through all the junk. A lot of it is crap the lads picked up on tour, people give them pendants, arm bands, all sorts of souvenirs. Old stuff gets chucked out to make room for new, they bring more back whenever they go anywhere. There are reels of film and old video tapes; no one can be bothered to find out what's on them.

'That rock opera was long before I went on the payroll. A mate who worked for them in the sixties told me about it. He said Quick fancied some bird who was supposed to be a High Priestess. The rumour at the time was he got her pregnant. Most likely, in the end, the whole rock opera thing had got too big and complicated for them. I expect the lads couldn't handle it. They'd have needed someone who could bring it all together and stage it – an impresario, if that's what they call them. What they've got stashed away in the villa may be junk to me of course, but, who knows, one day someone might pay a fortune for it as band memorabilia. If you want, you can hunt through it to see what you can turn up. Teef would be pleased to see you.'

Dale and I were both so tired by the Friday evening of that week that we went to bed early. At about three o'clock in the morning, the phone rang. I woke first and answered. A flustered Handyman said he had been summoned by the manager of a night club in Soho that Quick frequented. A new relief barman was saying he needed to contact Quick urgently with a message from an old friend. The club manager was suspicious and had his bouncers search the new guy; they found pills and capsules, too many to be for his personal use. The manager had rung The Handyman straight away.

'Is this barman called Toby?' I asked.

'You admit you know him then?'

'I did mention some stuff about the Egyptian sect. I know it was stupid, but he knows nothing about me having met Quick or Teef, or about the biography.'

Mercifully The Handyman accepted this explanation calmly. He said, 'At this moment, Toby's being held in the manager's office. You understand now how dangerous it is to talk about the band to people who are not in the loop, especially if it involves Quick. To anyone dodgy it's like waving a thick wad of money in front of their eyes. Your friend Toby says he's met somebody who used to be in the sect. He claims to have an address in the States for this bird who Quick got pregnant all those years ago, but he admits there was never any message, he just made that up. He is going to have to be taught a lesson, that old mate of yours.'

'We were friends once. He doesn't know anything important, honestly. He's nobody. How did he get into the club anyway?'

'The regular Friday night barman called in sick at the last minute, said he knew someone who would cover for him. Normally they wouldn't take anyone on without checking them out thoroughly, but they were already short staffed. Toby's a crafty bastard, persuading the guy to call in sick. Trouble is, it's the crafty ones you have to watch. And he's picked the wrong time. Quick's itching to get nasty with someone. You've seen those spiked cricket pads in the cupboard. He hasn't blistered anyone's legs with them for months.'

'You could just give Toby a warning, frighten him, let him know what will happen if he tries anything again. Maybe he did have pills on him, and he might have tried to sell them, but you've caught him before he's made any real trouble.'

'You've got your job to do, writing Quick's book. My job is dealing with shits like Toby. You get back to that boyfriend of yours and leave this to me. Bye for now.'

He rang off. Dale by this time was sound asleep again. I felt worried for Toby, and guilty. We might not be boyfriends any more, but he would not be in trouble now if I had kept my mouth shut about the sect. Was Quick really going to torture him with the pads? The anxiety kept me awake for a couple of hours, but my fretting was of no help to Toby. What more could I do?

Over a week passed before I learned that The Handyman's threat had been carried out, surprisingly enough from Jake. He turned up at the Give and Take one night and came over to Dale and me to say hello. 'I know you're thinking *Oh god, not him again,*' he said. 'But how would you feel about making a fresh start? See this?' He held up a half-pint of lager. 'Two of these will be my lot for tonight. No more getting totally off my head, all that is past, over and done with.'

'And you're drinking in a gay bar,' I commented.

'Yes. Jayde and me have split up. You're the one who made me face up to being bisexual. Well, I knew all along really, just never did anything about it. The time had come for me to be honest with myself.'

'You seen anything of Toby lately?'

'Yes. He was in a terrible state the other morning. Jayde had me go up to the flat to help her with him. He'd gone to some club in Soho with his usual menu of pills, been grabbed by some heavies who blindfolded him and drove him off somewhere. He claimed they'd strapped something to his legs that gave him electric shocks. He was put in the boot of a car and driven out to Dartford, where they dumped him in the mud on the river bank.

His legs were so bad he could hardly walk. He had these horrible blisters, nasty red blotches and little puncture marks, the tops of his thighs were red raw. Jayde had to go and rescue him, clean him up and bring him back home in a cab.'

'He didn't go to the police?'

'He can't, can he? He's been done for drugs before. They'd know what was behind it.'

Smiles came over to show me some leaflets about the school disco nights. There was a picture of a handsome young guy in school uniform, smiling broadly and holding out an apple. The heading was *New Skewl Disco on Thrusday* (sic) *Nights*, and under the picture it said *boys in uniform get a first drink free wiv dis ad*.

Dale pulled a face and said, 'The bar is fine like it is. People come in here to meet friends and talk. Why go in for this type of thing?'

'I'm trying to bring in more business,' Smiles replied. 'No one has to dress up if they don't want to. Give it a chance, Dale, it will be good fun.'

'It's not for me,' he answered.

Smiles looked at the floor, then at me, then back to Dale. 'Is there really a problem? Are you worried somebody might put his hand up the leg of your shorts or something? Come on Dale, you and Ben are together, everybody knows that. Let's not worry about it.'

Had something gone on between them in the past I knew nothing about? For Dale to be prickly over the school disco theme night was not like him. To break the silence I picked up one of the leaflets and said, 'I love the spelling of *skewl* and *wiv dis ad*. Clever.'

'Jake did them. He's helping me out.'

'Smiles is helping me out would be more like it. He's taken me on part time at the bar, and put me onto another part-time job selling sports trophies and medals. Since I don't have much of an employment record, it gives me a start. I'm doing some certificates for school disco nights on his computer, with a bit of artwork and fancy fonts, one for best school uniform, and one for the scruffiest. There could be others, let me know if you've got any suggestions. They'll be impressive done up in a scroll and tied with a bit of rainbow ribbon. We could give one to Smiles for being best bar manager. What do you think? Worth a go?'

'Yes. Good for you.' Dale said, and not really interested he went to talk to someone else.

I asked Jake, 'Do you see much of Jayde nowadays?'

'Not really. Her having someone else's kid was a show-stopper. My vasectomy was her idea. It's not right, is it, getting me to go through that and then letting some other guy get her pregnant?'

'You know she and Toby claim that I'm the father?'

'What? She told you that? She and Toby must have cooked that one up between them. Don't worry mate, she didn't fall pregnant until a couple of months after… ermmm… well, after that night we went to the fetish club. You're definitely in the clear. The bastards are trying it on. Sometimes I wish I'd never had anything to do with them. I bet that's down to Toby more than her. Living for kicks is one thing, but making trouble for you is completely out of order. Does Dale know?'

'Yes. Funny really, but he said he thought me being a father might not be a bad thing.'

'He could be right, I mean why not? You and Dale are pretty settled. Being gay doesn't rule out having kids, not these days, does it? You might love it, having a little lad calling you Daddy.'

'When I've grown up a bit more myself, like in twenty years, maybe.'

Previously, when Myrtle had helped print out and laminate Quick and Teef's palm prints, the congenial ambience in the shops was unaffected, but when she returned her tendency to challenge everyone and put them right could be extremely disruptive. Now and again she worked in the bookshop as well as helping in Hatshepsut's Pavilion. She made it vociferously clear to Jeremy that she disapproved of the way he ran things. 'Now let me see where everything is,' she said, and began a tour of the shelves, pausing to read out a title every so often, in an enthusiastic tone if the author was female, but in a very disapproving one if the author was a man. 'Jeremy,' she said at last, 'you've mixed up all the books by women authors with books written by men. They will have to be separated out.'

He thought for a moment and said 'There are some books, encyclopaedias for example, which include contributions from both sexes. In any case, in my view, a rigid classification by sex would itself be discriminatory. Both sexes cook; both cultivate gardens. And surely you would not want to deprive women writers of their male readers, or vice versa?'

'Exactly the kind of answer I expected. A lot of male-oriented, wishy-washy, liberal-minded tosh. The whole shop will have to be re-organized.'

'I'll get on to it tomorrow,' he said dryly. 'There are one or two practicalities that I need to explain to you in the meantime. For example, sometimes you'll find that customers want to haggle. Unless they're about to spend over fifty pounds, the answer is no. If they are spending that much, call me over, or if I'm out give me a ring, or just say no. Or someone may come in with books to sell. If they are mass-market paperbacks, refuse them. If you think what they've got is rare and potentially valuable, ask me about it. If anyone tries to leave books behind in the shop as a way of getting rid of them, tell them most of what we're given goes straight to charity shops.'

'If that's how you want it,' Myrtle said, reproachfully. 'If a poor woman, who has lost a dear one she has spent years of her life nursing, comes in with the deceased's books because she can no longer find room for them, your policy is to send her away with a flea in her ear. Of course, if that's how you like to treat people…'

Jeremy replied wryly, 'I'm sure you will treat all comers with equal delicacy and compassion, whatever I say.'

Dale hit on a brilliant way of coping with her. Whenever they spoke he would introduce the name of a prominent woman into the conversation. According to the topic being discussed he would praise Jane Austen, Florence Nightingale, Emily Pankhurst, Marie Curie or any highly successful and influential female. Myrtle could not fault his regard for them, and her usual stream of complaints and invective against men was, at least temporarily, curtailed.

Her manner softened after a while, and she was actually very good with customers, whatever their gender. Perhaps the pleasure of making a sale outweighed her desire for confrontation. The thing she could never cope with, though, was the computer. Within a minute or so of being at the keyboard she would be cursing, the expletives becoming louder and coarser until she exploded with a string of four letter words and accused the device of being a pernicious, malignant, twisted invention, obviously the creation of a man!

Once I was standing next to her, and saw her type in the capital letter 'O' in a space where the number zero was needed. When the inevitable error message came up, my explanation that she had pressed the wrong key aggravated her further, and she transferred her anger from the machine to me. 'What are you talking about,' she cried. 'Capital 'O' and zero are exactly the same! Anyone can see that. Didn't they teach you anything at school? How Alicia ever came to think you were gifted is beyond me.' It was easier to get her to write things down on paper for Jeremy or me to key in later.

She showed a better side when she gave Jeremy a thick brown folder of sheet music for once popular songs. She explained she had bought lots over the years from one of the second-hand bookshops in Hay-on-Wye. Each one was printed on a single sheet of paper, folded once to make four pages. The fronts had youthful photos of singers such as Frank Sinatra, Rosemary Clooney or Elvis Presley. The earliest of the printed sheets, with songs such as *Young at Heart* and *Bewitched (bothered and bewildered)* had cost one shilling. Thirty years later the price had doubled.

Jeremy handled them excitedly, reacting much as he had when the Larcher first editions turned up. He exclaimed '*Learning the Blues*, how wonderfully Rosemary Clooney sang it!' and *'It's Now or Never*, an emotional Italian ballad if ever there was one, but enjoyable, for all that.' He thumbed through them, utterly fascinated, and for several days sang softly to himself, stopping at once if he thought anyone other than me might hear him. After a week he became bolder. The baritone voice frequently drifted from the little office into the shop, making customers look up and smile. He sang well, seldom missing a note, and giving those old songs real charm.

'You should be on the stage, Jeremy,' I suggested, when he emerged after his swinging rendition of *Close to You*.

He answered wistfully: 'We used to perform at parties, Myrtle and I. She would play piano, and I would sing. Our little turns were quite popular, among friends. She had a piano in her flat in North Kensington, and in those days quite a lot of pubs had them as well, though they were often out of tune. She was, still is, a talented musician. I'm not saying concert pianist standard, but she had a feel for the beauty of a great variety of pieces. Not only the jazz standards we used to do together, but classical music… pieces by Mozart and Chopin. Many of the most famous soloists are men. I always think that could be part of the reason she's so strongly feminist, the sense that being a woman held her back her career in music.

'She and I were good friends back in the nineteen-seventies, long before she moved back to her childhood home in Hay, and before she met Alicia. We were both in the Gay Liberation Front. I think I was the only male friend she had. She used to love telling me that it would soon be possible to fertilize a human egg cell without the need for a male contribution. The whole male sex would, she imagined, be bred out of existence, if not humanely dispatched. At least she's not quite so hard on us these days.'

Her temper could still be fearsome, though. One Saturday, worried her car was being boxed in, she descended on the man who had parked too close. We could hear her scolding voice from inside the shop. She insisted that, if he would not move his car, he should give her his mobile phone number. Otherwise she would have a friend from a garage tow it away. When she had demolished him, she stormed in to us and screeched: 'Men, bloody domineering, stupid, thoughtless, inconsiderate men!'

Jeremy waited until she was calmer. When he judged she was ready, he slightly raised a finger and said, 'Something's amiss, Myrtle. I'm sure it isn't just that man out there. Come on now, tell me what this is really all about.'

It turned out that for quite a few years, during the week of the Hay-on-Wye literary festival, she had taken in lodgers. A children's book publisher had reserved all four of her rooms months ago, but yesterday had rung and cancelled. 'I'd stocked up with breakfast things for them and everything,' she moaned. 'They could not have left me in the lurch at a worse time.'

Jeremy made soothing remarks before tentatively asking if there was a chance that other lodgers might be found.

'I'm so fed up now I can't be bothered.'

'It would be a shame not to use it while the festival is on. That house of yours is a delightful place for anyone to stay.'

'Actually, how long is it since you have had a break outside London?'

'Must be a good six months,' he answered.

'You wouldn't fancy coming up for a few days? There'll be plenty to see while the festival is on. As a friend, of course, no question of money. If Ben and Dale liked the idea, they could come too. It would be fun, a little group of us at the festival together. Hay is only a small town, but it's well worth a visit.'

Sixteen

The small town of Hay-on-Wye, with its forty bookshops and international literary festival, was obviously an attraction for Jeremy and me as we were in the book trade. Alicia too was happy to spend another long weekend in her girlfriend's five-bedroom detached 'cottage' on the edge of the town. Dale was keen to go, if only to take a break away from London for a few days. Coincidentally, Loyd Larcher was due to speak at a festival event on Saturday evening.

Loyd and Alicia had finished writing their sections of Quick's biography, but Dale, Jeremy and I still had lots to do. Loyd's chapter was so professional, it set a standard that was hard for the rest of us to match. He even found some early photographs, including one of Quick and Teef as boys in their Sunday best on a school outing. Quick in particular was remarkably innocent and lovable. Hearing of our visit to Hay, Loyd gave us complimentary tickets to his talk.

The last part of Alicia's chapter dealt with Quick's experiences with the Oracles of Aten, her recollections from the nineteen-sixties reinforced by her recent visit to Sussex to see the sect's founder. She explained how members of the Oracles of

Aten sect arrived in England from North America, and they and the Boulders expected their collaboration to generate a flurry of news coverage.

Quick was determined to bed their High Priestess, the beautiful twenty-two-year-old daughter of a Texas oil magnate. She was said to have conducted his initiation ritual in person. This ceremony took place in the cult's premises, a building that had earlier been a small private school. The stuffed heads of deer that had once adorned the main hall had been replaced by wall paintings of pyramids and figures in the style of ancient Egyptian tomb paintings. The cult's services consisted of interminable monotonous chants, interrupted by brief prayers from priests and priestesses. Flowers and other supposedly sacred objects, such as saucer sized flat stones from the seashore, were dedicated to the god Aten. Flames from ornate candles flickered, and pungently scented smoke wafted liberally from censers.

Towards the climax of Quick's initiation he was given a pendant in the shape of the ankh, the ancient Egyptian symbol of life. After more chanting, bowing and kneeling, a sheet of flame whooshed suddenly upwards from the altar, and the youthful High Priestess conducted Rick through a concealed door into her private chamber.

At around this time, as Alicia had already told me, the band had begun work on a rock opera based on the cult's sacred texts. Only one song from this project was known to have survived, though no recording was ever released. In mood and style it was, as Alicia had said, quite different from the rest of The Rocking Boulders' music. Sensitive and melodic, it conveyed the sorrow of a priest over the death of a childhood friend, the subject of the final chapters of the sect's book.

Hopes that the cult might inspire the Boulders to take a new musical direction did not last. A paternity suit from the High Priestess' solicitor brought Quick the news that she was pregnant. The Boulders' involvement with the cult was terminated rapidly. The veracity of the cult's claim to be grounded in ancient religion was questioned, and the band engaged Alicia, as a professional Egyptologist, to investigate it. She reported that, aside from use of the name Aten and images of pyramids and human figures in the style of tomb paintings, the cult's beliefs, ceremonies and teachings were entirely of their own invention, without any historical basis.

The cult ran out of money before the paternity case reached court. The High Priestess returned to her oil magnate father and married one of his business partners. The founder of the sect remained in Sussex and became a dealer supplying antiques to customers in the United States. Work on the Boulders' rock opera was abandoned.

I gave Loyd's and Alicia's chapters of the 'auto'biography to The Handyman, who had to send them for clearance to the Boulder's lawyers, and then for final approval to a trusted music journalist who had travelled with the band on some of their tours. In passing I mentioned our trip to Hay-on-Wye, and Loyd's talk. He insisted on joining us: 'Larcher's giving a talk at a festival? He's not going to mention Quick's book, is he? You'd better make sure he doesn't. We'll all be in the shit if he lets on before the publicity moguls announce it.'

'Of course he won't. You would think that, wouldn't you? He won't be spreading gossip; in the past he's too often been the victim of it. He's a hugely successful writer. Quick's book is no big thing for him, we're lucky he agreed to help us with it. He's hardly likely to be a big fan of the Boulders. I'm not even going to mention what you've just said. He'd be very badly offended.'

'Well, what else has he got worth talking about?'

'Giving talks is something he does. He was on a lecture tour in the States not long ago.'

'Well, one of us must have the wrong idea about him. So in case it's you, we'd better make sure. Get me a ticket. Buy one, if necessary, and charge it on expenses. If your friend Loyd Larcher does decide to get himself a lot of free publicity by telling the world about Quick's book, the papers will be full of it the next day. Quick will go berserk.'

He had as much right to go to Loyd's talk as anyone, but his turning up at Hay meant that business would intrude on our few days' break. 'We're staying with Alicia's girlfriend, who lives up there. I can't ask her to put you up too, and all the hotels for miles around will be booked up for the festival.'

'What, do you think driving to Hay and back in a day and going to a talk while I'm there is going to be a big deal for me? What's the matter with you? Just get me a fucking ticket, will you? Be a good idea for me to see what this festival is like. When the book comes out Quick will want places where he can parade himself round, sign copies, and get his picture in the papers. Next year's festival might be perfect for it. I'll meet you up there, on Saturday afternoon before the talk, so I can sus it all out.'

If Alicia, Myrtle, Jeremy, Dale and I were to be away at the same time, cover had to be found for the shops. A friend of Jeremy's who had retired from the local council sometimes stood in if either of us was away. Jake was still working part time for Smiles at the Give and Take, and I suggested we also ask him to help. He had already made a good impression when he brought in some leaflets about his sports trophies and award certificates, and asked Jeremy and Alicia to display them. In return he offered to put round some leaflets about their shops.

On the first Friday in June, we set off for our long weekend in Hay-on-Wye. Myrtle insisted on providing transport, and drove down to collect us in an eight-seater minibus belonging to the Hay Girls Academy, where she taught music part time. A considerate driver, she would groan whenever she saw someone adopt the no-signal-so-guess-where-I'm-going attitude to road junctions. We took the motorway from Chiswick, and leaving London's congested streets drove past Reading towards Swindon, enjoying a sense of escape as we passed open fields. Then we took trunk roads to Gloucester and Hereford. Dale was delighted by the scenery, and kept saying, 'Wow, we're off to Hay-on-Wye, or should that be Way-on-High?'

'It'll be Gay-on-Wye when we get there,' Myrtle answered cheerily. For the final stage of the journey she turned onto country lanes to take us through the fine countryside near the border between England and Wales. On the outskirts of Hay, if such a small town can be said to have outskirts, we drew up at a gate bearing a sign saying Myrtle Cottage. This, presumably, was the origin of Alicia's pet name for her girlfriend. The 'cottage' was actually a large Victorian house in an eccentric Tudor style: white rectangles of wall were surrounded by heavy black timbers; the roof was gabled on three sides; a round tower was topped with a cone-shaped roof; and next to it was an old coach house with heavy wooden doors.

Myrtle had inherited the property from her parents, her father having prospered through the sale of agricultural machinery. Behind the lawns and flower beds of the front garden was a vegetable patch, and a chicken run with about twenty hens. The fowl were out in the open, scratching about. I noticed Phoebe, her cat, sitting on a ground floor window ledge snoozing, ignoring the hens, and wondered if she ever tried to get in among them.

Jeremy followed my gaze to the chicken coop and daringly asked: 'Do you keep a cockerel with the hens, Myrtle?'

'No, I bloody well don't. Those hens are perfectly happy as they are, without the male of the species pestering them and disturbing the neighbours with an awful racket in the early hours.'

Alicia showed Jeremy his room, while Myrtle took Dale and me up to ours. 'I've put you two in the bridal suite,' she said, opening the door of a large bedroom with an enormous window. The furniture was of the same vintage as the building; old blue and white porcelain plates and vases stood on every window ledge and shelf. You could understand how attached she was to this childhood home, and that Alicia would be put off living there, permanently surrounded by so much from her girlfriend's past.

When we returned downstairs Alicia was on the phone arranging to sell some of her magical realism pens in the marquee after Loyd's talk. She badgered me into helping. She had already borrowed a little folding table from Jeremy on which to set out the pens. Myrtle took the phone from her and rang the corner café in the town to ask them to keep a table free for us for lunch.

We were seated close to a couple with a toddler in a child-buggy, shaded by a parasol with prominent red polka dots. Alicia and Myrtle made rude remarks in low voices about the child being ugly, murmuring that it might do all right as a garden gnome, and that its parents might at least have put a mask over its face. It was a bit odd, for despite the afternoon sun it wore a woolly hat with flaps that were buttoned under its chin. Fortunately the couple were too absorbed in trying to stop the poor thing crying to pay any attention to us. Jeremy, offended for them, said 'Amazing how disdainful childless adults are of other people's offspring.'

'Don't be so bloody righteous,' Myrtle responded. 'We're having a bit of fun at the expense of straights, that's all.'

He shook his head sadly. 'As long as we're not being unfair to anyone.'

After lunch Myrtle and Alicia went to buy groceries while Dale, Jeremy and I visited some of the second-hand bookshops. They far outnumbered all other types of shop in the main thoroughfares. Many had silly names like Brought to Book, What a Bind, Rabid Reads, and B.O.O.K. – Best Overall Organizer of Knowledge. We wandered from one old-fashioned shop front to another, browsing the great range of second-hand volumes on sale. The town's 'Old Cinema' had been converted into a bookshop, and beyond it, through a gate in a garden wall, we found a house full of books, with a dozen bookshelves placed outdoors around the front lawn. Polythene sheets had been folded back, ready to use in case of a shower, but quite a lot of these unsheltered volumes were worn and faded, evidently getting their last chance of finding another home before they fell apart.

Jeremy had no time for these leftovers, but could not resist some of the rarities from specialist shops. A couple of hours later, when we went to find Alicia and Myrtle, our hands were full of purchases that he was convinced we would sell quickly at a profit in London. This was silly because Hay bookshops also sold over the internet, and the books would not magically become easier to sell from a London shop, but he enjoyed haggling over his purchases.

We found Alicia and Myrtle at the end of Castle Street, standing where a large plane tree narrowed the footway, apparently absorbed in conversation, but in fact deliberately blocking the pavement. They ignored the 'Excuse me's of passing book-lovers, forcing them out onto the road to get by. Myrtle responded to Dale's suggestion that we all move to where the pavement was wider with: 'This is a public right of way, we're entitled to stand here for as long as we want to.'

Jeremy said, 'You've picked this spot on purpose out of devilment. You take pleasure in inconveniencing the great and good people here for the book festival.'

Myrtle answered, 'Yes, we enjoy being awkward, and we're good at it; we've been specially trained.' She and Alicia then resumed their conversation. We walked on a short way to wait until they tired of being in everyone's way and followed us.

In the evening they cooked an excellent meal. Afterwards Myrtle brought out a large cardboard box of old things from the nineteen-seventies about the Gay Liberation Front. She had copies of the GLF magazine *Come Together*, and various hand-outs that must have been hammered onto wax stencils using a typewriter, and run off with one of those old duplicating machines that people used before the invention of photocopiers. She also had some photographs and about a dozen different badges with slogans like *Glad to be Gay* and *Keep Your Filthy Laws Off My Body*. She handed us various items to examine, but Phoebe, sitting in my lap, made it difficult for me to reach out for these treasures. Dale, leafing through a copy of *Come Together*, exclaimed: 'There's an advert in here for something called the Paedophile Information Exchange, P… I… E…, PIE!'

'Oh dear,' Jeremy said, 'those wretched ads have become a gift to everyone who wants to criticize the Gay Liberation Front. Naivety often goes with idealism. A lot of people in GLF were unhappy about them at the time, but others argued it would be more dangerous to force paedophiles into secrecy. There were grounds for saying that GLF should be willing to listen to everyone, since we had ourselves been persecuted, criminalized, and forced to lead double lives. GLF was anarchic, there was no membership as such, anyone could come along to a meeting and say whatever they liked. Society was much more repressive and authoritarian then. Lots of things were done to kids at home and in schools that would be unthinkable now, harsh corporal punishment, for example. Still, those PIE ads were a serious mistake. They got in the way of the important messages about coming out, being honest with ourselves, not being ashamed of our own natures, and treating others with respect.'

'PIE would never have had a chance if men had not been so dominant in the gay rights movement,' Myrtle said. 'It's nearly always men who abuse children.'

'There have been some very nasty cases where women played a part, or were the instigators,' Dale argued.

'Not many,' Myrtle insisted.

From the box she pulled out an envelope of photographs. Several were of her and Jeremy, then in their twenties, among groups of friends. They wore close fitting, richly coloured clothes, and flared trousers. The men had long hair, and everyone wore badges. How slim and attractive Jeremy was in those days, sporting a shirt with a pattern of autumn leaves above tight pinkish-grey trousers. 'You were on the pull that night,' I said.

'It's how lots of young men dressed at the time, straight as well as gay. We wanted to show ourselves off, all part of the new age of unashamed sexual freedom. There was a huge sense of shedding the constraints that our parents laboured under, of rejecting authority. We were striking out for a better world.'

'Where's that list of the groups GLF used to have,' Myrtle said, shuffling through the box. 'Here we are.' She read out the names of about half a dozen groups, including the Manifesto Group, the Counter-Psychiatry Group, and the Catering Group.

'And which group,' she asked, 'do you think Jeremy belonged to?'

'I belonged to the Catering Group,' he said laughing. 'Everyone helped in whatever way they could. We men in the catering group were showing our independence from the traditional male role. Some of us baked cakes, as well as making the teas and coffees. We also helped to get things organized generally. The Catering Group made its contribution, including raising a little money. Even in a radical group like GLF, some things had to be paid for. You feminists,' he said looking at Myrtle, 'had your own agenda… so did some of the others who turned up. The revolutionary socialists were another lot, with their background in student politics, sit-ins, and different flavours of Marxism. In real life putting up posters of Che Guevara was the nearest any of them were ever likely to get to violent revolution.

'All sorts used to turn up at the meetings, Vietnam war draft dodgers from the US, ex-hippy drug freaks. You remember that strange American with the ferocious black hair and beard? He used to stand up and deliver an impassioned diatribe at pretty well every meeting, but I never met anyone who could tell me afterwards what he had been raving on about. Yet we got accustomed to his harangues, meeting after meeting. There was excitement in the air, something exceptional about the idealism, about our crusading zeal against our oppressors. We were demanding our place in a society that had spurned us for so long.'

'You gay men were latching on to the women's rights movement,' Myrtle countered.

Alicia said, 'At least he stuck with it. He didn't go marching out in a huff.'

'My dear Alicia,' Myrtle said, 'we lesbian feminists did not go marching out in a huff. Huffs are something we were biologically not capable of. What we did was to register a proper and entirely justified protest against the domination of the meetings by men. We showed our rejection of their male chauvinist oppression by the only effective means open to us, by walking out. And how long did GLF last after we walked out?'

'It's true that it fragmented after a few years, but whatever the disagreements,' Jeremy reasoned, 'it did change attitudes. It led up to the Gay Pride events and many of the gay and lesbian groups that exist today. If the only thing we had done had been to stand in public view wearing badges that showed we were gay, we would have helped to end decades of secrecy, pretence, shame and guilt.'

'I'm not going to argue with that,' Myrtle said. She judged that we were all growing tired and began returning her GLF souvenirs to their box. 'Would anyone like tea or coffee now?' she asked.

Though it was not very late, we were all ready to turn in. Myrtle chased Phoebe off my lap, saying 'She'll be following you into the bedroom if you don't watch out,' before handing me my drink. 'Do you have any pets of your own?'

'We've got each other,' I said, smiling at Dale.

'Lucky old you,' she answered, in a tone that suggested she thought otherwise.

When Dale and I were on our way towards the stairs to go up to bed, she could not resist having a cheeky dig at us. She came over and said in pretended embarrassment, 'Before you go up, I hope you won't mind me asking, but I'm a bit concerned about the sheets, well, you know, stains from bodily fluids can be very persistent. I expect you two are too tired to be getting up to anything like that tonight, aren't you?'

Dale and I glanced briefly at each other. Guessing she must be joking, he answered, 'The trouble is, Myrtle, Ben can never

222

get off to sleep properly unless I give him a good seeing to first.'

'Oh well,' she said, 'in that case I suppose you must.'

I could, of course, equally well have said the same of him, if only I had thought of it first.

Myrtle need not have been concerned about her sheets that night. We were so sleepy that we settled for comforting sexual relief rather than giving each other a good seeing to. Having slept solidly, we went down for breakfast in the morning ready for an eventful day. Myrtle gave us eggs from her hens for breakfast, the yolks an exceptionally deep yellow-orange colour. Phoebe watched me eating. 'She doesn't worry the hens at all?' I asked.

'She gets as much food as she wants without having to run around after them. In any case, she can't get in, the chickens have to be well protected against foxes. I was wondering if, after breakfast, any of you might like to go for a walk by the river? It's lovely down there. Then we could have a picnic lunch before we go on to hear Loyd speak. I'm planning a barbecue for tonight, if that's all right?'

We all agreed. She loaned Jeremy a battered old copy of *The Observer Book of Birds,* saying, 'Take this with you. You'll be able to identify any that you see on your way.'

'This is a very dated copy,' he commented.

'Well,' she said, 'a blackbird still looks like a blackbird and a thrush hasn't changed much over the years, so far as I'm aware.'

She drove us four or five miles from Hay to the start of a path that ran through fields beside the river, then returned to the town on her own to put together the picnic, park the van at a spot near the town's bridge, and walked from there to meet us on the route. Jeremy, who was not fond of exercise, began to mutter about the fields being full of cowpats. Quite a lot lay beside, or even oozed over, our path. 'Myrtle should have given us *The Observer Book of Country Smells*, not the *Book of Birds*,' he grumbled.

We did not spot any birds more unusual than those you might see in London parks or gardens, but we saw wild flowers, butterflies and bees. In a couple of places, cows waded out into the river to drink or possibly to cool down as the day warmed up. Dale wore a pair of really sexy why-does-everyone-keep-staring-at-me jeans. He and I led the way, while Alicia and Jeremy followed behind. We were halfway to Hay when my phone rang. The Handyman was about an hour's drive away and wanted to know where to find me. Reluctantly I told him to park near the bridge and find us in the picnic area.

With only a few hundred yards to go, we came upon Myrtle sitting on a stile watching the river. 'The water's low at the moment,' she observed. 'We've had rain, but most of it goes to the reservoir. Still, it's nice when it's peaceful like this. The current can be very strong after a downpour.'

Near the bridge was a little park with a flower border, mown grass and some picnic tables. The day was warming up. Four or five canoes, hired out by the hour from a local boathouse, made their way slowly upstream. The Handyman, following my directions, came towards us, but none of us bothered to get up to welcome him. He squeezed himself onto the seat between Dale and me, resting one leg against mine under the table, and I guessed the other was pressed as firmly against one of Dale's. Myrtle offered him a sandwich, but he had eaten already in a pub. I tried to give him his ticket to Loyd's talk, but he told me to hold on to it, saying we might as well all go in together. He asked about festival venues where Rick might put in an appearance next year, but only Myrtle knew much about the festival, and she shrugged off his question by giving him the organizers' phone number.

To reinforce the message that he was imposing on us, I suggested he go into the town to see the posters for events for himself. Apologetically he said, 'I think I've seen the town, what there is of it. Look, this book of Quick's is an opportunity for me, the first time I've really got into the business side with the band. This could be my chance to edge forward a bit. I don't want to lose the initiative.'

He had helped me make friends with Quick and Teef, so maybe hoping for a little help from me now was not unreasonable. 'Okay,' I said, 'I understand that, but excepting Myrtle none of us has been to the festival before. Maybe Loyd could suggest how best to promote Quick's book, but he'll have a lot on his mind today. I can speak to him when we're back in London if you like.'

Dale suddenly stood up and called out: 'Look, they've got stuck over there.' The water being low, two teenage girls and a younger boy in a canoe had drifted away from the deeper channel in the river, and run aground on a little island in the broad river bed. We watched as they tried unsuccessfully to push themselves free with the oars. Then the boy took off his shoes and jumped out of the canoe. Pulling on a rope attached to the bow, he accidentally stepped off the rocks into deep water. His head went under. He surfaced, squealed at the shock of the cold river, and made his way up onto the little island. Dale walked down to the river's edge, kicked off his shoes, rolled up his jeans above his knees, and waded in. He could not persuade the girls to get out of the canoe to make it lighter and, even with the boy's help, their weight prevented him from freeing the boat. Seeing this, The Handyman ripped off his shoes and socks and went towards them, slowly picking his way over submerged stones. He was a strong guy, and he and Dale easily pulled the canoe back into the main channel. The boy clambered back in, and the two men pushed the canoe off downstream. Dale slipped, fell, and was soaked up to his armpits.

The Handyman helped him to his feet, and supported him as they regained the river bank. He held on to Dale firmly, and jealousy surged through me as I watched them. Why had I hung back on the bank instead of wading in to help? When The Handyman let go of Dale they came towards me side by side, Dale's wet jeans clinging to his thighs. I could not stop myself trying to see whether either of them was sexually aroused, and despite the cold water The Handyman definitely was. Our eyes met, putting me in a muddle of confusion and embarrassment.

Dale wandered over to the sparse cover of the flower bed, where he took off his T-shirt and wrung it out. He looked around for somewhere more private to remove his wet jeans, but there were no bushes or other possible cover. Unaware of my jealousy, The Handyman stood beside me, and for a moment we stopped watching Dale and looked at each other, reading each other's thoughts. He lowered his eyes. 'Like my boyfriend, do you?' I asked blandly.

'Fuck me,' he said, 'Sorry, didn't mean to… what is it about you two? You do this to me every time. It's seeing the pair of you together, knowing what you… I've got to pack this in. I'm going to go over there and cool myself down.' He walked back to the river's edge, knelt down and rinsed his hands and arms. I went back to the picnic table, leaving Dale to sort himself out, embarrassed by my own mixed feelings. Jeremy guessed something of my state of mind, for he tried to distract me with a poetry anthology he had bought the previous day. He flicked through it to find some lines by Maurice Baring he particularly liked, and read them out:

Because of you we will be glad and gay,
Remembering you, we will be brave and strong;
And hail the advent of each dangerous day,
And meet the great adventure with a song.

'Of course in those days the word *gay* would not have been used in a sexual context,' he said. 'Amusing though, to think of the verse with the old and the new meanings in mind.'

The tactic worked, for my attention shifted from jealousy and lust to the anthology. When Dale came over I was my normal self again. His trousers were still sopping wet, and Myrtle kindly drove him back to her house to change. The Handyman had not brought any spare clothing, but he had a small blanket in his car and dried himself as well as he could with that.

When we were all together again we still had an hour or two before Loyd's talk, and decided to call in at a pub in the centre of town. The bar was cramped, but at the side was a big room where half a dozen lads were playing pool. At one end of it was a little stage with a piano. Myrtle coaxed Jeremy to go up to perform with her. Fearing gross embarrassment in front of the locals, I prayed the lid of the keyboard would be locked, but of course it was not. Jeremy fetched her a chair. She sat bolt upright, looking not at the keyboard but straight ahead, and played a few runs of notes. The instrument's surprisingly rich tone echoed around the bare room. The lads at the pool table halted their game to see the show.

'We couldn't slip out and pretend we're not with them?' I whispered to Dale.

He and Alicia 'shushed' me as Myrtle played the opening chords of the song. When she began the accompaniment Jeremy sang in a relaxed, very cultured tone, like a vocalist from the era of Noël Coward or Ivor Novello:

> *'We hoped our love would find,*
> *Happiness with lives entwined.*
> *Friends simply could not see,*
> *We two were meant to be.'*

Despite the impassioned words of the song, his voice was marvellously cool and relaxed. The rich lilting sound of Myrtle's piano enhanced the mood of nostalgia:

> *'They said that like June snow,*
> *Our summer dreams would go,*
> *We thought we'd take our chance,*
> *Our love was no mere dance.'*

After several more verses they finished. We applauded, and surprisingly the lads at the pool table joined in. This being the week of the book festival, maybe they were not local yobs, but the cultured offspring of literati, schooled to be considerate towards ageing eccentrics.

'That was wonderful,' Alicia said, 'both of you. Will you give us an encore?'

'Best if we quit while we're winning, I think,' Jeremy said.

The Handyman added. 'You should send a demo around to music agents. You might not be chart material, but music of that era must have fans. What period was it, by the way?'

'That song is from long before we were born. I suppose we might have tried making a record, years ago, if we'd known how,' Myrtle said. 'A bit late now. One look at us would put people off.'

We left the pub to go to Loyd's talk, and entered a huge marquee on the edge of town. Our seats were a few rows back from the stage. The event had been well advertised and it was

228

packed. Press cameras began to flash as soon as Loyd strode onto the stage. When the applause faded he began his tirade.

'Earlier today I spent many delightful hours browsing the enchanting variety of second-hand volumes available in the famous bookshops of this delightful Welsh town. On first thoughts, the bookshops and the literary festival appeared to be an excellent match. The great range of works of every kind, in particular those hard-to-find titles, provide an excellent reason for holding a major literary event here, and the festival brings an influx of business to the town, and especially to the bookshops.

'How enjoyable it was to be able to see so many great books from earlier decades. What talent, what originality, what authorship, what sheer genius, beckoned to me from the crammed bookshelves. Without aids such as word processors, and all the other wonders of technology on which modern book publishing depends, the literary giants of the past opened up vast worlds of imagination and understanding, and brought to their readers a huge range of ideas.

'How quickly my enthusiasm faded when I turned my gaze to more recent products. However seductively they were presented, whatever the buzzwords used on the covers, 'products' is the right word for what is now issued by the global publishing conglomerates. Products is what they truly are, conceived and designed to meet known mass market demand, far from yesterday's carefully crafted works of art and invention that broke new ground and kept readers up with or ahead of the times.'

Witheringly he scanned the auditorium, from one side to the other. 'Save for a very few examples, there is nothing in the least *novel* about modern fiction. No one, apparently, has explained to today's authors that novel means 'new'. What depressing examples of re-hashed, over-familiar, hoary old detective stories

229

I found. What dreary yarns padded out with inconsequential minutiae, populated by, or should I say cluttered with, worthless characters leading trivial lives. What infantile fairy tales filled the pages of books ostensibly meant for adults to read, what daft imaginings that a clever eight-year old ought to dismiss as immature, and refuse to waste precious time on.

'Where today are the writers who can, like say Scott Fitzgerald, convey succinctly and engagingly the fragility of man's grasp of the essential influences that circumscribe his life? Where are the authors like Chekov, to touch us with their insights into the core of our beings, or like Orwell, to confront us with the momentous issues of the day?'

Loyd continued on and on in this vein, excoriating modern writers, their publishers, the critics, and everyone else. He condemned today's celebrity culture which, he said, had replaced talented writers with puffed up, preening, posing, posturing hacks, individuals whose most profound realization was that having their teeth whitened would help sell more of their books.

Only one man in the audience protested, twice shouting to Loyd that he 'belonged with the dinosaurs'. Maybe everyone else was dumbfounded by the ferocity of the attack, or were themselves secretly worried about the quality of modern fiction; maybe they were relieved to hear someone rail against what they themselves had not dared to criticize. After a final salvo at journalists, whom he accused of turning what had been an art form into a public relations circus, he sat down.

Jeremy immediately clapped loudly, and the rest of our little group did likewise. A little scattered applause began in other parts of the marquee, then more and more people joined in, and as the volume grew Loyd rose to take a bow. There were cheers and wolf whistles. Far from causing offence or resentment, his talk was a triumph.

Alicia nudged me and we stood and made our way towards the exit. While Loyd fielded questions from the audience, we set up the folding card table and put the magical realism pens out on display. Most people regarded us with mild amusement, and passed us by, but some stopped. Alicia caught the eye of likely customers and delivered her sales patter: 'The pens have been designed by someone deeply immersed in magical realism, who has added her own inspirational artwork to a top quality, twist-mechanism, retractable ballpoint. It has been scientifically proven that, for work in the magical realism style, a dedicated writing implement is an aid to the creative imagination.'

Some people were sufficiently gullible, or amused, to buy. A wire-haired woman picked up one of the pens and asked tetchily, 'But the symbols on these pens are all South American. My field is Scandinavian magical realism, though I will also do the Baltic countries. Have you anything for me?'

Alicia was not prepared for this question. 'Oh, Scandinavia... the Baltics... of course. I wonder... no. I'm not sure if the manufacturers... Let me give you my card. If you send me an e-mail I'll find out for you.' To Alicia's delight we sold several dozen of the pens in fifteen or twenty minutes.

Our second and last evening at Hay-on-Wye, or Way-on-High as Dale continued to say whenever he had chance, ended with the barbecue at Myrtle Cottage. As The Handyman wanted to begin his drive back to London by nine o'clock he was reluctant to come back with us, but Myrtle had bought in lots of food and talked him round. Loyd was due to have dinner with some of the literati, but he called at the cottage for half an hour, glad he said to have a break with friends away from festival activities. He had been reading through some of my section of the 'auto'biography, covering the nineteen-nineties, and before he left he handed the pages back to me. I saw he had made numerous comments and took them upstairs to put it in my bag for safety.

Phoebe saw me coming back down, and climbed slowly up towards me, purring and gazing at me, managing to block my descent. I petted her and picked my way carefully past her, but she followed me out into the garden. When I thought Myrtle was not looking I sneaked her a little piece of chicken from the barbecue, as a result of which she stayed with me all evening. She was a remarkably persuasive cat, sitting in front of me licking her lips, her big eyes staring. The second morsel I slipped to her did not escape Myrtle's notice. 'She's spoiled enough without you doing that. I don't want her pestering me for treats after you've gone.' she said.

As the shadows grew longer we all stood or sat around the lawn, eating, drinking and talking, until about nine when the temperature began to fall. Alicia suggested we go indoors. The Handyman decided it was time for him to set off for home, and I walked with him to his car. He said, 'This is such a different world to the one I'm used to. You're not still annoyed with me, are you?'

'Because Dale turns you on? No, as long as you're not trying to take him from me.'

'Not just that, is it? I was out of order, implying that Loyd was not to be trusted to keep quiet about Quick's book. You still friends with me?'

'Of course. You can't help having funny ways, you being straight.' He smiled and got into his car.

When the remaining five of us settled in the lounge, Alicia brought out a folder with pictures of a tomb in ancient Egypt. We looked at large glossy photographs of wall paintings that were four thousand years old. They were part of a huge funerary complex south of Cairo, excavated in nineteen-sixty-four. Two men, Khnumhotep and Niankhkhnum, were buried together, the size of their tomb reflecting their high social status. They were portrayed with the tips of their noses touching, their arms entwined. Only husbands and wives were usually shown in this way. The hieroglyphics, Alicia explained, identified the men as manicurists to pharaoh Niuserre. The ancients believed that the souls of a couple interred like this would be locked together in intimate embrace for all eternity.

Next she showed us pictures of a very remote oasis at Siwa, which had been visited by Alexander the Great, where the inhabitants had accepted gay love, including marriage between men.

'These must be among the earliest known examples of men loving men,' Jeremy commented. 'I've always loved the story of Hadrian and Antinou from Roman times. Antinou, the beautiful favourite of Emperor Hadrian, drowned while swimming in the Nile. Afterwards some of the cities of the Roman Empire had statues of him made to present to Hadrian, showing respect and sympathy for the Emperor's loss.'

A little later Dale and I went up to bed, full of thoughts of the ancient world's gay love affairs. When he was pulling his T-shirt over his head I jumped on him and pushed him over onto the bed. He pretended to struggle, but was giggling and clearly ready for some fun. Before he freed his arms from the T-shirt I pulled down his trousers; he grabbed me and rolled me over so that he was sitting astride me. I raised my head and shoulders from the mattress and kissed him repeatedly on the neck. One of the great things about Dale is that, since he is lovely all over, if you tire of kissing one part of him you can simply move on to kissing another. That second night in Hay neither of us was too tired to give the other a really good seeing to.

After breakfast the next day we returned to London. A few

days passed before I had time to read through Loyd's comments on my draft. He had made lots of detailed changes, clarifying the wording and improving the flow. Where I had used phrases such as *stunning electro vibes* and *early fuzzy guitar riffs* he had put in flippant comments in the margin like *How frightfully modern!* or *Totally with it, man!* I incorporated his improvements, and resolved to complete my part of the book over the next few weeks.

Jeremy and Dale were still working on their chapters, covering the nineteen-seventies and eighties. The Handyman reported that the lawyers and the music journalist had cleared Alicia's account of the band's involvement with the Oracles of Aten, and that the Boulder's management company were delighted that it was covered. The story might have been lost completely had Alicia not set it down for Quick's book.

Seventeen

Despite his soaking in the River Wye, Dale enjoyed the weekend in Hay. However, we agreed it would have to be our last break until the 'auto'biography was complete. After a couple of days back at work, the weekend seemed long past. Time was short; to maintain our momentum with the book, late nights out had to be avoided, even on Saturdays.

Takings in the shops had held up reasonably well while we were in Hay. Jake told me Jayde had contacted him again, and had admitted the story about her child being mine was false. She said Toby made her implicate me because they were desperate for money. Since then, she had gone back to her parents in East Kent, and she had asked him to visit her. He wanted someone to go down with him. I was reluctant because of the aggravation she had caused me, and asked if Smiles could not go.

'He doesn't know her, and it would be a bit awkward, taking my current boyfriend to visit my ex-girlfriend. They'd probably both feel uncomfortable. She has apologized for making out you got her pregnant. I could go on my own, but she would be less likely to try to re-start things with me again if you came with me.'

'Maybe I *could* help you keep out of trouble. How long were the two of you together?'

'Nearly two years. We saw a lot of life, maybe too much. We were bad for each other, you saw that for yourself; we overdid everything. The way I feel now is, it would be nice if Jayde and I could be friends, but nothing physical. Life's very quiet for her down there. Her old school friends have all moved away. You can imagine it… watching TV with her parents… dead boring. She always liked you, you know. She used to say you were one gay boy she wouldn't mind turning straight. Think about it, anyway.'

Though at first not happy to be reminded of her, later the idea of seeing her grew on me, partly out of curiosity to see how she was coping with becoming a mother. Dale was lukewarm because of the time it would take up, but left it to me to decide. He asked me again how I would have felt if the child had turned out to be mine.

I answered, 'I'm glad it's not. What kind of start in life would that be for a kid, having to rely on Jayde and me as parents?'

'It would be a better start than having Jayde on her own. Suppose it had been yours, what would that have meant for us?'

'Nothing, except for me having to support the kid and being skint all the time. You'd still come first.'

'Ought we to talk about how we see the future?'

'So much is going on right now, with our day jobs and Quick's book. The main thing is that we're together..'

'Okay, let's leave it for now, but not for too long.'

If he had told me definitely that a civil partnership was what he wanted, I would have agreed at once. Life with him was far richer and happier than it had been before. For me to do the asking would not feel right; he was more mature, and he owned the flat. Anyway, how do you decide you care enough for someone for a civil partnership? Lots of straight marriages end up in divorce. The Jay's experience showed how tricky long-term commitments could be; he had undergone a vasectomy so they wouldn't need contraceptives, only for her to become pregnant by someone else.

I decided I would go to visit her. We took the train to Aylesham, the Kent village near Canterbury where she had been brought up. Jake looked good in a long-sleeved T-shirt, dark blue jeans and one of the necklaces from Hatshepsut's Pavilion with a central cylindrical bead in rainbow stripes, a signal that he now thought of himself as gay. On the way he talked about Smiles' plans for the bar and his own future. Since Quick's book had to be kept secret from him I had little to tell him, so his being talkative suited me. He was thinking of buying a car or a small van so that he could drive around to sports clubs and show samples of trophies, medals, and key fobs, instead of leaving it to customers to contact him. He had with him a couple of certificates he had designed for the Give and Take's school disco night, to be awarded for best school uniform and best haircut. He asked me if I had any bright ideas for others.

'Teacher's pet, maybe?'

Aylesham was not as you might imagine a Kent village to be, an idyll of thatched cottages with ducks on the pond. Streets of uniform houses had been built for workers in a local coal mine, long closed. He phoned Jayde when we arrived and she gave him directions to the house. Five minutes later we walked down a front garden path, passing a pretty flower border and an incongruous, pretend water-well made of plastic. She was waiting for us at the front door, a bit plumper than before and wearing only lipstick, not the full coating of make-up she wore in London. In the hall she and Jake hugged and kissed lightly, and she pecked me on the cheek. I smiled and asked how she was.

'I never thought you'd come,' she said, 'not the way I was last time we met.'

I shrugged and shook my head to reassure her. She introduced us to her mother, who brought us tea and cakes in the living room. Jake found it difficult to know what to say at first, and to avoid a silence she said to me, 'You must have thought I was a right old slag, the way I was carrying on. It's nice to see you again. How's that gorgeous boyfriend of yours?'

'He's fine. Working hard, as ever. How's it been for you, coming back here?'

'Didn't have a lot of choice, like. It was hopeless sharing a flat with Toby. He's worse than I ever was, and that's saying something. Last I heard he was in trouble again. He went to Greece, humping the kit for some crap band, and got busted for drugs. He always had to be getting up to something. He wasn't so bad when he was with you. You probably helped to calm him down, like.'

I nodded. Was that how the three of them thought of me, as someone they asked to tag along to calm things down? There was another half minute of edgy silence, until Jake asked her about the child's father. She said she knew who he was, but that he was a happy-go-lucky type who never worked or took responsibility for anything. She was hoping that her mother would share taking care of the baby so that she could get a part-time job.

After an hour or so in the house we took her to up to Canterbury for a meal. She chose to drink mineral water rather than alcohol, saying, 'The baby has to come first now, as my mum is always telling me.' She and Jake chatted about people they used to know and bars they used to go to in London. She did not mention any worries about her future, and said, 'It's not what I set out to do, but p'raps it's what I needed to make me take a hold of myself.' She was standing up well to the challenge.

238

We saw her onto the train at Canterbury, and waited for one going in the opposite direction. On our way back, Jake was deep in thought. Maybe he was wondering how their lives might have been had the baby been his, or about how his future with Smiles would work out. We spoke very little. I was preoccupied by the thought that, whilst her life was now more settled, since my involvement with The Handyman, Quick and Teef my own had become increasingly unpredictable.

After we left the train and were walking up the platform at Victoria he asked, 'Do you think I was a cunt for walking out on her?' Unsure of himself, he avoided eye contact.

'No, I don't think that at all. Things had to change, didn't they? What would it have been like for the kid, especially it not being yours, with you two overdoing everything the way you used to? It would never have lasted. At least you've kept in touch with her.'

No relationship is immune to problems. Shortly after my visit to Jayde, Dale and I had a tiff over the Give and Take's school disco night. Without telling him, I went to a fancy dress shop that had school uniforms in adult sizes, for hire or to buy. The weather was warm, and as we already had white shirts, all we needed were shorts, socks and ties. We are more or less the same build so I bought two lots, thinking to save him the trip to the shop. When I showed him my purchases he said sharply: 'You should have asked me. I'm going to give the school disco night a miss. I hate the whole idea of it. You go if you want. I'll stay in, there are plenty of things that need doing. Adults fantasizing about being kids again strikes me as immature, not to say bizarre. And it feeds the stereotype of gay men being obsessed with superficialities like dressing up.'

Perplexed by this, I said 'No it doesn't. Most school disco

239

nights are hetero, organized by straight pubs and clubs. Just come for half an hour to be friendly. You've known Smiles longer than I have, you ought to give him a bit of support. Jake's doing his bit; he showed me a couple of certificates he's planning to give out. Don't dress up if you don't want to. We don't need to make a big thing of it, but they'll be expecting us.'

'I said no.'

'Why not? What's wrong?'

'I don't want to.'

'You could put up with going there for half an hour.'

'No.'

'All right, obviously I misunderstood. Since I promised to be there I ought to show my face, but I won't stay long,' I said, unable to hide my irritation completely, but holding back unspoken the words: *you miserable sod.*

He nodded and shrugged. 'Fine, if it's your kind of thing. It's not mine.'

We ate dinner in silence. As I started to clear the table he grabbed my arm and said, 'I had better explain. You know how free and easy Smiles is. We had a problem, before I met you. He knew my ex-boyfriend. They used to... play around... this is difficult for me to talk about. Of course what Smiles does is up to him, but he invited my ex and me to what turned out to be a sex party. He had this board game where you threw dice and moved a marker round the board. When you landed on certain squares you had to pay forfeits, take off an item of clothing, let someone grope you, do all kinds of stuff, and so on and so on. It wasn't for me, but my ex loved it. Curiously enough, though, when any of the others wanted to touch me he got jealous and was really nasty to them. Well, I went to two of these sex game sessions, people started taking their clothes off, and as the game progressed the real action started. Both times I dropped out early, which was what you had to do if you refused to pay someone a forfeit. Smiles and my ex, though, they stayed right to the end.

'Everyone took his turn at being host. When my ex had them all round here, half a dozen or more of them, I went into my room and shut the door. I'm not trying to condemn people for being promiscuous, some people have open relationships, good luck to them, but how can you stay a couple, if either of you walks off with someone else whenever they feel the urge? It's just not me. After a while my ex and I couldn't be in the same room without having a row. He found somebody who, as he put it, wasn't stuck with a Victorian outlook. The last I heard of him he had moved to Spain.

'Smiles was the one who had discovered the game, and got the little group of players together. You know what he's like – always has to know everything about everyone. I know school disco night is not going to be an orgy, exactly, but it may not be all that far off it, and with Smiles there as well it will bring back all those horrible memories. I'd hate it.'

Dale might enjoy the fooling around in the erotic computer game, but that was all on the screen and in the mind. Smiles' board game was obviously flesh on flesh, based on the gay-men-are-all-male-whores-anyway attitude to life. Dale's primary instinct was to find a long-term partner. The break up of his relationship must have been harrowing. I said, 'I had no idea at all what was going on in your mind. I do understand how you feel, but that all happened before we got together. Can't school disco night just be a bit of a laugh? Am I being naive?'

'We don't always have to do the same thing, do we? I accept you feel you ought to go. I never thought you intended to get off with somebody. You go, and have a good time – but you understand how I feel.'

'I never thought of the school disco as being a big thing. If it is, I suppose…'

'Go, have a good time. I'm not going to be resentful or anything like that. What counts is that you do come back.'

So, largely to avoid letting Smiles and Jake down, I did go to the Give and Take's school disco night. Also it would demonstrate to Dale I wanted to preserve some independence. As soon as I walked into the bar the atmosphere struck me as more sexually charged then usual. Attractive young guys always are ogled a lot, but that night some customers were staring constantly at anyone in school uniform. The sense of group lust was hard to ignore. Making my way through the crowd to get to the bar, several men deliberately brushed against me, rather than letting me through.

Smiles, who had watched this, welcomed me with a grin. 'Where's Dale?' he asked.

'He's got things he needs to catch up with tonight. I see you've turned the lights up.'

'Well, one or two guys were getting a bit over-excited. Dale's okay, is he?'

'Yes, he's at home. You've drawn in the customers all right.'

'Jake's put loads of leaflets around. Later on he'll be doing a raffle and giving out some awards. Keep your hands to yourself and you might be in line for a certificate for best-behaved boy.'

'Maybe. I might not stay that long. I told Dale I wouldn't be late.'

'Okay. I understand. Probably for the best. This is not his kind of thing. The get up suits you, you should be popular. Have fun while you are here.'

One group of three were fooling around playing supposed schoolboy pranks, like pulling chairs out from behind each other whenever any of them tried to sit down, something they

242

obviously found hilarious and repeated half a dozen times, the victim always managing to put his drink down safely before he landed dramatically on the floor.

At one point Jake grabbed me around the waist, somehow lifted me up and sat me on top of the bar. Grinning he picked up my glass, handed it too me and said, 'Drink up now, there's a good boy.' Then, more serious, he said, 'Better be careful, I don't want to make Smiles jealous by fooling around with you. Or Dale, for that matter. Where is he?'

'Does Smiles get jealous?'

'You know what I mean. Smiles has been good for me. What else have I got in life?'

'Don't think like that. You're fine, Jake, honestly, I mean it, you're fine.'

I went home, as promised, after about an hour.

Walking back along the street dressed like a schoolboy was itself a bit of an adventure. A couple of police officers came towards me, grinning. When they drew near one of them said, 'I hope your mother knows you're out this late.' Too embarrassed to know what to say, I laughed and hurried on.

When I got back to the flat Dale was waiting, dressed in a white shirt and the shorts he had been so determined not to wear to the Give and Take. 'You do look sexy like that,' I said.

'You do too. It would have served me right if someone else had got a chance with you tonight.' He held his arms out, his palms turned towards me. 'Help yourself. I'm all yours, Do whatever you want to me.'

A couple of months must have gone by without contact with Quick or Teef. They were busy, The Handyman said, with preparations for a charity concert at the Hammersmith Apollo, at three and a half thousand seats a small venue for a band that had played in massive sports stadiums. The tickets, though not cheap, sold out within hours of being put on sale.

The Handyman was worried that the return to live performance was proving too much for Teef. Practice sessions in the studio had gone badly. Whilst technicians could use the latest equipment and studio recordings to create the band's stage sound convincingly, Teef still needed to appear as though he was actually playing, not having to hazard a guess at where his fingers ought to be for the next chord. The Handyman asked me to go to the villa in the hope that I might be able to help focus the guitarist's mind.

When we entered the upstairs parlour Teef was sitting in front of the music stand, a Fender guitar resting on his lap. He did not acknowledge us until The Handyman asked loudly, 'Everything all right, Teef?'

He responded sullenly. 'Oh, yeah, I'm trying to rehearse. Seem to have got a bit rusty.' With a faint spark of interest he added, 'Is that you come to see me, Bendy? Been a while since we've had a chat.' Then he quickly rearranged the music on the stand.

The Handyman left us together. Teef sat silent and motionless, staring at the music. I said, 'I've been reading about the concert in the papers.'

'Oh, yes. Should have tried to get you in as a guest, but nobody listens to me any more, I'm only the fucking guitarist.' He sounded glum. 'Tell you what,' he continued, 'for a lark, you don't fancy another of our little duets, do you? You could try the guitar again while I tackle the vocal.'

'That would be great.' I moved up a chair so as to sit beside him in front of the music.

'Er, this time,' he said, 'sit over there and try playing from memory.'

He showed me how to hold down three chords, my clumsy fingers struggling to manage even that. Then he returned to his seat, fiddled with the sheet music again, and after counting to four, signalled to me to begin. I played the first two chords reasonably well, but my attempt at the third was dreadful. Nevertheless he launched into his monotone version of:

> *'Dancing dextrose, Oh what a rave,*
> *Dancing dextrose, that's what you gave,*
> *Dancing dextrose, I'll be your slave,*
> *Dancing dextrose, I'm out my cave.'*

After he sang the word dextrose he would pause, lean forward, stick out his tongue, and lick the sheet music on the stand in front of him. Straining sideways for a better glimpse of what was going on, I saw that he had stuck different kinds of his prescribed tablets, pink, blue, and yellow, over the musical notes on the page. He was licking a number of them after he sang each line of the song. Even more worrying, he was rubbing his crotch in obvious sexual self-stimulation. Could this be what The Handyman had meant when he had said that Teef did not 'have sex any more, well, not as we know it'?

I desperately wanted this demonstration of the joys of drugs, sex and rock and roll to end. Unexpectedly, it was brought to a close by Quick, who burst in followed by The Handyman. He marched over to the music stand, snatched the pages from it and threw them to the floor. 'I knew you'd be getting up to something, Teef, I could see it coming. You're too predictable. You know this is totally not allowed. And you've made things worse by involving Bendy.'

'I was only teaching him how to play the guitar.'

'Quick learner is he? Showing him what a prat you can make

245

of yourself, more like. What if Bendy had a little camera hidden on him? What would the press pay for pictures showing how much you love your drugs, literally.'

'Bendy would never do a thing like that.'

'He might if the money was right. What would the tabloids pay for the scandal, do you reckon? So we'd better give him a quick example of how we help people to see the error of their ways. You know what's coming next, don't you? Handyman, bring me the pads.'

For a few terrifying moments I thought I would be the one to be tortured. However, The Handyman grabbed Teef and wrestled him to the floor. Quick pulled off his jeans and strapped on the pads. 'Now, Handyman,' he said as he tightened the straps, 'quick, get me the itching powder.'

'No, Quick, not the itching powder, that's going too far. You know one of his knees is bad with arthritis.'

'He needs to be taught a proper lesson this time. Get me the fucking itching powder.'

Reluctantly, The Handyman brought a jar of white powder from the cupboard. Quick lifted the writhing Teef's feet up into the air and shook the contents out into the pads.

'Oh no Quick, you're overdoing it with that, not so much, now stop it!'

Quick ignored him. 'All right, let's hope you'll learn this time, Teef. And you, Bendy, if anyone else hears about this, if there's the slightest hint of a leak, you'll get the same. Don't even think about it, I'll be after you quick as a groupie can pull her drawers down, understand?'

Horrified, dumbfounded, I watched him walk out of the room. Teef was groaning in agony, but The Handyman grabbed my arm and said, 'We'd better go, too.'

'We can't leave Teef like that.'

'It may be a lousy thing to do, but you can't interfere in what goes on between those two, they've known each other so long. There've been so many battles between them. Sometimes things get nasty.'

'Can't we loosen the straps a bit? He might be able to get himself free.'

'They're special buckles, you need a key to release them. I know where to find one, but I daren't take them off yet. I need this job, I've got a wife and a kid. If I crossed Quick over this he would have me hung up by the testicles with guitar strings. I don't like leaving Teef any more than you do. Soon as I know Quick's properly out of the way chasing some chick or whatever, I'll come back, take off the pads, put some cream on Teef's legs, and give him some pain killers. That's the best I can do.'

Eighteen

Quick and Teef's deranged behaviour had surely shown the wild side of rock and roll at its worst. The Handyman and I were not much better, being far from heroic when we abandoned Teef to the agonies of the cricket pads. I was too ashamed to give Dale more than the barest description of what happened. Before going to bed I phoned The Handyman to find out if he had removed the pads. He had, but found Teef's legs were so red and swollen that he had to send for the doctor.

Before this episode, despite Quick's constant point scoring, I had felt friendly towards him, but after witnessing such unpredictable, bizarre and violent behaviour, warm feelings would be very difficult to rekindle. People in the rock and roll business do not mix much with outsiders, so maybe my contact with the Boulders would end anyway once the book was finished.

In spite of the pressures of our jobs and the 'auto'biography, Dale and I did somehow find time to prepare a couple of computer game scenarios for each other. His began with my avatar standing on stone steps that led up to the pillared portico of a museum. Clicking with the mouse took him to the entrance and into the first room, containing exhibits from ancient Greece in glass cases. Among them was a foot-high bronze statue of Priapus, the mythical goblin-like figure with an outsize erect penis. When I clicked on him he ran up and down his case and hammered on the glass as though determined to get out. More chaste bronze figures nearby recoiled in horror.

In another case was a large urn decorated with a handsome youth playing a lyre. Clicking on this caused two muscled, naked men to climb out of the urn and caress him, slipping their hands inside his robe. He ignored them and continued to play his lyre. Next, an older man carrying a staff climbed out. He whacked the two randy muscular men with it until they ran off to the other side of the urn.

The next room had full-size, marble statues, whose stone penises became erect when my avatar passed close by. At the end of this room was a doorway to the Temple of Dionysus. Inside was a collection of curiously shaped pottery vessels. A museum attendant appeared and handed 'me' one with a spout shaped like a penis. I clicked on this pot and a box popped up on the screen saying *Don't worry Ben, the contents are only white wine.* With the mouse I raised the pot to my avatar's lips and tilted it to make him drink. The brew must have been very potent, for the other pots began to change into lizards and snakes. They moved threateningly towards the on-screen me, teeth and fangs bared.

Running from the room and turning this way and that to escape them, I passed a statue of Dale. Clicking on it brought it to life. From a large stone chest he pulled out some nets with weights on the corners, and we flung these over the reptiles, eventually catching and entangling them all. Then, of course, my avatar thanked his saviour in the kind of way you would expect.

The scenario I devised for Dale began with his avatar walking along a deserted beach in a pair of long white shorts. Clicking anywhere on the sea made 'him' wade out, his shorts becoming almost transparent as they got wet, and revealing that beneath, he had on a pair of very skimpy swimming trunks. A dolphin appeared and swam around him. Clicking on it made it grab his arm in its mouth and drag him underwater to a hidden cave, where it released him. He surfaced near a small beach with partly submerged rocks. The cave had several branches that led off in different directions. A band of pirates arrived, ran to the water's edge and began to chase him. Clicking on the nearest rock made him jump into the water and climb up onto it. He went from rock to rock whilst the pirates continued to chase after him, until a sheer rock wall blocked his escape. A shadowy figure dropped a rope ladder from a ledge above. When he climbed up the ladder, he found his rescuer was the on-screen me, dressed as a marine and armed with a club. The pirates climbed up towards us, but clicking on the top of the ladder made us unhitch it to send them tumbling back down. The game ended with us going to a secluded inlet, where a rowing boat gently bobbed up and down. We climbed in, and the boat was soon bobbing up and down more vigorously to the rhythm of our movements.

Increasingly I wished that Dale and I had more time to enjoy doing things together, as we had before Quick's book came to dominate our lives, like taking out rowing skiffs on the Thames. Instead, however, a call from The Handyman added to the pressures. The doctored cricket pads and itching powder had so incapacitated Teef that he was unable go to the theatre to try out the stage set and do sound checks. They desperately needed someone they could trust to substitute for him. Since I had zero experience of stage productions of any kind, they must have asked me out of desperation. I could imagine Dale's voice in my ears imploring me to stay away. I told The Handyman I had no time, and would only be in everyone's way, but shortly afterwards, he rushed into the bookshop, saying the concert would have to be cancelled unless I went. Hearing his agitated voice and wanting to be helpful, Jeremy said he would be in all afternoon and it would be perfectly okay for me to take a few hours off.

This made it impossible for me to refuse. On our way to the theatre, The Handyman said all they needed me for was to make sure the stage lights would catch Teef in the right way while he was performing, and to ensure no wires or equipment had been put where they might be a hazard. He made it sound as though a mannequin, moved around the set, would have done. Nevertheless, the attraction of actually helping with a live music performance, even in such a small way, began to grow.

Our arrival at the theatre was the opposite of a glittering occasion. Vans were parked everywhere, and the only spot left was next to overflowing rubbish bins. The stage door appeared not to have been painted since the place was built eighty years ago. We climbed a bare concrete staircase and turned into a narrow corridor leading to the dressing rooms. We found the band's manager, Max, a big wire-haired man with a cigar who looked past me at The Handyman and said, 'You sure about this one?' The Handyman must have nodded, for Max rested his cigar on the edge of the table and pushed several sheets of paper towards me. 'Right-oh, sign here.'

'Er, what is it?' I asked.

'Confidentiality agreement. The essence of it is, if word about this gets out to the press, or anybody at all, we get to rip out your tongue and castrate you.'

I signed nervously. How much less anxious I would have felt if Dale had been with me. The Handyman led me towards the stage, but was called away to talk about food for the band the next day. He found someone to take me to a stage entrance, where I was to wait until called.

In front of me I could see the Boulders' drum kit, a backdrop of large screens stretching behind it. Dozens of people, hidden from the auditorium, were busily working at keyboards and control panels. No one took any notice of me. After hanging about in the wings for ten minutes or more, ignored and becoming increasingly bored, I meandered out and peered into the dim auditorium. Empty rows of red upholstered seats stretched away into the distance. Up above, the steeply raked seats in the balcony receded even further, disappearing into the gloom. The footlights in front of me glared suddenly. A voice from the stalls shouted, 'Give him a guitar somebody.'

One of the stage hands appeared with a Fender guitar. My pulse quickened, my stomach tightened, and a shiver of stage-fright ran through me. Terror must have shown in my face, for as he handed me the instrument he said, 'Don't worry, mate, you look really cool.'

My eyes adjusted to the footlights, and I saw The Handyman make his way along a row of seats towards Max, who was already in the middle of the stalls. He called out, 'We really appreciate you coming to help. You've seen Teef perform, on telly at least, haven't you? Maybe you could try a few of his moves, to help us adjust the lights and check the set. I'll give you a tip. The most important thing with the guitar is holding it right. Try this for us. Stretch your left arm right out forwards holding onto the neck… yes… bend your knees slightly as though you're ready to spring into action… that's good, now hunch your shoulders over the guitar, you've got it, we call it the battering ram, make like you're ready to charge into the audience with it. Swing it gently up and down a bit, that's it, great. Now another one of his favourites, straighten yourself up, bring your left arm up so the neck of the instrument is above your head... now move your hips back and forth. Yes, you've got it, we call that the space launch. It's like you're ready for lift-off.' He glanced across to The Handyman, gave him the thumbs up sign, and called out to me, 'That's how it's done, mate, the girls will love it.'

He again looked at The Handyman, who this time moved his hands forwards and down in front of his chest to suggest a female bosom, shook his head and pulled a face. 'Oh, right,' Max said, 'correction. The guys in the audience will really go for the next moves. Hold the guitar like you're trying to shake the chords out of it... terrific... turn sideways for me... a bit more... now back to face me... and again... yes, you're turning me on now.'

With more encouragement, I pretended to play the chords Teef had taught me, swung around this way and that, and strode towards a back corner of the set. 'Excellent. Now, Bendy, isn't it? Try that again. Let's have some backing music this time. Wiggle your arse for us a bit... not too much.'

Posing as a rock star, I must have struck everyone as utterly ridiculous, but they did not laugh, and Max continued to praise and urge me on. After about fifteen more minutes he said, 'Someone take him up to a dressing room, put a headscarf on him and slap on a bit of eye shadow.'

He explained: 'We have to make sure the image is right. So we need to get you made up properly.'

When he next saw me, in the headscarf and wearing eye make-up, he had me walk around under different combinations of lighting for a couple of minutes, then nodded his approval and said, 'Okay, you can go home. Unlikely we'll need you again, but be back here at four o'clock sharp tomorrow in case we do. The Handyman will take care of you.'

I learned on the drive back that Quick himself had not taken part in stage and sound checks for decades, because he

253

considered himself too important for them. When we pulled up at Fulrose Court, The Handyman dropped a brown envelope full of money into my lap. 'What's this?' I asked.

'Hush money,' he said gruffly.

Dale was very dubious about that brown envelope full of cash, money not duly recorded or signed for. 'For all we know,' he said, 'it could have come from drug dealing or organized crime. What are those guys up to? If they needed someone to prat about on stage pretending to be Teef, why couldn't one of them do it? Still, you're not going to hand such a big wadge of notes back, are you? I could go with you tomorrow if it would help. I can leave work a bit early to get there for four.'

He did not have to repeat the offer. The Handyman collected us from Fulrose Court, and during the drive to the theatre talked constantly of the need for strict secrecy. He said that Max, the band's manager, alone knew the grand plan, how and when all the elements needed for the show were to come together. Everyone else knew enough to perform their particular tasks, and no more.

All day, fear of what might be about to happen had caused me nervous inner twinges. At the theatre we entered through the weather-beaten door, went up the concrete staircase, and into a shabby room containing a couple of plastic chairs, a small table with mineral water and polystyrene cups, and a very old television monitor showing the empty stage. Dale was told to wait for me there. I was ushered along the corridor and into one of the dressing rooms. 'They'll dress you and put some stage make-up on you next,' The Handyman said.

'What's going on? Yesterday they thought I probably wouldn't be needed.'

'Same kind of thing, the performance has got to feel right.

Image is everything these days, everything has to be just so. Little details you or I would never think of... how the guitars and outfits appear in different coloured lights... clothes having a particular style, not what the kids might wear, but not dated either. Nothing is left to chance, everything is thoroughly tried out, checked and re-checked, so even if you don't know the reason for some of the things Max asks you to do, just go along with him. He even fusses about how visible the knot at the back of Teef's headscarf is, and how close the guitar strings are trimmed back to the machine heads. Shouldn't need you for long. You'll be performing a few moves under the dark spotlight.'

'The dark spotlight? What the hell is that?'

'It's some newfangled thing. The Rocking Boulders are the first band ever to use one. It has a sort of silhouette effect, makes people seem a bit fuzzy. It creates a sort of Goth aura, no matter how bright the other stage lights. Someone tried to explain how it works to me. Something to do with low-frequency energy fields. A professor at Pottsville University in the States invented it.'

I remembered Alicia speaking of a professor at Pottsville when she had been banging on about psychics and low-frequency energy fields. Perhaps they were not just mystical mumbo-jumbo. After the dresser and make-up artist had finished, they handed me a mirror. The face that gazed back was more like Teef's than it was my own; patches of a rubbery substance had been stuck on to create wrinkles, and my colour was ashen enough for a deathbed scene. Was all this really necessary to get the stage lighting exactly right?

I went down to the wings of the stage where an earpiece was fixed under my headscarf. Through this Max gave me instructions, evidently able to see me, though this time I could not see him. He had me cross from one side of the stage to the

255

other several times, turn to face into the wings or move back towards the drum kit, and then twirl around and strut to the front of the stage, then go a little to the right of dead centre. He stopped me a couple of times because I was encroaching on Quick's centre-stage space. After that came an exercise in which I had to lean back whilst pretending to pluck the guitar strings rapidly. 'Go on, further, lean right back as far as you can, bend your legs more, not too much with the right one, remember Teef's right knee is a bit stiff,' he ordered. Worried more about the guitar than my own safety, I lost my balance and fell down, banging my head. 'That might have stretched you a bit, but you're getting to know your limits, well done,' he said. 'Let's try you in the dark spotlight next. Be extra careful. It will make you appear shadowy and mysterious to the audience, but for you everything more than a few yards away will become indistinct. You may see weird coloured patches of bright light. They can be confusing... try to ignore them, they're a side effect of the equipment. Always check the guide marks on the floor when you're moving around on stage; keep at least three feet away from where the others will be. It would be a disaster if the spotlight suddenly made them look like Goths as well.'

I practised a few more of Teef's moves as directed, trying to drag my right leg a bit to make it appear stiff. Then the dark spotlight came on, and except for what was directly in front of me I could make out nothing at all, not the footlights, the edge of the stage, or the rows of seats in the auditorium. Random patches of colour appeared, as if part of a light show. Following Max's commands, his voice constantly in my ears, I moved as though blindfolded. After several minutes the spotlight was extinguished and the stage became visible again. 'How was that?' I asked.

'Great... little bit of adjustment... no problem. Tell you

what, we'll take a break now and you can meet a few of the people backstage. Not sure if we'll need you any more, but you may as well see what goes on. Give you some impression of how the show is put together. The technology we've brought in is fantastic – terrific sound system, top class lights, hologram projections, the dark spotlight – but you can't put on a concert with technology on its own. Not yet, anyway, you still need flesh and blood artistes up on the stage, unpredictable buggers that they are.'

The Handyman waved to me from the wings and took me back up to the room where Dale was waiting. 'Is that really you in that disguise?' he asked. 'Was that really you on the stage? I can hardly believe it.'

'I can hardly believe it myself.'

'You're like an octogenarian pirate. Hang on to those clothes, they would do you for fancy dress parties.' The Handyman took us backstage, where the technicians, hidden from the audience, controlled the show. He introduced us to a couple of them, who told us how the stage effects and sound system worked, for instance that the phase of sound waves from more distant loudspeakers had to be altered to avoid spoiling the acoustics. We moved on to see where body guards would be waiting in case anyone climbed onto the stage. Next, we made our way up to a cubicle on the balcony from where the lights were controlled. It was so cramped that the woman at the desk had to squeeze past banks of electronics to greet us. 'They don't leave you much room,' I commented.

'It's not usually as bad as this. They've brought in whole racks of stuff for the dark spotlight. You can see the main unit over there.' She waved towards a special caged-off area at one end of the balcony. There a huge cylinder, with half a dozen or more thin tubes attached to the outside, pointed towards the stage.

'It's big enough,' I said.

'Yes. It doesn't actually produce light itself, it works by generating low-frequency energy fields that interfere with the light from other sources. You see those tubes fixed to the outside? They're telescopic sensors. The output is constantly varied with every change in the main stage lighting. This is the first time I've seen one. They're horrendously expensive. Only a mega-group like The Rocking Boulders could afford one. Worked a treat on you, though, made you so spooky, like a real creature of the night.'

We returned to the shabby room where Dale had to wait. As it was late and Max wanted me to stay longer, The Handyman sent out for takeaway food. When we were alone, Dale said, 'I don't want to sound melodramatic, but in case they do want you again, you have got your phone with you, haven't you? If they push you too hard, call me. I'll come running.'

'Thanks. You're sure you don't mind hanging around here?'

One of the stage hands came to take me back downstairs. Before he led me away Dale hugged me and mouthed 'phone'. Off a short corridor I had not noticed before was a first aid room, where a man with a stethoscope around his neck said he would give me a quick check-up. He had me sit on a couch, move my arms and legs this way and that, and told me to follow the light of a little torch he held in front of my eyes. Then he checked my pulse and blood pressure. 'You'll do,' he said.

With his fingers he moulded two plugs of a cotton wool-like substance around a couple of tiny earphones and fitted them into my ears. He clapped his hands. The sound was barely audible. Then he plugged the earphones into a small amplifier and snapped his fingers close to a microphone. The thwap of his finger and thumb came through loudly.

'Very good,' he approved, 'Now, take a couple of deep

breaths through here for me.' He put a little perspex mask over my mouth and I breathed deeply. I felt a burning sensation in my sinuses and lungs. My muscles relaxed totally and I slumped onto the couch. If I had been standing I would certainly have fallen. My eyes shut, but I had the impression of seeing a brilliant flash of light that quickly faded. When I was conscious again he helped me straighten up, and said, 'Now, one more good breath, and we'll be finished.'

'But…' He pressed the mask over my mouth and nostrils hard, forcing me to inhale another dose. This time I blacked out. I have no reliable memory of what happened next. A kind of consciousness, or the illusion of consciousness, returned. My impression was that I was standing in the wings of the stage holding a Fender Stratocaster guitar. I could hear Max's voice in my ears, ordering me about. Next, the dark spotlight's deep shadow enveloped me, and its chromatic patches of light appeared. I have no idea know how long it was before I became properly awake. Whether my impressions were distorted memories of actual events, or weird imaginings induced by the inhaled gas, I cannot say.

I have a clear memory of going back to the room where Dale waited. He removed the headscarf, pulled the earphones from my ears, and washed my face with warm water from a plastic bowl. Then he helped me change back into my own clothes. Holding my arm he led me down the concrete staircase to a waiting taxi. On the way home I blacked out again.

Dale had watched the concert on the small screen of the closed circuit TV, but the picture was poor and the fixed camera revealed no detail. All kinds of things might have gone on under cover of some of the light-show effects and hologram projections. Teef, in particular, was very heavily made up, and was frequently under the shadowy influence of the dark spotlight. He also quite often disappeared behind the screens for a minute or two.

We bought newspapers the next day to read the reviews. They were of two kinds: those that praised the band effusively, and those that, whilst saying it was amazing they had continued to perform live for so many decades, suggested their material must sound dated to younger ears. All the reviewers loved the strange Goth aura that followed Teef around. There were no suggestions of anything amiss, or questions about how much of the music was actually live, or comments about the use of holograms or the special spotlight. A famous rock and roll band was expected to put on an expensive stage show, and the showmanship, mostly, was what interested the press.

Dale and I discussed whether the audience might, briefly, have seen me impersonating Teef, rather than the man himself. Was it possible that a holographic image of me, acting under Max's directions, had been shown for a few minutes to allow him to rest? My own vague, uncertain memories proved nothing. We might as well speculate that the whole performance had been generated by the banks of computerized equipment, hologram projectors, and so on, without any human performers being on stage at all. No one would take such outlandish ideas seriously.

But if they had not used me during the concert, why had they dressed me up like Teef, and why had Max been directing me under the aura of the dark spotlight? Even if my role had been bigger than giving a little help with preparations, none of The Rocking Boulders' entourage would ever reveal the truth. Why should they risk losing their highly paid jobs, or being tortured with the doctored cricket pads, for a story that could never be proved and was unlikely to be believed? If, during the band's long history, a lookalike had ever been used in performance, the

The Rocking Boulder's loyal circle knew better than to tell.

There were, though, clear signs of a change in attitude towards me. For over a week The Handyman phoned every day to ask how I was. Teef and Quick each called personally to thank me for helping with the show. Quick, instead of fobbing me off with the usual terse statement that he could not talk for long because he was on his way to some exclusive gathering, talked for ten minutes about how the band had struggled to get bookings in their early days. He promised that I would be the special guest at a big party on a river boat in a month or so. Twenty places were to be reserved for anyone I wanted to bring along. The Handyman gave Dale and me another brown envelope full of money for expenses, even though we had not claimed any.

Finishing Quick's 'auto'biography again came to take up much of my time. After several weeks more work, only a final batch of comments from the music journalist brought in by the band remained to be considered before the book was complete. Busy with our day jobs and our own routines, Dale and I soon stopped worrying about what might or might not have happened at the theatre.

The date of the party on the boat was confirmed. I easily filled my quota of guests by including those who had worked on the book and friends from the Give and Take. When anyone asked about the invitations, I gave an explanation suggested by Max, that they were a thank you for some papers and pictures belonging to Quick and Teef that I had discovered at an auction of celebrity memorabilia.

The party on the boat began with lunch. We joined the boat at Millbank, near a stubby pillar marking the place where, long ago, a prison hulk was moored, full of convicts awaiting transportation to Australia. The boat for the party, in contrast, was a luxury river cruiser with a gleaming white hull. The forward of its two large cabins was filled by tables set for a four-course meal, and the rear one, with a small stage, had been cleared for dancing. Once aboard we were directed to the free, already crowded, bar. As the cruiser cast off we went in to eat.

My friends and the band's people did not mingle much. Open bottles of wine were already on the tables, but the Boulders' guests were soon calling for more. The traffic between bar and tables was constant. Everything was paid for, so there was no reason to hold back. A few of my group did their best to keep up, but alcohol consumption on the Boulders' tables was hard to match.

At the end of the meal, when coffee had been served, Max stood up to speak. 'First off,' he said, 'thanks to all of you for coming along. Well done to everyone who helped make the concert at the Apollo such a success. I'd like in particular to extend a special welcome to Ben and his friends, who discovered at an auction some material from a rock opera that, sadly, was left unfinished a long time ago. For anyone who would like to know more, a song from it will be performed in the aft cabin after the meal.

'A question I am often asked, but can never give a definite answer to, is where the name The Rocking Boulders came from. Various ideas have been put forward, but none of them has ever been confirmed. The lads themselves are always very coy about the band's origins, as I'm sure you know. One thing we can be completely sure of is that they did not start out as a tribute band to The Rolling Stones. My favourite story is that The Rocking Boulders was chosen from a long list which included gems like The Quaking Shoulders, The Party Holders, The Paper Folders, and The Do Az-ure Tolders.'

He was answered by noisy, drunken laughter and a cry of 'Should have called them The Sex Soldiers.'

'Finally, would you all raise your glasses, please, to the forthcoming work of fiction to be known as Rick Schwagger's autobiography, subtitled: *Quick: Fore, Aft, and Everything in Between*. To the autobiography, your glasses please!'

Later, as we made our way to the rear cabin, we passed the toilets. A long queue had formed outside. I thought at first this was a result of all the wine and beer that had been consumed, until Dale came up with a more likely explanation: Peruvian Marching Powder. Three lads confirmed his theory by coming out of the loos together, one rubbing his nose, all of them unnaturally alert and pleased with themselves.

The Handyman saw them and said quietly to me, 'I'd better make sure there's no risk of Quick shoving any of that stuff up his nostrils. We don't want him flinging his clothes off and jumping into the river. By the way, Max wants to have a word with you. You'll find him over at the bar.'

He was talking to a couple of people when I approached, but seeing me he quickly disengaged from them. He ordered me a drink, put an arm around my shoulder and walked me to the now deserted gangway where we had boarded, so that we could talk privately.

'Party all right for you?' he asked.

'Yes, fine. Terrific.'

'Okay. Now, if Quick's book goes as well as we expect, there will be others in the business wanting to have a book of their own. There will be an opening for someone who can be trusted to put their stories together for them. Give me a ring in a couple of months' time. If anyone is sniffing around I'll hear about it, one way or another.'

'Wow! Would you do that for me? Thanks.'

'In this business loyalty is paramount. There are times when working for the Boulders is a bit like being a secret agent, or possibly like working for the Mafia. You get to hear about things that are definitely not for the press or public. You got as close as you did because The Handyman vouched for you. Now I'll be willing to vouch for you too, if I can be sure you won't let me down.'

'Count on me, not the slightest hesitation.'

He gave me his card, we shook hands, and I went back towards the rear cabin. The Boulders had taken up their positions on stage and were ready to begin the song from the rock opera. A couple of chords from Teef's guitar got everyone's attention, and Quick began to sing in a voice so tender it surprised us all:

> *There's nothing wrong with the sunshine,*
> *Sun and sky are a perfect blue,*
> *But, with you oh so far away,*
> *Here's one more weary, lonely day.*
>
> *Days break and fade as they used to,*
> *But pleasure is too hard to find,*
> *Sun, sand and sea, but miss you so,*
> *Love him, respect him, let him go.*
>
> *Those sweet love songs we like to hear,*
> *Whispered words meant so to endear,*
> *For my ears, they've nothing to say,*
> *Can't ease this weary, lonely day.'*

Without the aid of backstage technicians, they delivered a moving and expressive performance. Teef's guitar solo was great.

The song lasted for perhaps ten minutes, and was very different from the raunchy, rebellious hits that had made them famous. They bowed and quickly left the stage, not returning to acknowledge our applause. A five-man vocal group took over to sing rock and roll standards, with no instrumental backing. Most guests began to dance.

Jeremy, Alicia, Myrtle and Loyd left the cabin to sit in the open area in the stern of the boat, whilst Dale, Smiles, Jake and I danced together in a little group. Listening to the words of the songs, I realized the singers had adapted the lyrics to give them a gay flavour; for instance, The Drifters' 'Like sister to brother, We'll wave to each other, We don't want all the world to know, We are really lovers,' had become 'Like brother to brother, We'll wave…'

After nearly an hour of singing, the vocalists came down from the stage and cleared a space for themselves on the dance floor. A deejay took control of the sound system and played hits from the sixties and seventies, whilst the five-man vocal group went into a dance routine. The youngest of them, who had white streaks in his dark curly hair, began to strip. He unbuttoned his shirt, rolled up a sleeve to expose one arm, and slowly revealed his upper torso. He took off his shirt and handed it to one of his mates, who dropped it onto a nearby empty chair. Predictably the audience began to clap and shout 'Strip… strip…' He reached down to the zip of his trousers, and made as though to undo it, but his friends moved to block our view, and when they moved away from him his zip was still done up. After a couple more feints of undoing his trousers, his friends grabbed him, and removed his shoes and socks. They released him, and he stood up and danced barefoot. Next his friends wrestled him to the floor, removed his trousers, released him, and he danced in his underpants. The next time they got hold of him they removed those too. Naked, he pretended to be embarrassed, and ran around trying to recover his clothes, which were snatched away again several times before he could reach them. Eventually they were given back. To enthusiastic applause, the entertainers lined up in front of the stage, bowed, and then ran off to the bar.

Dale hugged me, said the party was terrific, and that he was going on deck to get some fresh air. For a while I danced with Jake and Smiles. The cabin was becoming very hot and I went to the bar for a cold drink. The boat slowed, and through a window I saw we were approaching a jetty where some tough-looking men, bodyguards I supposed, stood waiting. Quick and Teef stepped off the boat and walked towards them. They were leaving before I had had a chance to thank them for the party, and I realized that my role in their lives had ended: they were, quite simply, moving on. I took my drink outside to where Alicia, Myrtle, Jeremy, and Loyd were sitting, the breeze ruffling their hair, or in Alicia's case a great confection of lace she had piled onto her head. Seeing me, she said, 'It's much cooler out here.'

'Yes. Not getting bored, I hope?'

'No. We were just saying it's ages since any of us have been on a boat on the Thames. You forget how good it is. I've been telling everyone about this archaeological dig in the Nile delta I'm going to join. It'll mean being away for six months.'

'Six months! What about the shop?'

'A friend of Jeremy's is interested in taking it over. They will make it more of a party goods kind of shop, fancy dress, room decorations, party novelties, you know the kind of thing.'

'Will you be going too?' I asked Myrtle.

'On the dig? Not bloody likely. I might fly into Cairo or Alexandria to meet Alicia and have a break.'

After this the conversation settled into a curiously disjointed dialogue between Myrtle and Loyd. Each spoke on their favourite themes; Myrtle would say something about how men had been lording it over women for thousands of years, holding them back with the burdens of childbirth and rearing the next generation and so on; Loyd would wait for her to pause, then weigh in, putting the blame for the world's problems on modern writers, saying they had no grasp of grammar, could not even spell, had never learnt to think logically, and wrote such dense, impenetrable prose it was amazing anyone persevered beyond the first few pages. The two of them looked set to carry on like this indefinitely.

I struck up a conversation with Jeremy by saying quietly: 'Can I ask you a question?'

'Of course you can.'

'With your background in the Gay Liberation Front, what do you think of civil partnerships? Do you approve of them, or do you think they are too much an imitation of straight marriages? I mean, would GLF have said they were a cop-out from spontaneous gay desire and affection?'

'Good heavens, how should I answer that? I don't think they're a cop-out, it all depends on who we're talking about. If you mean you and Dale, you two might make a go of a civil partnership. He is already closer to you than breathing. He's the one you need to talk to. If you both like the idea, I'm sure everyone would wish you well. Why not discuss it between yourselves, and plan to make a decision in, say, a year's time? If you both still feel the same in twelve months, then why not?'

'A sort of engagement period?'

'Yes, if you like. Where is he, by the way?'

'I'm not sure. Thanks Jeremy. Maybe I should go and find him.'

I wandered through the boat, eventually seeing Dale in the bow. He was standing on his own, gazing ahead as we surged forwards on the rising tide. Central London's concrete and glass towers were behind us, and we were passing the riverside path near Hammersmith where we had often walked together. There were pubs with busy tables outside, and on the opposite bank was a line of great poplar trees, in front of school playing fields. He looked fantastic – his skin glowing in the light of the afternoon sun. He saw me out of the corner of an eye and turned towards me. 'Hello, Ben. Sorry, I was about to come and find you. This stretch of river always appeals to me. We've been rowing here a few times, haven't we, and walked along that path over there? It must be much the same as a century and more ago. I wonder how far up river they'll take us today. Remember that island ahead planted with osiers?'

'Yes. It is a beautiful stretch.'

He smiled. I wished it were possible for me somehow to become physically joined to him for a while, to see the world through his eyes, to feel his blood pulsing through my veins.

'Should we be going back to the others?' he asked.

'Maybe, in a minute.' We each put an arm around the other, ignoring the sounds of the party behind us. We were coming up to the next bend in the river, and a broad vista opened up as the boat turned. The dappled blue of the water's surface rippled constantly.

'Everyone will be wondering where you've got to,' he said.

'No they won't,' I answered. 'Quick and Teef went ashore without saying goodbye. Or even hello, for that matter. Being here like this is perfect.'